The
7th Man

An Urban Horror
Part One

MARCUS T. JONES

Outskirts Press, Inc.
Denver, Colorado

The 7th Man
An Urban Horror Part One
All Rights Reserved.
Copyright © 2010 Marcus T. Jones
v3.0 r.1.1

Cover Photo © 2010 JupiterImages Corporation. All rights reserved - used with permission.

Outskirts Press, Inc.
http://www.outskirtspress.com

ISBN: 978-1-4327-5633-8

Outskirts Press and the "OP" logo are trademarks belonging to Outskirts Press, Inc.

PRINTED IN THE UNITED STATES OF AMERICA

Prologue

The day was harsh and the night was uneasy on the Travis plantation. He had almost worked his field hands to near death, which was common with Joseph Travis because he was known as being a hard slave owner, a malignant master especially when he was trying to meet his quota. This was common at least twice a month but this night would be far from usual, it would be the beginning of a small but significant battle of good using evil to fight evil.

It was 10:14p.m. August 13, 1831 and the field hands were tending to their personal and house duties. Some were taking in eggs, some were sewing their tattered clothing, and some were tucking in their children. Sam picked out of his 8ft. by 10ft. garden (a turnip here, two tomato plants there, a few potatoes and a couple of peas) when he noticed a bluish-green light shimmering off the sweat on his arm. He gazed up and with a trembling voice and said. "Jesus Lord my savior!"

What he saw was the moon, but it was not the normal grayish-white he normally saw, it was like a bluish-green emerald. It sat in the sky shinning so bright that he could only stare at it for a few seconds. He dropped his sack of pickings and ran as fast as his scarred bare feet could move. He came to the last slave quarter on the plantation and full of panic he banged on the dilapidated door.

Doom-doom-doom. "Nat come quick!" *Doom-doom-doom.* "Nat you in 'nare!" *Doom-doom-doom.* "Nat!"

"Okay-okay, I'ss coming!" He shouted getting out of his straw and chicken feather makeshift bed and putting on his ragged trousers. "Let me get my britches on first. I soe hope you da Black Moses her-self here to point me to freedom raisin' all dat fuss."

"Naw it's Sam, Nat you gotta come see dis!"

"Sam!" Nat responded with disappointment. "Boy you better have a hot skillet of hens and taters wit'-cha." Nat opened the door to see a wide-eyed Sam standing in his doorway sweat glistening a bluish-green. "Dis better be good or I'm goin' beat chew worse than masser."

"Look." Sam said pulling Nat out of his shack and pointing up to the moon. In a deep and heavy tone, Nat whispered.

"Almighty God! Sam go rally Henry, Hark, and Nelson and tell 'em to meet me at the old dead dogwood tree by the pile of stones; it's time."

Sam hurried and gathered the men just as Nat had asked and the four men with just the rags on their backs ran through the thick woods. When they arrived they found Nat standing by a circle of white sand, in it was a strange drawing of a twelve pointed star, with a white sand drawn eye in the middle. Outside of a twelve-pointed star but inside the circle were snake like trails that ran throughout the diagram and surrounding the circle were six black candles.

Nat greeted them with an embrace as if they were brothers in arms going into a bloody battle, which they would not survive. "Yall know what we's 'bout to do here ain't Godly nor Christian like and we'll damn our souls fo'-ever. But remember this here is bigger than us, this is the night we send a message to are so called earthly massers, that we are men and we will be free. This is for ours childwen and they's childwen. Now if'en one of yall men got any doubt about what we's doing tonight then return to yo' chains and whips, I won't be bitter." The men looked amongst each other then Henry stepped forward.

"Well we's here ain't we, we knows what we gettin' ourselves into, we's wit-cha' all da way Nat."

The men lit the candles in front of them and sat Indian style around the circle, Nat then picked up an old kitchen knife he'd stolen from Master Travis four months ago and said loudly.

"This is our blood and we give it willingly to give life to the powerful Zeinoch so that he may strike down our enemies." Immediately after Nat spoke the words the wind picked up just enough to tremble the flames of the candles. He then made a small cut in his left palm and squeezed a few drops of blood in a small wooden bowl and the ground began to rumble as if the earth itself growled. He passed the knife and bowl to his right to Sam and he did the same.

"This is my blood and I offer it willingly to give life to Zeinoch." Sam cut his palm and dropped in his blood then passed the knife to Henry who did the same, and from Henry to Hark, and from Hark to Nelson. The bowl returned to Nat a quarter full and he said.

"Zeinoch, we offer our blood and in doing so we denounce our God above so that you may have power and walk the earth to do our will, and to do are work. So come Zeinoch through the gates of hell and into our services where you shall dwell."

Their words set off thunder and lightning and the winds howled like a pack of wounded wolves; panic set in the four men as they gazed up pass the trees and into the sky with fear in their eyes, except Nat who sat emotionless. Calm. Tranquil. He held the bowl of blood, which now bubbled like cooking grits. He then poured the blood on the eye in the circle and it immediately began to flow through the snake like trails, like blood pumping through veins, upon the blood running its full course a tremendous cracking sound in the sky thundered as if God himself had cracked his knuckles. Following the sound a bolt of lightning shot down from the sky striking Nat then like an arc of electricity, a smaller beam shot out of Nat and into Sam, then from Sam into Henry then into Hark, and then back into Nat (in the same order the bowl was passed). Once the complete circle of light formed, the beam of energy shot out of Nat and into the eye of the circle releasing an earth-shaking, *boom*.

Complete silence covered the woods and the five men found themselves lying on their backs exhausted, bewildered, and nauseated. A few moments passed and Nat finally sat up slowly followed by Sam, then Henry, then the others.

Nat struggled to his feet feeling weak from the episode they had just experienced. He balanced himself using the old dogwood tree until he felt strong enough to walk off in the direction they had came, staggering like a drunk toddler. The others struggled to their feet and looked amongst each other confused, waiting on further instructions.

"So what we do now Nat?" Sam asked in a weak voice. Nat stopped, exhaled exhausted and without turning around as if to hide unbearable shame he replied.

"Now, we sleep."

They reached their quarters and gave each other a look as if it would be their last time meeting, before going into their shacks. The men got into their beds and almost simultaneously drifted off to sleep. Then it began.

It felt like it was more than a dream: An empty room with blood colored walls that lit up bright from some unknown source of light. Then it was dark. Then it was light. The light began flickering on and off with less than a second between each flicker. Then a figure appeared in the distance, too vague to make out by the dreamers. As it approached it seemed to be a man but it was too large. Deformed. It was not human. It stood six inches from the dreamers face.

It was a hideous creature: It stood nine feet tall, massive muscles, bluish-green reptilian skin and lightly covered with brown coarse hair on its back, arms, legs, and head. It had large hands that even with its huge body structure they seemed larger than normal. Each hand had six fingers with the sixth digit at the wrist, each one containing six-inch black claws. Its feet were similar to its hands with a sixth digit at its heel. Its face was the most grotesque: Its ears were long hairy and pointed, K-9 like. Its nose was black, wide and slimy similar to a gorilla's. It's bottom jaw protruded further than the top and had two four inch sharp teeth curving up like a warthog's which were surrounded by two rows of two inch sharp teeth, the top were the same and all its teeth were covered with a puss colored slime. Its tongue was a foot long, black, forked and covered with thousands of razor sharp scales. Its eyes were symbols of pure evil: They were dark yellow with red veins running throughout them with white irises and crimson pupils, truly hellish.

The dreamers and the creature stood staring at each other, letting out vague growls as it breathed. Though it was a monstrous being, the dreamers however, were not scared but nervous.

The room began to spin causing the dreamers to become disoriented. Then it stopped and the dreamers were now looking from another view, they looked at their hands and it were the creature's hands, they looked down at their feet and they were the creature's feet. They were the creature and the creature was them.

The walls fell and the beast was now standing in a familiar place in front of a familiar house. It walked up the porch steps, approached the door, and grabbed the handle. It was locked. It stepped back and with a horrific sound, coughed up and spat out a gruesome puss onto the cast iron handle immediately melting it away. The beast pushed its way in and sniffed the air in search of something. It caught a pleasing scent at the foot of a winding staircase and despite its huge stature, it moved with stealth like movement up the stairs.

At the top of the stairs, it caught some noises, which became clearer and louder as it proceeded down the oak-wood-floored hallway.

"Yes-Yes-ooh-yes daddy-like that just like that!" A woman's voice uttered in passionate yelps. "Do it to me harder please-yes just like that!"

"Yea you like that, huh baby you like the way master fucks you!" A man's voice moaned.

The creature followed the sounds to a door where it pushed it open to find a white man in between the legs of a pale white woman. She scratched his back as he bounced up and down on her.

The beast approached the bed and stood over them, its shadow casting over her caused her to open her eyes from bliss. When she saw what horror that stared back at her she let out a scream that was not a scream of passion, but of fear. Terror. However, Joseph Travis was so engulfed in his sexual bliss that he could not distinguish the difference, he continued his sexual aerobics.

The creature quickly raised its massive right arm, dropped its claws into the lower region of Joseph's back, ripping through flesh, bone, and muscle then into the woman's stomach. The beast pulled its hand back along with a claw full of Joseph and the woman's innards and watched as they spasm to their deaths.

Satisfied, the beast left the room and continued down the hall where it picked up another scent. It came to another door, opened it and saw two young girls (which were between the ages of nine and eleven) asleep in their beds. It walked over to the smallest one and with a quick swipe of its claw, decapitated her leaving her headless body holding a Dixie doll. Her head rolled off the bed hitting the floor making a solid, *thump*. The sound only slightly disturbed the other girl causing her to turn over onto her stomach. The creature walked over, thrust its hand into her back, and pulled out her spinal cord, her skull still attached.

It continued, back down the hall following another scent that it followed to a room occupied by a young man (between the age of 18 and 20) sleeping. Feeling the presence of someone or something in his room, the young man awoken to find himself in the presence of evil. He sat up in terror and just as he did the beast grabbed the young man's face completely covering his head, lifted him up, and with a quick swipe of its claw separated the man's torso from his bottom half, holding him by his head as his guts spilled out onto the bed. The creature then tossed the empty torso against the wall and made its way outside.

It walked through the woods until it came upon another plantation, where it entered the house of the slave owner and repeated its carnage. From plantation to plantation the beast slaughtered slave owners and their families in their sleep until the dreamers woke up.

The morning came and brought confusion to the slaves, the majority of them were lined up for their usual head count that was normally carried out by Master Travis or his overseers, but there was no sign of Master Travis nor his head overseer and there was no ringing of the work bell to start the days laboring. Nat, Sam, Hark, Henry and Nelson all came out of their shacks putting on their ragged clothes with a sluggish effort, exhausted and fatigued. Nat walked to the house steps and addressed the confused.

"Listen up brothas and sistas, there ain't no mo' massa, it ain't no mo' whips, it ain't no mo' chains, it ain't no mo' raping our women, it ain't no mo' taken our childwen-it ain't no mo' brakin' up our families. God gave me a sign and work has been done. Today you's free."

"Quit tawlking that foolish tawlk. You can't give nobody no freedom you ain't even got no freedom. Massa just tessen us to see if we goin' do somethin' stupid. We need to sit right here until he shows up." A man spoke from the crowd.

"Yea Nat." Another man spoke out. "We's tired of hearing 'bout cho' foolish signs. You sick in da head. Just hush that fuss befo' you get's all us a beaten."

Henry quickly stepped up onto the steps next to Nat. "No, you hush up. I know it to be true Massa and his family is dead, punished for their cruel ways. Them and every other Massa 'round here." The crowd of slaves still not convinced gave Henry an unsure look. "If ya'll thank we lies then see fo' ya'self." Henry said as he ran up to the door and pushed it open.

"The sun done cooked yo' head boy that fool is crazy." A man said.

"I'sa go in there." A huge prime buck named Paul said in the crowd. "If massa in there dead, then that's a sight I gots to see." Paul slowly made his way into the house and a moment later, he came out with a blank expression on his face, he then sat down on the steps next to Nat. "It's true massa and everybody else in the house is dead. And whatever killed them wasn't no man."

A strange silence fell over the crowd for a moment until a woman spoke out. "Well what we goin' do now? If some white folks come and see massa dead we's all gettin' da rope."

"I know some of ya'll is scared, but if we work together we won't ever have to worry 'bout da rope." Nat said. "Now I ask yall to join me to fight for our freedom. Yes, yall lives will be in danger, but it's for our childwen's freedom. But if you too scared then you need to leave now and find you a new massa with new chains, new whips, and new ropes."

"Nat." Paul said. "I believe we's all wit'-cha', just tell us what we need to do."

Nat and the others went to work. They burned the bodies, buried what wouldn't burn, and cleaned the house then all of the able body men gathered all the garden tools and anything that could be used as weapons (shovels, pitchforks, knives, etc.). They took all of the overseer's horses and organized; the women sewed blankets and prepared meals and traveling bags for a few selected men, they then rode to every house and small town and killed a few selected white people and let a few go so that they would tell officials of what was going on. When they would arrive, while Nat and his men slept, the creature would be waiting and would slaughter them with plenty of night left to go ahead to the next town or house to perform its carnage. The paddy rollers would arrive at towns where grocery stores would be full of dismembered bodies, taverns and saloons with mangled men hanging from the ceilings by their intestines tide into nooses. Black smith shops with their owners and customer's heads neatly stuck on the walls like decorations. Before leaving these places of horror, Nat would leave messages in blood: *White devils free us niggers.* A few men (outside the circle of five) would ask how is it possible that, that many people could be killed in such a brutal way. Nat would respond. "It's God's work."

One day around sunset the men had set up camp in the woods and was cooking supper when they heard the sound of dogs and men approaching. "It's a lynch mob, what we do Nat!" Sam urged. Nat looked upon the faces of his men, all had their weapons at the ready, some had faces full of fear.

"Well, this is it men. You can run, or you can stand and fight it's yo' choice. Either way I'ss thank yall greatly fo' comin' this far." A few of his men ran off while Hark, Nelson, Sam, Henry, and the loyal few stood their ground.

"Nat Turner." A man shouted from a short distance. "We know where you at boy, we got-cho' nigger ass surrounded so you bets come on quietly!"

"Come and get me you white devils!" Nat shouted back and a few seconds later the mob came into view. It was a little more than a hundred, some with guns, knives, torches, and dogs. A heavyset white man (obviously the leader) with his left thumb pulling his overalls spat out some black tobacco and wiped his chin. "Where the rest of 'em!"

"It ain't no mo' just us." Nat replied with anger.

"Bullshit, yall handful of dumb niggers ain't kill all dem white folks. But it don't matter none, we'll catch-'em. Kill-'em all, except Nat. I want his black ass alive." Nat and his men put up a small fight but were quickly killed off. The mob apprehended Nat and knocked him out. He awoken to find himself with his hands tied behind his back, a noose around his neck, and standing on a barrel surrounded by his captures. The heavyset man stood before Nat.

"Now I 'on't know how in the hell you and that bunch of measly niggers was able to kill more than three hundred white folks in a few nights, but chew 'bout to go to hell in a few minutes. What chew got to say about that?" Nat looked the man in his eyes and said.

"I wish I would of killed mo' of yall."

"Got damn you nigger!" He said as he cocked his leg back. Just before he kicked the barrel from under Nat, Nat shouted.

"FREEDOOOOOMMM!" The rope snapped his neck and his body twitched a little then swung stiff.

"Skin 'em, then burn 'em."

Dedicated to Marcus T. Jones Jr.
...I'm sorry...

Chapter 1:
The Crew

May 5, 2006

"Slow down Will, it should be right up here." Tracy said from the front passenger seat of the blue Ford Explorer.

"Man this party better not be lame." Larry said from the back seat. "I'm tellin' you if I go to one mo' lame ass party I'm snappin'. And it better be some whoes up in here cause I'm tryin' to get my pimpin' on."

"Come on now LL, you know Chris' parties be off da chain." Tracy replied then frowned as he gave more thought to Larry's statement. "And what chew worried about the females fa' ain't like you finna pull none."

"Okay." Michael agreed.

"What, man please I'm snatchin' up all da whoes, that's real talk. And stop calling me LL I done told yall my name is Larry."

"Naw yo' name is Lyin' Ass Larry." Michael corrected.

"Man fuck you Mike, ole John Madden-ass-boy. Watch, when I leave this party the girls is gonna be callin' me LL alright, but it's gonna stand for Lovely Larry." Larry bragged as licked his two index fingers then smoothed down his eyebrows.

"Now ya' eyes stank." Michael said.

"Hater."

"Shiiiiiitttt, Lame Ass Larry is what they goin' be callin' you." Said the driver causing everyone in the Explorer to laugh.

"There it is right there." Tracy said interrupting the laughter and pointing to the house they were approaching on their left. It was a line of cars parked along both sides of the street and a few new arrivers exiting their cars.

"Shhhhiiiitt. This jank is crunk." Will said as he parallel parked a few houses down from the party.

"I told yall." Tracy said. The six got out of the SUV and made their final and minor adjustments to their outfits. Larry sprayed his mouth with some breath freshener and then popped in a piece of gum for extra freshness.

Michael laughed. "You know that'll work a lot better if you brush yo' teeth a little every now and then."

"Hater. Yall better get cha' game tight cause I'ma' 'bout to pull every shawty up in this jank."

"The only thang you gonna be pullin' tonight is when you get home and pull on that lil baby dick of yours." Mike said while brushing his hair, the others laughed.

"He ain't got no dick dat nigga gotta we-we." Will added to the laughter.

They all were dressed for the occasion, putting on their best and newest stepping-out-threads, except one. Michael wore a red and black horizontal striped polo collar shirt and a pair of black Girbaud shorts with lettering, that was a size too big and sagged slightly. He wore black ankle socks with red Nike emblems with a pair of black and red Michael Vick Nikes and to complete his outfit he put on a black cap with a red Atlanta Falcons logo on top of his freshly cut hair.

Larry had on a pair of South Pole blue jeans shorts that were two sizes too big, a white and blue South Pole shirt that was also too big, and a pair of white and blue Nikes. Though his outfit was new it looked ridiculous on his skinny frame, even his blue and white Colts cap was too big.

Tracy wore a pair of Raw Blue, blue jean shorts, a black and gray shirt that bared the likeness of Tupac Shakur, a black fitted cap and a pair of gray and Black Nike Air Force Ones.

William also wore a pair of black and gold lettered Girbaud shorts one size too big, a pair of black and gold Air Max and a black shirt with a white snowman on the front. He wore no cap to show off his neat and long cornrows.

Deshawn wore a pair of PJ Mark khaki shorts, a white and cream Clench collar shirt and a pair of cream and brown F-13 Fila Bucks.

Kevin kept it simple with a pair of black Dickie pants, a new white T-shirt that still had the new crease and a pair of black Nike Air Force Ones. No cap to cover up his kinky braids. His attire was simple for a reason, a reason that troubled his comrades.

"Look Kev." Deshawn said with slight worry in his tone. "Please don't go up in here and act a fool. We just gonna have a good time, get fucked up, and holla at some females. Don't start with that gangsta-thug shit, bustin' heads and what not. See Chris is good peoples and he ain't use to all that thug shit, so be cool, alright." Kevin smacked his teeth and twisted his mouth.

"Yeah Kev the last party we went to you started fightin' right when I was 'bout to take this red-bone around back to do my thang, messin' me all up." Mike added.

Kevin was a rough one, known for getting into altercations everywhere he went that contained a crowed. He was fearless and refused to back down from anyone no matter the size or the number of his opposition. It was his nature and it created a reputation that preceded him and conceived his nickname 'Killer Kev', the troublemaker in fact Chris specifically asked Shawn not to bring "that fool Kevin". Shawn said that he would not bring him, but Kevin is Big Will's cousin and since Will was the only person in their crew with a ride, it was automatic that Kevin would tag alone.

"Yall need some napkins? Cause yall cryin' like some whoes."

"We just sayin', we wanna have a good time with no trouble…" Shawn tried to explain.

"-Yeah-yeah-yea, I hear you dawg but hear me. I ain't goin' start no shit but Chris go to Butler (Butler was one of twelve public high schools in Augusta and was actually athletic rivals of the school that the crew attended, Glenn Hills) and you know half of them pretty muthafuckas at Butler don't like me and if an-one of dem fuck-sucks look at me funny, I'm swangin' first, I ain't 'bout that bull-shit, I'm tellin' ya."

"Alright cuz I hear you and we got-cha' back you know that, just don't be the one to start it and swangin' on innocent bystand-ers. That's all I'm sayin'."

"Yeah I hear ya."

As they walked towards the house the loud music of the lat-est rap song from Lil Jon and The Eastside Boys grew louder and clearer as well as the distinct smell of marijuana. "Damn, yall smell that?" Will said sniffing the air. "Smells like that good-good."

As they walked through the yard they passed by four teenage males passing around a blunt (A cigar that has been split open, emptied of tobacco and filled with marijuana) the one passing it was coughing and the others gave the usual greetings as Shawn and the crew passed.

"What's up?"

"What up folk."

"What's happenin' fellas?"

As they walked up to the door two females were coming out laughing. "Girl that snaggel tooth fool tried to holla at me." One of them said. "I was…"

"What's up ladies, why yall leaving so early?" Mike interrupted.

"Oh naw we ain't leavin' we finna go to the car real quick."

"Good, because I wanna grind with you later on." He said with a smooth smile.

"Alright." She said returning the smile.

Michael Johnston was not only a good athlete, but he also was good with the ladies. He had clear smooth pecan tan skin, silky wavy hair that he kept trimmed, and straight white teeth. His eyebrows were thick but not bushy, deep dimples, full lips that were a shade lighter than his face, and a slight mustache that was just starting to develop. He had a confident walk full of swagger and always knew exactly what to say to the ladies, and his brown eyes and long eyelashes helped hypnotize any female he conversed with. He was 6'2 162lbs. with almost no body fat. He looked over at Larry and said. "See LL you gotta be smooth with the shawties, show confidence and interest."

"I'm smooth, I'm confident, I show interest you just wait until we get in here I bet-cha' I pull mo' whoes than you, I bet-cha'!" Larry said with confidence.

Lawrence Watkins could be considered the complete opposite of Michael. He was short and boney 5'5 and weighed a measly 112lbs. He was the same complexion as Michael however puberty was being cruel to him causing his face to be polluted with pimples. His nose was wide, his lips were big, and often cracking and pealing and he had big bulging eyes, which made him look as if he was always surprised. He had black curly hair that could be considered as "good hair", but since he never maintained it nor kept it trimmed, it always looked dry and spotted with dandruff flakes and his head was long in the back creating nicknames in junior high such as; Egghead, Hammerhead, Heady Kruger, Heady Murphy, the Head Doctor, Battery Pack, etc… But due to his constant lies his comrades caught him in, their nick name stuck, Lying Ass Larry. Larry was also far from being a ladies-man as any man could be, he had no swagger though he tried, miserably.

"Matter-of-fact let's bet."

"Bet what?" Michael asked confused.

"Let's bet on who gets the most numbers."

"You can't be serious?" Tracy said.

"Hell yeah I'm dead ass serious. How 'bout we bet five dollars on who gets the most phone numbers and five mo' dollars fa' each number the person lost by."

"What?" Michael said still surprised. "So you sayin' if by some miracle I only get two numbers and you get four I'll owe you five for loosing and ten mo' for the two numbers you got over me?"

"That's right."

"Okay then, bet it up." Tracy, Shawn, and Will shook their heads in pity.

"Larry." Kevin said. "You stupid." Just then a teenage boy burst out of the house followed by another.

"Not in my house!" Chris shouted pushing him out. The boy pushed Tracy and Shawn out of the way, ran down the steps, lend forward, and puked. A thick pink and cream color vomit poured out of his mouth and splattered onto the pavement causing chunks in it, that looked like pieces of potatoes and raisins, to bounce a little.

"Ewe shit! Nasty bastard." Shawn replied.

Will laughed after recognizing the boy. "Hahaah hell naw that's Tron! Ole baby-belly-ass boy, you can't drank." While still vomiting Tron held up his middle finger.

"What's up fellas?" Chris greeted after realizing who they were.

"What's up Shawn." He greeted with a pound while holding a Budweiser twelve-ounce bottle in one hand.

"What's up Chris." Shawn replied.

"What up Big Will, T-Murray, MJ." Chris greeted with pounds, daps, and fives. "Ole Lyin' Ass Larry, what it do?"

"Man chill wit' dat shit my name is Larry."

"Whatever, don't run off all the females. All hell." Chris said with worry as he looked at Kevin. "Yall brought crazy ass Killer Kev. Look cuz, don't fuck up my party and tear up my momma's crib."

"There you go wit' that shit, I came to have a good time just like everybody else."

"Yeah you say that but I'm still goin' be watchin' you. Shit if I knew you was comin' I would of called Richmond County's most finest to pull security. Naw I'm just fuckin' wit'-cha'. Come on in fellas."

They walked in bobbing their heads as the DJ mixed the Lil John and The Eastside Boys' music into the latest Pastor Troy song. They scanned the living room that was impressively transformed into a carpeted dance floor: the house furniture had been removed and the only furniture in its place was dozens of white plastic lawn chairs that lined the walls. Chris had even removed his family's pictures from the walls earlier that day. It was an end of the school year party and he knew it would get wild so he planned ahead and decided to remove anything breakable, expensive, and important which was a good idea, so he thought.

The scene was wild; there were fellows dancing up against females that popped their backs and threw their butts against the boy's pelvises and some girls were sandwiched between two guys. There were some girls pushing boys off them in disgust and a few lesbian couples, studs and fems dancing together in one corner while two boys took pictures with their camera phones. "This shit here is goin' on MySpace!" One said with glee. A female sat on a boy's shoulders with her crotch in his face jerking her hips as her female friends cheered her on. The chairs were occupied, some with boys too cool or too clean to get all sweaty dancing and some with females that were overly dressed-to-impress and did not want to mess up their new hairdos. A few chairs were occupied by males with females on their laps performing lap dances, minus the stripping. The majority of the party carried the usual red plastic Solo cups that were full of liquor while others carried bottles or cans of beer. The living room was lit up by a red light bulb except the area where the DJ mixed, which had a white light bulb lamp behind him to see his equipment.

The crew was being greeted by varies people in the crowd and by some that walked by. "What's up Shawn?" A boy shouted grinding against a female.

"What's up Steve?" Shawn replied throwing up two fingers (known as chunking up the deuce).

"What up Big Will?" A boy said walking by William.

"Nothin' much."

Two girls approached giggling and said in sync. "Hey MJ."

Mike responded first with his hypnotic smile then followed

through with his response. "Hey what's up Keisha, how you do Monique?" He then put his arms around the both of them. "Let me holla at chall ladies for a minute. A fellas I'll catch up wit'-chall later on."

"Go ahead and do yo' thang boy." Tracy smiled.

Kevin then looked at Larry then shook his head in pity. "You finna lose."

Larry stared at MJ as he walked off with his two acquaintances. "A, that shit don't count wit' girls you already know either." He shouted over the music.

Chris looked confused then asked Shawn. "What in the hell is that clown talkin' 'bout?"

"Oh, LL and MJ gotta bet going on to see who can get the most numbers tonight."

"Haaahha, what!" Chris laughed at Larry. "You finna be broke."

Larry smacked his teeth. "Man whatever yall haters just watch and take notes. Matter-of-fact I'ma' get mo' numbers than you and you da one throwin' the party, that's how much game I got."

"Anyway." Chris responded to Larry's ridiculous statement. "Yall some lying asses, I thought chall was comin' early to help me move all the furniture and help me set up everythang."

"That's Big Will's fault." Shawn quickly pointed the blame. "He ain't get out the house 'til nine and after he picked all of us up he rode around damn near the whole Augusta lookin' for some weed and you know it's a drought."

"Weed? Why the fuck was yall lookin' fa' weed I got weed, it ain't no drought 'round here."

"Yeeesss! That's what I'm talkin' about." Will said.

"Well I guess yall didn't find none."

"Hell naw." Shawn answered with disappointment.

"Don't even trip I got-cha'." Chris said then took a swig from his bottle of beer. "Now it's a cooler of beer in the kitchen, it might be some wangs left but I-'on't know, you know how high niggas act when they get around some chicken wangs. The liquor is on the kitchen counter, now check out how I did it. I put the Hennessey in a Royal Club bottle, the Couvossior in a Canadian Mist bottle and the Canadian Mist is in the Couvossior bottle, the Seagram's gin is in the Glenn Moore bottle and then Glenn Moore gin is in the Seagram's bottle. To make a long ass explanation short, all the good shit is in the cheap shit bottles and vice versa. That's to keep these fools from drankin' up my good-shit, but keep that on the low, don't nobody know but yall. Oh and it's a girl here named Kelly T. out of all the mothafuckas in here she's the only one that knew the difference, wit' her drunk ass. Girl just turned seventeen and already been to AA."

"Damn!" Tracy replied.

"Now if yall run into a freak and you wanna beat, the fuckin' room is the last door on the left. I got paper towels in there so it ain't no need to be nuttin' on the bed or on my flo'. Now if yall boys wanna blaze yall smoke in the garage."

"The garage?" Tracy asked. "I thought you was lettin' people post up and burn outside."

"Hell naw! This may be Pepperidge but police ride trough here too."

"Well shit you better tell that to them cats chiefin' in yo' drive-way." Tracy informed.

"In my driveway!" Chris eyes widen from the info.

"Yep it's 'bout fo' of 'em out there chiefin'." Will said.

Chris hurried to his front door, opened it and shouted. "A man, what the fuck ya'll doin'!"

"Whaaat's up man?" One of the smokers said in a slow manner.

"What's up!" Chris said rhetorical, dismayed at the fact that the smoker would even ask that, he should have known what was up. "Take that shit to the garage police be ridin' through here. Yall tryin' to get me locked up."

"Oh my-bad folk we aint know." Another smoker said. The four complied and headed to the garage.

"Ole disobedient ass mothafuckas. See, see why I 'on't like yall thugs." Chris complained to Kevin. "Yall just don't give a fuck, yall get niggas locked up."

"You need me to get some tissue?" Kevin asked.

Chris looked confused. "Some tissue?"

"Yeah some tissue for all that cryin' you doin'… Oh shit who is that DJin'?" Kevin squinted through the crowd of dancers across the room to the DJ. "That aint my boy is it?"

"Yeah that's Carlos." Chris answered.

"Damn I thought that nigga was still in the hospital."

"Naw he got out about three days ago."

"Let me go holla at my dog C-Los real quick, I'll get back up wit'-chall later. And don't smoke wit'-out me, I know how yall do." Kevin departed from his comrades and shoved his way through the crowd of dancers over to the DJ.

"Shit I'ma' 'bout to get up on these whoes" Larry said licking his two index fingers then smoothed down his eye brows once again. "You might wanna peep the technique."

"What technique?" Will asked with a grin. "The only whoes you gettin' wit' is those holes in yo' draws. You might wanna follow me LL and hit these bottles and get fucked up wit' me cause you aint finna pull nothin' tonight, wit' that big ass funny lookin' hat on."

"Hater, you say that now Big Will but watch, watch when we leave here, I might even have enough whoes to let you barrow a few." Larry then began to walk off with a stride as if he was the coolest person in the party until he tripped over his own foot. A few people that were close enough witnessed the fumbling fool laughed. A distant voice shouted from the crowd of dancers.

"You alright cuz?"

"A fellas I'm about to fix me a drank I'll holla at chall." Tracy said.

"Hold up T-Murray I'll drank wit'-cha'. Anyway I do need to show yo' ass how to drank."

"Shit look how big you is, it'll probably take a half gallon of gin just for you to get a buzz."

"Shiiiitttt, don't let that be da reason."

"We'll holla at-cha' later Shawn."

"A, A, C-LOS!" Kevin shouted over the music at the DJ. "C-LOS. Damn this nigga can't hear me." He mumbled then attempted to walk around the table that held up the equipment until he tripped and almost fell. He looked down to see what had almost sent him tumbling and saw a pair of legs that belong to a boy that sat on the floor with his back against the concert speaker asleep with vomit on his shirt. "Damn, now dat don't make no damn sense to be that fucked up. C-LOS." He shouted again and was about to wave his hand to get the DJ's attention, but Carlos had just turned his back to dig through his crate of CDs. Kevin walked around the table and was about to tap on Carlos' shoulder when he turned and noticed a finger in his peripheral.

"Oh-shit, what's up Killer Kev!" Carlos shouted pulling his headphones down off his ears to rest around his neck. "My mothafunkin dawg, what's going on man?" Carlos greeted Kevin with some solid dap and a quick short but meaningful embrace.

"Nothin' much, what's happenin' wit'-chew?"

"Trying to get this cheese, you know me."

"True-true I hear you. I see you outta the hospital, you alright?" Kevin said with modest concern.

"Yeah-yea I'm alright. Walk wit' me let's get somethin' to drank." Carlos took off his headphones and pushed a few buttons on his Numark CD Mix 3, turned and retrieved a mahogany cane that rested against a speaker. As they made their way into the kitchen, Kevin noticed that Carlos was still in pain from his ordeal seeing that he was almost totally dependent on his cane. "Yeah cuz I'm doing alright, I mean, I'm alive and shit, I ain't in no wheelchair, thank God. I'm still dealing with pain and I'll be walkin' with my pimp stick for who knows how long, but it's cool. My doctor got me poppin' Percocet like Skittles, the strongest kind made, so I get a lil buzz out of it, but I'm alright."

"I feel ya-I feel ya. But what really went down I'm hearing all kinds of rumors?"

"Like what?" Carlos asked with a sneaky grin as he reached for a Hennessy bottle.

"Oh naw C-Los you don't want that shit, get the other bottle."

"Which one?"

"The Royal Club bottle."

"Hell naw, I don't drank that cheap shit."

"Naw C-Los that ain't Royal Club in that bottle, that's Hennessy."

"Then what's in here?" C-Los asked still holding up the half-full Hennessy bottle.

"That's cheap ass Royal Club."

"For real?"

"Yep, that nigga Chris swopped it out so everybody won't drank up all the good shit."

"Hell naw, Chris wit' his slick ass, and I'm the DJ he could at least told me. That's alright it's gonna come back on his slick ass, that cheap shit is finna have people in here fightin' and tearin' up shit, watch. So what chew heard Kev?" Carlos asked with a sneakier grin on his face.

"Man I heard all kinds of shit. First I heard yo' girl caught chew cheatin' and unloaded a clip in yo' ass. Then I heard you got shot up breakin' in somebody's crib. Then I heard you got shot tryin' to rob Frank's liquor sto'." With his cup to his mouth about to take a sip, Carlos gave another, yet less defined sneaky grin. "What chew smilin' fa' one of 'em true?" Kevin asked as he poured gin into his cup from the Glenn Moore bottle.

"Naw, hell naw. I made all that shit up, none of dat shit is true. I spread all dem rumors to keep people outta my business, you feel me?"

"Yea, I feel ya'." Kevin took a sip of his gin. "Well can you tell ya' boy what really went down?"

"Yea-yea, I can tell you." Carlos said as he took a strong gulp as if to drown out the pain of his ordeal. He then began his tale.

"You know I was fuckin' 'round wit' T-Money?"

"T-Money, Terrell Samuels use to call 'em 'Rell?

"Yea."

"Naw I aint know that."

"Yea I was gettin' weight on the weed tip from that nigga."

"Fo' real, I heard you shouldn't fuck wit' dat nigga cause he dirty as hell."

"Yea I know that now, but I ain't know that then I had to learn the hard way. He had the weight fa' the low-low, I'm payin' forty bones fa' an ounce and they was weighin' thirty-two grams not no damn twenty-eight."

"Damn that's a lic."

"I know that's why I was fuckin' wit' 'em and it was good weed. I was sellin' QPs (quarter ponds) in a day. One time I sold a QP in like two hours. I was boomin' that erb. Then I decided to move on up to pounds. I went to go holla at 'em fa' two of 'em right." Carlos took a sip of his Hennessey and continued. "He sat me down and started talking to me, he was like.

'Damn Cuz you movin' dem trees pretty good.'

I was like yea, I damn near got two high schools sewed up. He was like.

'That's what I'm tawkin' 'bout, you know how to get that money, dat's da kinda' nigga I need on my team know what I mean.' I was like yea agreein' wit' 'em and shit, but in my head I was yellin' man just hurry up and serve me so I can go." Kevin nodded with a grin then sipped his gin. "Then he said.

'If you wanna make some real money instead of that slow dough, then you gotta' move on up to the big leagues, like this here.' That's when this nigga dropped a brick of that thang on the table."

"Damn how much was it?"

"Half ah key."

"So what chew do?"

"Shit, I tried to get out of it smooth cause I ant won't no dealins' wit' no dust or no hard, I can't do that type of time and that nigga was known to act stupid. So I shot 'em a quick lie, I said. A cuz I 'on't know too much about that coke, I 'on't know how to cut it, break it down, weigh it up, nothin'. He was like.

'I'll show you, it ain't that hard, no different than weighin' up that weed. It ain't that hard.'

Then I shot 'em another lie, I said. It ain't just that, it's my brother, he's a heavy snawter and he might fuck around and find my shit and dip in it, or hit me up fa' da whole thang and that's a whole lotta' shit to be tryin' to replace. I ain't got it like that and I definitely ain't tryin' to fuck up yo' money. He was like.

'You know somethin' 'Los, I can respect that and since you been real wit' me I'm still goin' look out fa' ya'. How 'bout chew be my runner? Pick up weight, drop off money, you know shit like that.'

I thought to myself that sounds easy and then I thought about that cat Lil Tech and how he came up and started ballin'."

"Lil Tech from Sunset?"

"Yep."

"But he sold dope didn't he?"

"Yeah, but first he was runnin' dope fa' dat cat Gunswanger."

"No shit, I ain't know that."

"Yep he stacked his paper and got wit' a few of Gunswanga's connects and came up. That's what I planned to do, 'til shit got fucked up."

"So you said yeah?"

Carlos nodded and took another sip. "I said yea, he left the room and came back wit' a book bag and gave it to me. I opened it and it was two Glock nines wit' two extra clips and a box of bullets, he was like.

'That's fa' you cuz, just in case you ever get into some shit.'

I should of known right then that this shit was 'bout to get ugly."

"Damn. So what went down?"

"I started makin' pickups and drop-offs fa' T-Money, only a few times I would drop shit off at a trap, most of the time it was to older cats wit' families, good ass jobs, business men, and even doctors it was almost never a street nigga. It would be a quarter-key, a couple of ounces, shit like that, nothin' more than a half of kilo. Then one day this nigga' calls me up for a drop, I gets to his house and this fool got two keys on the kitchen table, I said.

Damn man this is a lot of shit here. He said.

'Yeah Los, now if you can't handle it I'll get somebody else to do it.'

Now in da' back of my mind I was like, I shouldn't fuck wit' it but like a dumbass I said yeah I can handle it. So he tells me where to go, the Red Carpet Inn."

Kevin's facial expression changed to a concern one. "Oh hell naw."

"Yeah I felt da' same way. So I'm comin' up Gordon Highway and the Red Carpet is on my left, I scope it out and I see the police over there, off da' rip I get scared and nervous so I pulled into the Waffle House across the street and parked facing the motel, and just watched it. It wasn't nothin' just a couple of young niggas out there fightin'. So I got me somethin' to eat while thangs cooled down, you know waited 'til the police left. So I drive over there, parked, got out and strap up 'cause you know da' Red Carpet, anythang can happen. I knock on room 116 and this big ugly ass nigga wit' fucked up braids and a gold grill open the do' and just stared at me, didn't say shit. I said.

What's up man, T-Money sent me, he finally said.

'Oh come on in shawty.'

When I heard dat I knew where he was from."

"ATL." Kevin said.

"Hell yeah you know dem Atlanta niggas call everybody shawty males and females. I walk in da' room and it's 'bout eight niggas crammed into that little ass room, all of 'em had on white T's and Dickies, gold grills, braids and dreads, and all of 'em was strapped. I even saw a shotgun leaning against the bed, I was nervous as fuck. I thought that was it these niggas is finna rob me, I was ready to shot it out wit' these niggas, but they was real cool. All of 'em was smokin' and they had a pound of purple on the table, they even offered me to hit the blunt but I was like naw. See I wanted to be on my P's and Q's just in case somethin' went down. But nothin' happened, these cats was real cool gave me a dub of their weed fa' free, told me to be careful it's that thang and even made a joke about Augusta niggas ain't ready for that ATL Assassin, some kind of fye ass weed they got in da' A. They was some ole courteous-ass-thugs. Big dude showed me the money, I gave 'em da dope and I was on my way, that simple. Now I'm drivin' back down Gordon Highway when it hits me. Why in da hell is niggas from Atlanta comin' to get weight from little ass Augusta, it's usually the other way 'round and dope in Atlanta is cheaper, the shit didn't feel right."

"Yeah that shit is kinda odd."

"So at this point I'm paranoid as hell, every thirty seconds I'm checkin' my rearview mirror fa' da County, Feds, jakers anybody, Glock in my hand. I make it to South Side and instead of parkin' in front of his buildin' I parked in da' back 'cause somethin' was tellin' me not to park in da front, it still didn't feel right. I walked around da buildin', spoke to the three niggas that's always in front of T-Money's buildin' shootin' dice. I knocked on the do' and T-Money let me in. He asked me.

'Everythang straight?'

Like he always do, I said yea and gave him the money. I sat on da' couch while he sat at the kitchen table and counted the money, like always. I was watchin' Half Baked and thankin' 'bout that 'purp' while I waited for him to finish countin' and pay me like he always do." Carlos took another sip of his Hennessy while Kevin sipped his Gin. "Then all of a sudden I heard this nigga shout.

'What da' fuck!'

Right then my stomach turned and I dropped my head, somethin' was wrong. I said what's up T-Money? And in a hard as voice he said.

'Come here C-Los let me show you somethin'. I walked into the kitchen up to the table and I asked 'em what's up? He handed me a stack of money and said 'count it'. I started countin', one hunned, two hunned, three, four, five up to a G. I put that stack to da' side and picked up another one and started countin'. One hunned, two hunned, three... Then I got to a hunned dollar bill that didn't feel or look right. While I'm starin' at da' bill this nigga T-Money pulls out his nine and lays it on da' table and said.

'Umhum.'

See Kev what it was, you remember last summer when all that funny money came from Atlanta and niggas was gettin' ripped off wit' that counterfeit shit?"

"Yea I remember, I bought some from Moony, he sold me two hunned for a dub. So the money was fake?"

"Yep. Now when I saw da pistol on da table I knew what time it was, so I started tryin' to reason wit' 'em. I was like. Look T-Money man... I ain't know man... I ain't know man... I ain't have shit to do wit' this. He just nodded his head and said.

'I Know.'

I mean you know how I am 'bout cha' shit, man... I, I, I'm careful. He kept on noddin'.

'I know. But what I don't understand is why in da hell you

didn't count da shit befo' you left da motel?'

I was scared as hell Kev, my voice was tremblin' cuz. I said, 'cause T-Money man, man it was like eight mothafuckas in there and all dem niggas had heat, shot guns and shit, mean muggin' me and shit. I-I-was I was nervous as hell, I thought dem niggas was gonna fuck me up or somethin'.

'Nigga I'll fuck you up or somethin'!'

I know man but, but I'll get-cha' money back, all of it, I'll replace every dollar cuz.

'I know, I'ma' give you a chance to make this money back.'

Now when he said that Kev, I thought I was straight, I thought everythang was cool, until this nigga said.

'But first I gotta give you somethin' to let you know I don't bullshit when it comes to my money.'

"I said huh, and as soon as I said that he was reachin' for da pistol, that's when I snapped and just reacted. I pushed dat nigga hard as I could, he started fallin' back over da chair, Kev I ain't even stay long enough to see him to da flo'. I turned and started haulin' ass to da' front do', the whole time I was starin' at the do' knob waitin' for da first shot cause I knew it was comin'. Sure enough he started bussin'. Pow-pow-pow and as I was runnin' I could hear them bitches flyin' pass my head I mean whistlin' pass me, shush-shuush-shuush. Pow-pow-pow-pow, my heart was pounding, this nigga was still missin', but soon as I grabbed the do' knob, pow. I felt one of dem bitches hit me in the back of my left arm." Carlos turned slightly, lifted his sleeve to reveal the barely healed bullet wound in his tricep.

"Damn C-Los!" Kevin said getting a close look at his arm.

"Yea it's alright though, it ain't hurt as bad as I thought it would. Kinda' felt like a cigarette burn, it's straight. Anyway, I opened the front do' and da' three niggas that was out front shootin' dice was runnin' up to da' do', I pushed open da screen do' hard as hell just as the first one had ran up to da' do' knockin' him into da cat behind him puttin' both of them niggas on the ground, then pow. T-Money caught me in the back." Carlos turned and lifted up his shirt to reveal another barely healed bullet wound just below his left shoulder blade. "That one felt like somebody had pushed da' shit outta me, it knocked me forward and I would of fell if it wasn't for da' other nigga. I ran into him knockin' him down but I stayed on my feet and on kept on runnin' and that's when all of 'em started bussin', I heard all kinds of gunshots. I ain't look back fa' shit I was Mike Vickin' it up-out dat bitch and as soon as I got ready to turn da' corner and get to the back street where I was parked, pow. One of dem mothafuckas shot me in my ass cuz, right on my left ass cheek. I ain't finna show you that one."

"I-on't wanna see it neither." Kevin said with a grinning frown.

"But it didn't stop me, I made it to my ride, jumped in, crunk it up, reversed outta the spot, and as I put it in drive as they was comin' 'round da' corner, bussin'. They shoot out my back window and I could hear da' bullets hittin' my trunk as I mashed out. I ducked down so they wouldn't hit me, I couldn't even see where I was going, then they just stopped shootin'. I sat up confused, scared, crunk, adrenaline runnin' I ain't know where to go. My first thought was to go home, cause I ain't even feel da' bullets except fa' da' one in my ass cause I was sittin' on it. I wasn't even thankin' 'bout 'em 'til all of a sudden I got real tired and I couldn't catch my breath. I was takin' real short breaths and the left side of my chest had started hurtin'. I said to myself I probably gotta collapsed lung or somethin', I better take my ass to da' hospital. So I hit

MARCUS T. JONES

Fifteenth Street haulin' ass I'm swervin', hittin' mailboxes and shit, wide open. Then I hit MLK (Martin Luther King Boulevard). I flew cross dat jank, ran the light and all. So now I'm comin' up to Josey High School and I started feelin' dizzy and woozy like I was about to pass out so I thought I'll go through Sunset projects and get pulled over by da' police 'cause you know how da' police be deep out there in hot ass Sunset. I figured I'll go through Sunset wide open get pulled over, and da' police would see a nigga bleedin' and would rush me to da' hospital. But guess what?"

"What?"

"Not one damn police."

"That's how it is, they ain't never around when you need 'em."

"Yea, out of all nights. They be everywhere like roaches when you doin' dirt, when a nigga needs help they're like cats around a Chinese restaurant, missin'."

Kevin smiled at the comparison and took another sip. "Hell yea."

"So now I'm swervin' tryin' to stay up, mothafuckas out there grindin' start runnin' 'round and tryin' to get outta da' way and shit cussin' me out and yellin'. Kev, I'm all up on da' curb and shit, on da' other side of da' street, side swipin' cars and shit. Then I finally makes it outta Sunset and almost hit two crack heads comin' out of that corner store..."

"Lee's." Kevin answered.

"Yea that's it. I took a sharp turn, you know, where Wrightsboro Rd. meets R.A. Dent Boulevard."

"Yea at da' train tracks."

"Yea, I got right there and tried to make that right and lost it. The car started flippin' all over Wrightsboro Road, then I gets thrown from the car. Kev, it seemed like I was in da' air for about

22

thirty minutes cuz, then. Baaamm! I hit the ground, landed on my back. I ain't even try to get up, I just laid there, tryin' to breathe and lookin' up at da' stars wit' a loud ringing in my head. I said fuck it, this it, I'm finnna' die right here in Gilbert Manor projects. I closed my eyes and waited, the ringin' in my head stopped and I could hear people talkin'. I guess the whole neighborhood either heard or saw what happened. I heard people sayin' shit like. 'Buddy dead!' 'What happened?' 'Man you saw dat?' 'Man dat nigga was flyin' cuz.' 'Oh dat nigga fucked up.' I even heard a nigga say. 'Check that nigga pockets."

"Damn, heartless ass niggas."

"Naw, they was cool they helped me. A cat came over and said. 'Cuz you alright?'

I opened my eyes and guess who was standing over me."

"Who dat'?" Kevin said pouring another cup of gin.

"You remember dat cat Black Pat?"

"P-funk, use to hang wit' Hammer."

"Yea that's him. He helped me up, him and one of his homeboys, I guess they was out there grindin' and saw da' whole thang. They helped me to my feet, well really they had to hold me up because I couldn't stand on my own. And guess what I said when they stood me up. See when they was helpin' me up it was this female standin' in front of me askin' was I alright, I lifted my head and in my face was two big ass, juicy ass, huge ass, titties. They sat in a white tank-top and her nipples was hard. Then I said weak as hell, damn you got some big ole titties."

"Hell naw you 'bout to die and all you can thank about is some titties."

"Hell yea, that cat Pat laughed and said. 'You don't need to be worried about no titties right now cuz.'

One of his homeboys drove over to where we was at, they put me in da' back and drove me to University. I woke up three days later wit' tubes and IVs and shit all in me. My momma, sisters, and my brother was in my room. They had me hooked up to a machine that helped me breathe 'cause I had a collapsed lung. I was in intensive care fa' fo' days and you know what, the whole time I was hooked up to them machines and couldn't talk, these dumb ass detectives kept askin' questions like. Who shot me, was my accident related to gun shots heard in South Side, do I know a Terrell Samuels aka T-Money. Shit like dat. One of 'em was a rookie, I could tell cause da' cat looked too damn young to be a DT. I lied and told them that some niggas down on Eastbound had robbed me and nope I wouldn't be able to identify 'em. The doctors they kept me for about two and a half weeks after I got outta ICU. So all together I was in that bitch damn near a month cuz. When I got out I looked at life a whole lot different now. I said fuck these streets, they ain't goin' do nothin' but end up killin' my black-ass. So I'm leavin' that shit alone and focusin' on this music thang. You know, do this DJ thang, parties and what not, stack my paper move to da' ATL, and get me a studio together. Shit I actually had stacked up enough paper to do that runnin' fa' T-Money but I had to spend all that on doctor bills."

"I feel ya cuz, these streets is cold than a mothafucka. I hope you come up on that music tip. But let me ask you somethin'. You don't be thankin' 'bout gettin' that nigga back?"

"Hell yea, every damn day. I wanna kick in his do', rob his ass and slap his fat ass around wit' da pistol, you know what I'm sayin'."

"Shit you should do more than that, kill that nigga, shit he tried to kill you."

"Naw, I would just rob his ass, that'll be enough, 'cause you know dat nigga is sittin' on about six mill."

"…What!" Kevin said in the midst of a swallow of gin causing him to choke. "Are you serious, six million dollars, you bullshittin'."

"I bull-shit-cha-not Kev. I heard he was sittin' on two befo' I started fuckin' wit' 'em, then I heard he robbed dat Jamaican last year."

"You mean the one they found behind the old Regency Mall?"

The Regency mall was a huge and popular shopping center in Augusta that is now closed and abandoned. It was a major hang out spot for teenagers and young adults in the early eighties and mid ninties.

"Yep. The rumor is that he robbed 'em, cut his throat, and dumped him on JC Penny's front do' step. They say T-Money got 'em fa' fo' mill, two and fo' is six."

"Damn! That's mo' reason for you to get his ass. Shit if you need some help I'm wit' it, I got-cha' back, just let me know when ya' ready, fa' real."

Carlos smiled. "I hear ya' Kev, but you know wit' that kinda money ain't no nigga finna just hand it over, ain't just finna lay it down and let you take it, not wit'-out a fight. You gotta burn dat cat, and to be real wit'-cha', I ain't no killer Kev."

"Shit, you ain't gotta do it, I handle that part fa' ya', ain't nothin', for that kinda money it's whatever wit' me."

Replying with a slight laugh. "Yea I know you would Killer Kev, yo' crazy ass. But naw, I ain't finna fuck around, I'm leavin' them streets alone and focusin' on this music thang."

"I feel ya' and good luck on that to cuz."

"Preciate that Kev. But shit while we talkin' 'bout music let me get to my mixin' befo' my program end. I'ma' holla at cha' later Kev, get fucked up and shot da' shit."

"Oh hell yea that's a bet, go on and do yo' thang C-Los. I'll holla at cha'. It's good seein' you folk."

"You too Kev."

After giving each other dap and a masculine shoulder to shoulder embrace, Carlos walked off with the help of his cane and his cup of liquor in his other hand. He tried to hide his limp with a cool stride but his temporary handicap was too overwhelming. Kevin watched as Carlos walked off with a feeling of pride and admiration for his friend that had survived such a dangerous and life threatening ordeal. He put Carlos on a new level. Then he thought of T-Money, a man he didn't favor too much himself due to his part in the destruction of his family. However, he would later find out that T-Money had contributed to more of the destruction of his family's life than he could have imagined. With his cup to his lips he said to himself. "Damn, six million muthafuckin' dollars, the thangs I could do wit' that."

Across the room, Larry was trying with extreme desperation to win the bet that he had made with Michael earlier. Sitting uncomfortably next to a pretty girl he struggled with lame pick up lines.

"A shawty where ya' man at?"

Responding with obvious attitude she said with her face twisted up as if she smelled something awful and fowl. "At home where yo' ass should of stayed."

"Damn baby why it gotta be like dat?"

She stood up and before she walked off she said. "Damn nigga why yo' breath gotta be like dat!"

"Oh dat's fucked up, you ain't gotta be all loud wit' da' shit." Larry quickly shook off the insult and tried again with an even prettier girl, way out of his league, about ten feet away. "A, A."

Larry shouted over the music. "A lil momma, what's up?"

She looked at Larry with a mean stare and shouted as she walked off. "Fool I ain't cha' mamie, and if I was I would of locked yo' ass in da' basement."

Larry stood paralyzed by the insult while he watched her disappear into the crowd. He then leaned over and said to a boy dancing with a girl. "Shit she wasn't that fine anyway." Larry continued his hunt. He scanned the floor of dancers and within seconds he struck gold. A tan colored petite female, with shoulder length glossy and wavy hair, tight and revealing clothes, and a cup in her hand dancing by herself. Larry ran over to her as if his life depended on it and began grinding on her from behind. The girl turned around with a smile that was pretty as her body. The DJ began mixing into the song 'Soldier' by Destiny's Child, which excited the obviously drunk girl, causing her to throw her hands in the air, wasting liquor in the process and yell out.

"Woooohhhh Shhhiitt! That's my shhoung! Youuh goin' be my-my shoulder bahaby?" The girl fumbled over her words.

"Hell yea, I'll be whatever you want me to be baby."

"Ouuhhwee, thhhattsss whaaat I'm tawlkin' about bahaby! Wiilll..." The girl stumbled and if it wasn't for Larry holding her, she would have fallen over face first. "...Wiilll you be my freeaak, nasty?"

"Hell yeah, I'm down for whatever." Larry said as he gripped her bottom with both hands. "You must don't know what they call me?"

"Whhhaaat's dat?"

"They call me LL."

"Whhaaat, what... dat stand fa'?" The girl said as she took a moment to swallow some vomit that had rose up in her throat.

"Lick 'em Larry, 'cause I'll lick you like you never been licked befo', lick you dizzy." Larry was completely surprised to have gotten as far as he did. She was digging him and even with her alcohol and vomit polluted breath that was invading his nostrils, it didn't stop his noticeable erection that was poking her in her pelvis.

"Oooh La-Larry I se-seee you already ready! My name is Kelly dey call me Kelly T. Youuou goin' show me why they call you luh-lick 'em Larry?"

"Hell yea we can go in one of dem back rooms and I'll show you somethangs you ain't never heard of." Larry couldn't believe how much success he was having with Kelly T. He felt that he needed to act fast before she changed her mind or something messes up the moment and his plans but before he could react, it happened.

"Oohh come on let's go to da' back ro…" Kelly pushed away only an inch then. *Huuaacwkaawwack!*" Kelly released warm vomit all over Larry's shirt, some even got in his face. Couples that were dancing nearby hurried out of the way as if someone had pulled out a gun. Kelly continued to empty her belly on Larry and all he could do was stand there and accept it. Everyone that saw the embarrassing action was in complete laughter. Some held their stomachs bent over in laughter, while some were on their knees unable to stand because they were laughing so hard. Even his comrade Kevin that was on the other side of the room shook his head and laughed as he poured himself another drink. The girl seemed to be finished and as Larry began to walk off in shame, she asked.

"Baahhbay can yooouu walk me outside, I need some air."

"Hell naw, look at what chew did to my new shirt." Just as Larry uttered that, a boy snapped a picture with his camera phone.

"Oh shit I'ma' put this on my, MySpace page!"

Then a girl did the same and said. "Facebook, hell yea."

"You nasty bit..." Before he could finish another stream of vomit shout from her mouth, this time landing on Larry's new sneakers. The laughter erupted even louder and more cell phones were pulled out and more pictures were snapped. Larry yelled out. "Gurl!" Then stormed off heading to the bathroom to clean himself off. He ran pass Kevin that yelled out.

"Go-head playa-playa." As Larry hurried down the hall, people laughed as they jumped out of his way. He grabbed the doorknob but only to find it locked.

"Shit!" He uttered wiggling the handle.

"Hold up somebody is in here!" A male's voice shouted from the other side. Larry stood at the door in the crowded hallway impatient and embarrassed.

"Hurry up man!"

"Wait man, shit!"

People walked by him staring, some laughed while some frowned in disgust as they caught a whiff of his new odor. Some shot insults at him. "Damn, that nigga smell like cottage cheese!"

"Boy you smell like a three day old fart!"

"I like yo' shirt!"

Trying to reply with a come-back Larry shouted. "It was a gift from yo' momma!" Not noticing Michael standing behind him writing down a female's phone number. He tapped Larry on his shoulder. "What!" Larry uttered in frustration as he turned around. The quick turn threw a gust of funk in Michael and the girl's face he was talking to.

"Ewe shit! What happen to you?"

"Oh, um some fool couldn't hold his liquor and threw up on me. I was about to whip his ass but everybody was like naw, buddy is just drunk he 'on't know no better. But I was like fuck that shit, this fuck-boy just threw up on me! So I cocked back gettin' ready to knock his ass out, 'cause you know me I don't take no shit. But then this fine ass girl jumped up and was like naw baby don't do it. So, I was like cool I 'on't even wanna mess up Chris' party, so I let it ride." Just as Larry finished his obvious lie, a boy approached him.

"Damn cuz, that's fucked up how Kelly T. did you, she's a freak too you could of hit dat. Better luck next time."

As the boy walked off Michael began shaking his head. "Lyin' Ass Larry." He said as he walked off with his arm around the girl.

"That's alright 'cause I'm still gonna get mo' whoes than you. They goin' call me Pimp Puke, 'cause I'm too damn cute…"

In the midst of his rhyme, a boy came out of the bathroom and immediately caught a whiff of Larry's shirt. "Damn you stank."

"I know you ain't talkin' Shit Stains I bet-cha' didn't wipe yo' ass good. I bet-cha' got shit skid marks all in yo' draws." The boy gave Larry the middle finger, as Larry entered the bathroom.

"We finally did it Shawn, we're finally leavin' that jank." Chris said as he leaned against the wall in the hallway.

"Hell yea, my momma is happy as R. Kelly at a girl-scout meetin', she thought I wasn't gonna graduate."

"Me too, my momma was panicking this year."

"What chew mean Chris you always balled out in school, you kept good grades."

"She was worried about that mothafuckin', graduation test. I kept on failin' the math and social studies parts."

"Damn, I ain't know that."

"Hell-yeah." Chris took a swig from his beer. And the crazy thang about it, it was cats that was takin' general math acin' the math portion, I was ballin' out in advance algebra and failed the math portion twice. It was like everybody that was skippin' school, comin' to school high and bullshittin' in class, was the ones passin' the whole test while honor roll cats was failin' different portions of it."

"I know what-cha' mean I took all five parts of the test high and passed wit' high scores. I amazed myself... Oh!" Shawn said snapping his fingers as he remembered something. "You remember Satash Stolkley that went to middle school wit' us?"

"Yea I remember her, what adout 'er?"

"That girl tried me. See she was in my three thousand level citizenship class. On the day we got the test scores back I walk in the class a lil late and she ask me did I pass. I said yea, then she asked, all of 'em. I said yea all of 'em and she was like, for real, all in shock like I wasn't supposed to pass or somethin'. Then she looked around at all of her lil clique of brainy bitches then looked at me like a mothafuckin' museum exhibit or somethin'. I was mad as hell, she was lucky I was high 'cause if I was sober I would of snapped on 'er ass and cussed her out. See later on I found out a lot of them high level niggas was failin' different parts and it was eatin' they ass up to see a regular nigga like myself do better than them." Chris gave Shawn a slight mean stare.

"Yea I'm one of dem high level niggas."

Shawn laughed and replied." Please, don't hate that's just how thangs work."

"Naw that's just how the Richmond County school system is, but fuck it, I graduated with a diploma and not a certificate."

"I feel ya' cuz, me too."

"So now that we're outta that hell-hole what-cha' gonna wit-cha'-self?"

"Shit I 'on't know, I wanta go to school, but you know I got a seed on the way. So I'm just goin' snatched up a plant job until I get some money saved up to make some moves. My momma's friend got me a job at Carole Fabrics. I start Monday."

Chris nodded as he sipped his beer. "How about you come in the army with me." Shawn quickly turned his head and stared at Chris.

"What! You going in the military?"

"Yea."

"Why?"

"Shit, why not. It ain't shit here in Augusta but trouble. You should come in wit' me cuz."

"I ain't in the streets like that, and I ain't no military person."

"I know you ain't in the streets like that, but look at the company you keep."

"What?" Shawn sounded slightly offended. "What-chew you mean man?"

"I don't mean no disrespect, I'm bein' real wit-cha', them cats you hangin' wit' ain't nothin' but trouble." Shawn's expression revealed that he was on the defensive. "Look at cha' boy MJ, he's hell on the football field and on the court but with him chasin' females all the time, he fuckin' up his grades and on top of that if he keep on messin' with those slut- bucket whoes he goin' catch somethin', or a case fa' messin' wit'-ah young girl. I know he's ya' boy and all but that don't mean you gotta go down wit' 'em. Then it's ya' boy Larry, not only is he a big ass liar but he's a rape case in da' makin'."

"What! Come on Chris, I understand why he lie like he do, his home life ain't too pretty and Larry wouldn't hurt no female. Hell I 'on't know a female he can beat up wit' his fragile ass."

"Right now he wouldn't, but give 'em two or three mo' years

wit'-out gettin' some ass, oh-yea, he goin' end up takin' it one day. Okay now ya' boy Tracy he's straight, he's good people he's graduatin', he comes from a good family and he gotta good head on his shoulders. I'll give you him, he's cool to hang wit'. But then you got-cha' boy Killa Kev. I shouldn't even have to explain that one, his name says it all. He don't give a fuck about nothin' or nobody and you know how knuckle-head-ass niggas is these days, they ain't wit' takin' no ass-whippin', it's all about pistol play now. He goin' end up beatin' up the wrong person and get his self burnt. I hate to say the obvious but dat nigga got one foot in da' grave and another in the pen. It's just a matter of which one comes first. And last but not least ya' boy Big Will, I shouldn't have to say what's up wit' him either."

"Man I ain't even tryin' to hear that bullshit, it's just a rumor."

"Cuz, you ain't gotta accept it but it's real, he been kickin' it wit' Peaches from Sunset."

"That's because he's hittin' it."

"Shawn, Peaches only give up da' pussy fa' two reasons, for some money or coke, and if you payin' for it then you in and out in a couple of hours. I hear that cat Big Will be over there three and four days at a time, so you know what time it is. Face it dawg, your boy is a powder head. And you know what's next, sooner or later he's goin' be a rock star and it's fucked up because his folks is some educated successful people."

"Well I ain't never seen 'em do it or seen 'em geeked up. And if he is doin' it that's his business and he's still my boy, all of 'em my homeboys and all of us got problems and imperfections. I ain't finna turn my back on none of them."

"That ain't what I'm sayin', what I'm mean is sometimes you out grow ya' homeboys. I've known you since when, elementary, you've known them only since high school."

"So what that mean?"

"That means I know yo' ass a little bit better than they do, which means I wanna see you do good wit'-cha'-self. Know what I'm sayin'?"

"Yea I hear ya'. But that army thang, I ain't wit' going off to some country I 'on't know shit about, killin' folks that ain't did shit to me. I mean you got cats 17, 18,19, 20 years old going to war not knowin' when they're comin' home, or knowin' if they're even goin' make it home. They're old enough to die fa' this country but not old enough to buy a beer in this country." Shawn said thumping Chris' bottle. "That shit don't make no sense to me, that ain't no government I wanna die fa'."

"Yea you gotta point, but don't look at it like that. Look, you can go in for about two or fo' years and get out befo' anythang pop off. I gotta cousin that did six, never seen combat, he's a registered nurse, gotta degree in electronics, and they gave him twenty stacks. Thank about it Shawn, you can get paid to go to school, plus you gettin' in shape and you can travel all over the world. You can fuck women from Hawaii, Tibet, and Brazil. How many cats you know can say they fucked a Brazilian chic."

Shawn smiled and replied. "Not many."

"None. Or how about ah Indian woman, it's some fine ass females over in India, you can fuck all kinds of women in the army."

"You ain't finna fuck nothin' over there if you blowin' up their country, homes, husbands, brothers, and kids. And all that yellin' in ya' face and shit."

"So what, all they can do is yell at cha' it ain't like they can put their hands on you. And thank about it, what if you ridin' wit' cha' homeboys and somebody that Kevin done swung on sees 'em and start shootin' at chall, and let's say, God forbid, you get hit and killed. Do you got money put up fa' ya' momma our ya' seed on the way?"

"Nope."

"See, now if you was to get killed in one of those countries you don't know shit about or in a car accident two miles from yo' house in the Army, at least ya' folks get two hunned stacks. You gotta baby on the way, yo' decisions you make ain't gonna affect just you. And check it out, we can go in on the buddy system. Which means we'll go everywhere together. I'll watch yo' back you watch mine, that way it won't be so hard. At least thank about it for a couple of days."

Shawn pondered on Chris' advice and at first was almost offended to bitterness because of the way his old friend downgraded his other comrades. But, he did see the honest and genuine concern from his long time friend. "Alright I'll thank about it but I ain't makin' no promises."

"I ain't askin' you too."

Shawn was feeling uncomfortable and decided to change the subject. "Man where da' weed at, I'm at a party tryin' to relax, celebrate graduation, have a good time, and get fucked up, but here you go talkin' 'bout da' future, stability and responsibilities. Fuckin' up the atmosphere, and it's yo' party. Where the trees at?"

Chris started laughing. "Oh my-bad man, come on." Chris led Shawn down his crowded hallway and just as they got to the bathroom door, Larry was coming out wiping off his shirt with a nicely decorated towel. "Lyin' Ass Larry what's up man? Ooh-shit! Is that you smellin' like that?"

Shawn quickly added his insults. "Ewe! You stank ass lil-boy, you threw up on yo'-self, you supposed to aim that shit in da' toilet, or a trashcan not on yo'-self silly-ass boy."

"How you get that drunk that quick when you just got here?" Chris asked.

"Naw it wasn't me yall know I can handle my liquor." Chris and Shawn looked at each other. "It was some ole weak, baby-belly ass boy walkin' 'round here. See he was lucky that I respect ya' crib Chris 'cause I was 'bout to whip his ass."

Chris shook his head with a smile but it quickly disappeared quicker than it appeared when he noticed the towel Larry was using. "Fool! I'm 'bout to kick yo' ass! I know you ain't cleanin' that shit off wit' my momma good towel!"

"Oh my-dad folk, I thought that since you was throwin' a party you had put all the good shit up."

"Fool, do that look like a bad towel! Damn!"

Shawn shook his head. "Larry, you always fuckin' up... Oh yea, give me yo' five 'cause I'm 'bout to get the weed."

"My five?" Larry said somewhat confused.

"Yea yo' five, you did say you got five on da' weed."

"Yea, I did but um, I had to um, you know."

"Naw I don't know."

"Man I ain't got it."

"See you always do this shit, every-time it's time to put in on the green you either ain't got it or you pullin' out two funky-ass lil dollars."

Chris added to the insult. "I wouldn't smoke wit' 'em if I was you."

"I shouldn't."

"Come on Shawn don't act like that." Larry pleaded.

"You should smoke the whole blunt in his face and don't even let 'em hit it, then blow the smoke in his face."

"Hell yea." Shawn agreed.

"Come on Shawn you know I got-cha'. When that check come in from that wreck I was in, I'ma' be sittin' on stacks so high that I'm goin' get dizzy!" Shawn dropped his head in shame as he shook it, another one of Larry's lies. He continued. "Then I'ma' get a pound of dro' and you and me is goin' smoke until we forget how to breathe. Real talk. We goin' smoke so much weed that..."

Shawn quickly interrupted. "Shut up Larry! There you go wit' that bullshit about a wreck, you ain't never been in no wreck, it ain't no check comin', quit lyin' all the damn time. Shit. Just go get everybody else and tell 'em to meet me in the garage."

Larry hurried off, he looked back at Shawn and said. "That 'dro, a whole pound!"

As Chris led Shawn down the hall he looked back and asked. "So what chew want?"

"First of all is it any good?"

"Hell yea it's that Georgia Pine, that pretty green like the grass in ya' yard."

"I hope it don't smoke like that grass in my yard."

"Hell naw, it's some fye, why you done smoked the grass in ya' yard befo'?"

"What?" Shawn looked confused.

"Nothin'. But it's good, bet-cha' can't smoke a whole blunt by ya'self."

"We'll see, how 'bout you let cha' boy get the dime fa' da five."

Chris gave a slight laugh. "Ha-haa-no buddy, this weed is so good I should be chargin' ten dollars a blunt. But I'll let-cha' get the quarter for the dub."

"That'll work."

Chris took Shawn to the last door on their right, dug a set of keys from his pocket, and unlocked the door. "Close that behin' ya." He said on his way to his bed, he reached under and pulled out an old Nike shoe box. Shawn immediately started sniffing the air.

"Damn, I smelt that soon as you lifted the top. What's that a QP?"

"Yep a quarter pounder wit' cheese." Chris said as he picked out one of the four sandwich bags.

"Sale me an ounce."

"Oh no my brotha'. Chris said with a grin. I'm smokin' all of this, I'm just lettin' you get a quarter 'cause you my boy but that's it, that's all I'm sellin'."

"Why?"

"Cause, I gotta get clean before I take the physical and it's gonna be a long time before I taste Mary Jane's sweet pussy again. So I wanna go out wit' a bang and this is some of the best smoke I done had in months, makin' it even better."

"Where you got it from, so I can go holla at 'em?"

"Some cat form Burke County I met through Courtney Wells."

"Fine ass Courtney Wells from Hephzibah?" Shawn asked surprised.

Chris pulled out two long buds from the ounce as thick as his thumb and about two inches long. "You know it."

"That's you?"

"That's right."

"Damn Chris how you pulled that one, I heard she was stuck up?"

"Oh, that's just a front she put on 'cause cats just be tryin' to hit. See wit' females like her all you gotta do is be friends with 'em show no type of sexual intensions, treat 'em almost like a homeboy, and let it take it's course and in due time the panties will fall."

"So have the panties fell yet?"

"Hell naw." Chris said with frustrated disappointment.

Shawn chuckled. "Well how long yall been talkin'?"

"About three months."

"Oh that ain't too bad."

"Naw it ain't, and it ain't even 'bout that, ole girl is cool, she likes football and she's a hip-hop head, none of that shit they play on da' radio either. I'm talkin' Andre 3000, Field Mob, Nas, Dead Prez, Common, Mos Def, all kinds of underground cats I ain't even know nothin' 'bout, shit I like." Chris gave Shawn his bag of buds which was a lot more than what he was paying for.

"Okay then, so she's not like everybody say she is." Shawn said smellin' the bag. "Oohhwee! That's what I'm talkin' 'bout. You lettin' me get this fa' da dub?"

"Yea, you my boy and I want-chew to thank about what I told you and this shit will definitely have you thankin'."

"We'll see, I mean it looks and smells like that good but I had weed that looked and smelled good but smoked like pine straw."

"Damn Shawn how do you know how pine straw smoke?"

Shawn gave a guilty look and said. "Don't ask."

Chris laughed. "You's a fool. But on the real side it's some good shit. And to make it even better all the ounces weighed thirty-two grams not twenty-eight."

"Man! You need to hook me up wit' buddy, that's a good ass connect."

"I'll see, but you gotta do me a favor first."

"Like what?" Shawn said with a tone of suspicion.

"Let me take you to holla at my recruiter."

"There you go, I told you I'll thank about it."

Chris closed the shoebox, pushed it under the bed, and stood up. "Alright-alright I got-cha, I ain't finna rush you, but I'm takin' the physical in September. I want-chew to be wit' me."

"We'll see. You got a cigar?"

"Nope, but Corey sellin' 'em in the garage."

"You talkin' 'bout hustlin' ass C-Rock?"

"Yep."

"Man that cat can get his hand on anythang to make a profit."

"Hell yeah and I should be chargin' his ass rent for settin' up shop in my garage." Chris said closing and locking his room door.

Well shit I'm 'bout to get the rest of these fools and blaze up. You comin'?"

"Naw I'm straight, I finna go and try to talk Courtney into spendin' the night."

"When yo' momma comin' home?"

"Monday."

"Oh you set, do ya' thang cuz. I'll holla at-cha'."

Larry found it hard working his way through the floor of crowded dancers as he headed towards Tracy and MJ that danced with two females. It became even more difficult to make his way through when the DJ began mixing in a Lil Wayne hit 'Go DJ'. The crowd amped up more and people was bumped and pushed into Larry and each other. However, Larry made this work in his favor. As he walked through he manage to pinch, rub, and grip the butts of the females he passed, a skill Larry had mastered since eighth-grade from attending parties and clubs.

"A, T-Murray, Tracy-Tracy!" Larry shouted but Tracy's concentration was on the waist and bottom of the female that grind his pelvis. Larry got closer and tapped him on his shoulder, hard. "A-Tracy!" Tracy's attention was interrupted and he turned and answered with frustrated hostility.

"What man!"

"Shawn got the green man, he said meet 'em in the garage."

"Alright I comin'."

"A a MJ." Larry shouted tapping Mike on his shoulder.

"What's up?"

"We finna blaze man, meet us in the garage."

"Alright."

"Tracy, a Tracy, T-Murray!" Larry shouted in Tracy's ear.

"What now man!"

"You seen Big Will?"

"Naw, oh yeah-yeah I thank he's outside shootin' dice."

Larry maneuvered through the dancers while getting thrills on the way until he made it to the door. He found Will on one knee in the driveway in a half circle of four, and three standing around with money in their hands side betting. Big Will had the dice in his hand shaking them and talking loud over the others. "Okay-okay-okay what's my point-what's my point."

"Nigga you know what-chow point is, just roll the dice!" The boy on William's left argued.

"Yeah I know what it is, I just wanna hear yall say it so it won't be no confusion when I win all ya'll's money."

"Whatever rich boy, the point is eight." Another said from Will's right.

"Naw I ain't rich yet, but I'm finna be rich after I roll this eight, so don't hate, 'cause after these dice shake, yo' money I'm goin' take."

Larry was just as excited as Will, he was watchin' his comrade in rare form. William was hardly the one to be excited, he was calm, cool, talked calm, and seemed to walk without a purpose. Maybe it was his huge stature that he carried around that made him unenthused. Or it could have been that he was always high or drunk that gave him the sloth mentality. But right now he was alive and having a good time.

"Man just shot the damn dice, man!"

"Give it to me!" Will yelled out, as he tossed the dice against the garage door. Soon as they stopped rolling he snapped his fingers. "What dat is-what dat is-what dat is? Five!" He picked up the dice, blew in his hand and begun shaking them again when he noticed Larry approaching and watching. "A Larry come here and watch me take these fools money." He tossed the dice and snapped his fingers. "Uhhh-what dat is-what dat is. Nine. Okay-okay here it comes here it comes, get ready I'm finna send you niggas home broke!" Will boasted as he picked up the dice. "Here it come. A Jeff." Will said looking at the guy on his left. "Get ready to make up a lie to tell yo' girl why you can't get 'er hair done cause I'm finna take it all, uuhh!" Will tossed the dice. "Shit!" He shouted when the dice stopped rolling and displayed seven. The whole group of boys erupted into laughter.

"Aaaaahhhhahaha!" Jeff laughed as he scraped up money.

"Aaahhaha that nigga crapped out!" The boy on Will's right uttered.

"That's what-cha' get, talkin' all that noise. Now it look like I can get her hair and her nails done, and buy her some panties. Don't worry Big Will I'll let you smell 'em after she wear 'em. You know that's the least I can do since you payin' for 'em."

Big Will now back to his normal calm demeanor tried to save face. "Don't worry 'bout buyin' 'er none, cause she look better wit' none on."

"Ahh don't get mad rich boy."

Will shook his head in defeat as he watched the pile of money being collected and the laughs, jokes, and insults were being distributed. Then he looked at Larry. "Damn Larry you bad luck, I was breakin' them fools off befo' you came out here, what-chew want man?"

"I came out here to let you know we 'bout to blaze up."

"Alright, I'm comin, ya'll niggas' lucky I'm 'bout to go smoke, I was 'bout to bankrupt all you clowns."

"Yeah right." One of the winners said.

"Matter-of-fact, if ya'll still out here when I come back it's over, I'm gettin' those fresh Jordan's off Jeff's feet."

Jeff looked down at his feet then back at Will and Larry as they were walking off. "Oh don't worry we'll be right here, so make sure you come on back so we can win some mo' of that rich boy money."

"Damn I gave them clowns forty dollars." Will said full of disappointment as they walked in the house.

"Damn Will, forty." Larry replied.

"It's alright, 'cause after we finish smokin' I'm going back out there and win all my shit ba… What da fuck is that smell!" Will said with his hand over his nose. "You farted?"

"Naw that's my shirt, some fool threw up on me."

"You need to go and jump in a tub of bleach and Lysol or somethin' that shit is ridiculous."

"Well thanks for noticin', friend." Larry said shaking his head and walking.

"Hold up, let me fix a drank real-quick." Will said.

"Yea me too."

As they walked into the kitchen they noticed Kevin leaning

against the counter sipping from his red plastic Solo cup. "Look at 'em Larry, he's already fucked up. Cuz-o, how many cups you done had?"

"Shit, this my third."

"Oh so you 'bout straight huh?" Will said pouring from the Glenn Moore bottle while Larry poured from the Royal Club bottle.

"Hell yea, I'm tight." Kevin replied in a relaxed tone.

"We 'bout to head to the garage cuz, Shawn got the green."

"Alright, I'll be there in a minute."

Shawn opened the door and a cloud of marijuana smoke rushed out at him. "Damn." He mumbled as he walked into the garage, which was lit up by a green light, it was as if he had just walked into a different party. He walked by a card table where four teenage males played a game of spades while they passed around a marijuana blunt. He noticed in the center of the garage Corey sitting at a table with six boxes of different brands of cigars. He passed by a small couch positioned askew to his left with three girls sitting on it. The one closest to him gave him a flirty look with a mild smile. "Hey ladies how yall doin'?" The other two couldn't respond being that the one in the middle had the lit end of a blunt in her mouth and blowing smoke out of the opposite end, into the mouth and nose of the other girl (known as a shotgun).

"We doin' fine, how 'bout-chew?" The flirty one asked then snapped a picture with her cell-phone.

"Oh I'm 'bout to be feelin' good in a minute, what's da' picture fa'?"

"I hear ya'. Oh, MySpace, I want to remember the people that

I want to be my friend.

"Alright." Shawn said with one of his most swagger tone. He continued over to the table, passing a larger couch with a boy laid across it asleep, obviously unable to handle his intoxication. Shawn walked up to the table and with a deep tone trying to hide his natural voice. "A man let me get a strawberry Philly and a chocolate Swisher." Flipping through a bundle of twenties, fives, and ones the tall red skin male with dreads answered without looking up.

"Two dollars."

"Two dollars, them bitches ain't but 75 cent at One Stop."

"Well take yo' ass to One Stop." Corey said as he lift his head then noticed who it was. "Oh shit Whitney Houston done left Bobby, what's up man! Long time no see!" Corey stood up and greeted Shawn with some dap and a quick shoulder to shoulder.

"What's been up wit-cha', what cha' doin' for it?"

"Shit, you know me. Tryin' to keep a dollar in my pocket while I make five mo'."

Corey was a natural born hustler, anything that could be sold at a profit, he'll go out of his way to get it. It wasn't just the love of having bundles of everything from ones to fifties in his pocket but he also loved and fed off of, 'being da man' that had or can get anything you needed, he thrived on being 'da cat to holla at'. This reputation made him popular in school as well as a growing one in the South Augusta area.

"I hear you got a seed on da way?"

"Yep ole-girl fo' months now." Shawn replied with a hint of stress in his tone.

"Well cuz you ain't the only one, my shawty is three months."

"Dawg, what's goin' on, seems like everybody is loadin' their shawties up."

"You on point wit' dat shit. But how ya' momma' doin'?" Corey asked with a little more concern in his words.

"She's doin', workin' her life away fa' them crackers, tryin to pay the bills. But one day I'm goin' be payin' all of 'em for her."

"I hear dat cuz. So, how did she feel about da baby?"

"Mad as hell, and hurt. She wanted me to finish college first, or at least get in there good befo' I had a child."

"Well, at least you told yo' momma." Corey said dropping his head.

"Yo' momma' don't know?"

"Nope I'm too scared to tell 'er."

"Cuz, you need to go 'head and tell 'er, get that part out the way, that's the first major hump you gotta deal wit'."

"I know. I just don't know how to break it to 'er, how did you tell yours?"

"Oh, I was lucky, my momma got it crunk first, she popped it off. See 'round the time I started hittin' my girl on a regular, I notice I was always sleepy, I'm talkin' 'bout all day long. I'll take a nap soon as I got home from school then wake up when Big Will or MJ would hit me up. We'll smoke and I'll go right back home and go to sleep. Then I started being hungry all the time. Then after 'bout a month of that my girl hit me up and told me she's pregnant. Then, all that shit got worse, my back startin' hurtin'. After 'bout a month of bein' sleepy all the time, eatin' up everythang in the house and cryin' 'bout my back hurtin'. My momma said. 'Boy what's wrong wit'-cha.' I was like I 'on't know ma', I just ain't been feelin' right. She gave me this crazy ass look, stared at me fa 'bout five minutes and said. 'You done got that girl pregnant.' Shocked the shit out of me. I thought to myself, this was the best time than any and said. I thank so ma'."

"Damn, then what she said?"

"She shook 'er head and said. 'I knew it, that's why I been dreamin' about fish."

"Yea you got lucky. And I feel ya' on that sleepy and back hurtin' tip. My shit been killin' me cuz."

"That's that baby. Believe me she'll catch on, mommas know, grandmommas too, they can always sense a major change in a family, especially if yall close."

"True-true-true, so what's up wit'-cha' clique?"

"Oh they here matter-of-fact they supposed to meet me in here to smoke. Oh yea, let me get two cigars." Shawn said handing Corey two dollars. Corey shook his head.

"Naw man you straight, you know we go back like lil Lees wit' da knee patches." He handed Shawn two cigars without taking the money.

"Damn CJ you wouldn't hook us up and we go to the same school." One of the girls on the couch complained.

"That' because yall fine-asses is dikin' and ya'll won't let a nigga hit, and I know it's good, all three of yall." Corey began to perform his fake cry. "Especially you Rashika!" Corey now pointing at the girl sitting in the middle. "All you got to do is let me smell yours and I'll be happy, then you can get anythang you want."

"Boy you crazy." Shawn laughed at Corey's proposal.

Rashika blushing replied. "Maybe one day Corey, maybe one day."

"Baby why not today?" Corey begged. The girl sitting on Rashika's right, the one that smiled at Shawn earlier said.

"But not tonight baby tonight is a girl's night."

"See Rosalyn that's why yall gotta pay full price, 'cause yall won't share." The girls giggled.

Shawn scanned the garage and noticed a couple sharing a beanbag and a blunt. Next to them, he saw three guys sitting on milk-crates. Two of them was bobbing their heads and rocking back and forth to the rhythmic words that was flowing from the other's mouth. He was rapping, free-styling. Shawn's eyes then fixed on the fellow laid out on the couch with his right leg and arm hanging off the edge and a thick string of drool hanging from his bottom lip. "A CJ what's up wit' this cat, why he takin' up the whole damn couch?"

"Oh that fool came in here earlier talkin' loud about how he can out smoke everybody in here. He started drankin' wit' this girl Kelly T. and twenty minutes later he was out. Ole girl tried to wake 'em up to dance wit' 'er but he just started snoring. She got up and stumbled up out this jank. I can tell dat he don't go to Butler 'cause everybody know drunk-ass Kelly T."

"Why you ain't dance wit'-'er?"

"Because she'll end up passin' out on yo' ass or throwin' up on ya'. It never fails, she'll end up doin' one of the other, she need to stop doin' dat shit befo' somebody rape 'er ass." Just then Larry walked through the door followed by Big Will. Larry approached the girls on the couch.

"What's up tenders ya'll lookin' real tasty."

The trio looked amongst each other then burst into laughter as Roslayn pulled out her phone and snapped a picture. Larry asked. "What's dat fa'?"

"MySpace."

"Okay then hit me up. What-chew taggin' me as?"

"Ladies, what not to holla at."

Larry smacked his teeth as if to be expecting the insult. "What's up CJ?" He greeted as he gave Corey some dap.

"Nothin' new, tryin' to trap a dollar." Corey replied and was about to give Larry a shoulder to shoulder when he caught the smell. "Ooohh Shit, that's you smellin' like dat?"

"Naw, it's my shirt some fool threw up on me."

Corey dug into his pocket and pulled out a pack of gum. "Here give this to yo' shirt LL."

The girls on the couch laughed and Jennifer taking pulls from the blunt and exhaling thick smoke asked. "A, why they call you LL?"

Larry quickly shot a deep lustful eye at her with a ridiculous smile of desperation and answered. "Oh, baby that stands for Lick 'em Larry."

"Oh so you know how to lick 'em huh?" Roslayn said accepting the blunt from Jennifer.

"Hell yea."

Corey, Shawn, and Big Will looked at each other with grins on their faces knowing the truth behind his tails. Larry walked over to Jennifer. "You should let me demonstrate fa' ya'."

"I might if you act right. Ewwee hell naw take yo' stankin' ass back over there!" She uttered after getting a whiff of Larry's stench. "You smell like a spoiled tampon."

Everybody in the garage erupted in laughter; the boys playing spades stopped their game to laugh, the couple on the beanbag held each other in laughter. The boys on the milk-crate stopped rapping and started laughing while Corey, Shawn, and William bent over in laughter. Everyone indulged in the humor of Larry's insult except the boy asleep on the big couch. "Damn shawty, you ain't have to bust me out like dat." Larry said in a flat tone.

"Believe me shit-water yo' shirt been told on ya'." Larry walked back to Shawn who was now staring at the boy asleep on the couch.

He noticed it had plenty of room for his clique if he could get the drunk boy to move.

"A yall, watch I get-'em up off the couch." Shawn bragged.

"Just roll his ass on da flo'." Corey advised.

"Naw check it out." Shawn walked over and started shaking and shouting in his ear. "A, a, a dawg-a cuz!"

"Huumm?" The boy said bewildered as he sat up slow.

"Chris got dem strippers out there butt naked, it's 'bout twelve of 'em and six of 'em done started suckin' and fuckin'! You better get up man!" The boy struggled to his feet and stumbled on his first step.

"Chris got dem whoes, I'll holla at chall." He said with his eyes slightly open, he stutter-stepped all the way to the door and at one moment he had to catch his balance by grabbing the back of the chair of one of the spades players. He barely made it to the door, opened it, and in a polite manner he closed it, then followed a huge *thump,* which was followed by laughter from the other side of the door.

"He'll be alright." Shawn said sitting at the end of the couch as he peeled off the plastic wrapper from the cigar. He split the cigar down the middle and dumped the tobacco out in a small trashcan next to the couch. "A Corey what's up, you gettin' up out of that school house?"

"Hell yea, I'm walkin'."

"Yea I'm gettin' that paperwork too."

"That's good folk, how 'bout chew Big Will?"

"Shhiitt, man I need two mo' credits."

"Damn. What about chew LL?"

"Man you know I got another year to go."

"I thought you was in the sixth grade wit' me?"

"I was, I had got skipped in the fourth grade, but then I fucked up messin' wit' them whoes and got kept back in the ninth." Larry said as he sat next to Shawn.

"Man you gotta move over, I 'on't mean no harm but you don't smell too pleasant."

Sliding down a little Larry continued his lie. "But yea Corey I was skippin' school wit' them whoes and messed up my grades."

Shawn now braking down the buds into the dissected cigar, cut Larry off. "Quit lyin' Larry and tell that man the truth."

"That's real talk, them whoes."

"That wasn't the reason CJ, that fool gotta job and couldn't maintain his grades. And he had just started smokin' weed."

"Hater." Larry pointed hard at Shawn. "Real talk CJ it was them whoes." Corey nodded and fed Larry's obvious lie with some sarcasm.

"Yea them whoes will do all the time. So what's up wit'-cha' lil sista Shawn do she be still be sangin'?"

"Hell yea, be gettin' on my nerves too." Shawn said doing his finishing touches on the blunt.

"I remember when she sung at that Christmas play in middle school, man yo' sista' can blow, you need to be the one to put 'er out there, she'll make yall rich."

"I wish."

"A Will, where yo' crazy ass cousin at?"

"Oh he here." Will answered sitting next to Shawn who was now lighting and taking pulls from the blunt, then suddenly Shawn let out a loud and violent series of coughs.

"Aaaauuhhack-auuugghac-auuguugh."

"Damn Shawn you alright man?" Chris asked, while Will aided by slapping Shawn on his back with an unnecessary amount of force.

"You alright man, that must be the shit." Shawn nodded with teary eyes as his coughing eased. He then tried again to take a puff and immediately had the same affect however, this time he tried to hold in the cough, which made his reaction a lot more embarrassing. Snot shot out of his nose, drool hung off his bottom lip, and tears fell down his cheeks. The three on the other couch along with Will and Corey laughed. He struggled for air as he shook his head and passed it to Will.

"Let me see what the fuss is all about." Will said accepting the pass. "I'll show you how to handle this thang." Will put it to his lips and took a long pull and held it in for two seconds before he erupted into a series of harsh coughs almost as strong as Shawn's.

"Damn that must be that killer." Corey replied.

"Chris wasn't lyin' this shit is crucial."

In the midst of Big Will's struggle for air, Tracy and Michael walked in the garage. "A ya'll, Tracy announced as he walked over to the couch, some fool just passed out on the flo' in front of the do'." Corey, Shawn Big Will, Larry, and the three on the couch that were now standing, all laughed at the inside joke. The girls walked pass Tracy and MJ, Michael giving the eye to all three.

"Naw ladies don't leave now, the party ain't over. You might miss out on somethin' good."

"Oh we ain't leavin' yet we finna get somethin' to drank." Jennifer said with her arms around Rashika and Raslayn.

Tracy gave Corey some dap and a shoulder to shoulder then sat next to Larry. "Damn, gotta sit next to Dr. Smell Good." MJ sat next to Tracy and noticing Big Will still slightly coughing while passing the blunt to Larry, he had to say. "That weed must be the truth."

"Yeah you bet-not hit it too ha…" Shawn's advice was stopped by Larry's loud and rough coughs. "See what I'm sayin'."

"Excuse me." A heavy-set female said to Kevin as she reached for a cup, he moved over to his left to allow her to reach the cups, all the while his eyes were fixed across the living room (dance floor) at three guys sitting in lawn chairs.

"Is these niggas lookin' at me?" He mumbled into his cup. "I know they ain't starin' at big girl right here she just walked over here. Yea they muggin'. I'ma' give-'em a minute of muggin' and it's finna be some nuckin' in this bitch."

"Damn that's some good smoke, where you got it from?" Corey said passing the blunt to Shawn.

"Chris."

"I need to holla at him, get 'bout two onions of that."

"Two ounces, don't waste ya' time, I had to bribe 'em to sale me a dub, he said he smokin' the rest."

"Ole selfish ass, did he say where he got it from?"

"Some cat from Burke County he met trough Courtney Wells."

"Fine ass Courtney Wells?" Michael said sitting up from his stoned sloush.

"Yep."

"Ole Chris is bussin' up Courtney?" Shawn only nodded as he struggled to hold in a lung full of smoke. "Oh dat boy done caught him an impressive piece."

Larry smacked his teeth. "She's alright, I could of hit it, real talk."

MJ, Shawn, and Tracy shook their heads while Will stared at the side of Larry's face as if he was the most aggravating person on earth. Corey noticed their reaction to Larry's words and realized the lie, and decided to encourage him some more. "Oh real talk?"

"Real talk."

"When was this?"

"About tenth grade. She wanted to give me the pussy, bad too."

"O-yeah, why didn't you take it?"

"I had to baby sit my lil sista at the time."

"So why you ain't hit later?" Corey continued to encourage him.

"'Cause I had so many whoes at the time I couldn't fit 'er in the schedule."

"Oh that be happenin', I know how it is, it's hard bein' a playa."

"Larry." William said exhaling smoke. "Please man stop bullshittin' I ain't never seen you wit' no girl, not even a ugly one."

"Me neither, I'm startin' to wonder 'bout-cha'." Tracy added.

"I 'on't remember seein' you wit' a female in so long, that I 'on't thank you even got female cousins." Shawn said.

"Hater, yall don't be everywhere I be, I got plenty of shawties."

"Like who and where they at?" MJ asked. Larry received the pass from Will and said.

"I had one named Debra."

"Debra Gray?" Tracy asked.

"Naw Debra Fields man."

"Who else?" Shawn asked.

"I had one named Crystal."

"Crystal Smith?" William asked proving his guess that they were thinking of the same mutual girls they all came up with. However, Larry was swift with changing the last names.

"Crystal Williams. Yall don't know her neither."

"Name another one." MJ said.

"I had one named Stephanie?"

"Stephanie Cooper?" Shawn asked.

"Naw, Stephanie Hicks. She lived in North Augusta, ya'll wouldn't know her."

"You know what LL, can I tell you somethin' that the oldest cat I ever met in my life told me?"

"Go-'head."

"He said that if you lie on your dick it'll get smaller."

"You know what, I heard one of my Uncles say somethin' like that." Tracy said receiving the pass from Larry.

"I ain't lyin', this here is real-talk I don't bullshit 'bout my mackin'." Larry said with worry in the back of his mind. "A, MJ is that true what dat old cat told you?" The stress in his voice was loud, Will, Tracy, MJ, and Corey started laughing.

Tracy then passed the blunt to MJ while exhaling smoke. "You know what Larry, you should be happy that you don't get no ass."

Corey completely curious to Tracy's comment. "How in the hell should he be happy?"

"Yeah, please explain this one?" MJ added.

"For one Larry, you 'on't have to worry 'bout diseases…"

"That's what condoms 'r fa'." MJ answered.

"Be real right now, holla if you never went raw." T-Murray waited but only got snickering from both Corey and Shawn. "Like I said, no STD worries. Two, you ain't gotta worry about no babies on the way like eighty percent of the cats we know, no offense Shawn."

"You straight." Shawn said.

"Uugghg-uugguh." Corey cleared his throat.

"You too?" Tracy asked, Corey simply gave a sad face and a simple nod as if all hope was lost. "My-bad, but it proves my point. And three, pussy is just as strong as the most addictive drug known to man. Once you get some, the right some, you are hooked and you'll do whatever it takes to get mo', it comes in all different flavors, textures, sizes, temperatures…"

"-Chill-out T-Murray you finna make me walk to my shawty's house, now." Shawn said.

"Fa' real man, ease up." Corey said staring at his cell-phone with lustful intent."

"He serious ain't 'e." MJ said."

"…See my point." Tracy continued. "And when you can't get it you go crazy."

"T-Murray, you too damn high, you 'on't need to smoke no mo'." Big Will advised.

"He's gotta a point." Shawn said.

"Yea right, I got it." Big Will replied. "See Larry you gotta get that pussy smell on you first. Once the smell is on you then it'll start flyin' 'round you like gnats in the summa' time at a watermelon eatin' contest. So just get 'bout forty or fitty-dollas' go down town to Broad Street and get-cha' one, get dat smell on ya' and you'll be straight."

"Yea he'll be straight alright, walkin' straight down Laney Walker to the health department tryin' to find out what's wrong wit-'em."

"Look yall, I gets plenty of pussy, you and Will don't know what da hell yall talkin' 'bout."

"Don't listen to Will, unless you wanna turn into some sick trick that gotta go through life payin' for pussy or companionship." Tracy subtly stressed.

"A, what's wrong wit' payin' for it?" William said slightly offended. "That's what ya'll fools be doin' when ya'll take 'em out on dates, to the movies and feedin' them. Gifts and shit, that is the purpose of all of it, ain't it?"

Michael coming out of his utopian state to agree with William said. "Yea he is speakin' the truth."

"Not really." Tracy began his argument. "If you gettin' her nails and other shit done just to hit it, or givin' her money fa that, then yea you're payin' for it. But if you really feelin' shawty I mean diggin' 'er. I'm talkin 'bout on the phone until one or both of yall fall asleep on the phone, or one of ya'll's momma pick up the other phone and fuss at-cha' to get off the phone it's late." Shawn nodded agreeing from experience. "Or-or if you don't mine walkin' down the hall hugged up while everybody ya' homeboys, teachers, ex'es, and girls you wanted to get-wit' is watchin'. Oh and check it out-check it out, this is the shit here." Tracy strongly expressing the importance of his next statement. "Or when that day come when she finally go down on you, after yall been freakin' for a while of course, and the question comes up amongst you and ya dawgs... And you lie to 'em."

Corey, Will, and Larry stared at Tracy in a confused and gaped-mouth stare, Shawn still nodding his head in complete agreement as he began rolling the next blunt. Corey was the first to break the three seconds of silence. "What?"

"That's right, when ya' boys ask you do she gives you head, you say no."

"That's true there cuz, if you really like 'er, respect 'er, and plan on wifen 'er, you wouldn't even want your boys to know." Shawn agreed.

Will now in amazement at his two comrades' revelation. "Yall hear this? So you sayin' you wouldn't tell us?"

"Nope." Shawn answered as he finished rolling the next blunt. Not wit' somebody I'm feelin', hell naw not wit'-chew clowns."

"You serious, you wouldn't tell us?"

"I'm serious, I wouldn't tell until we broke up and a good minute done passed, or if she did me dirty."

"Man I'm hurt. I told yall about Debbie given me head and I really liked her."

"How did yall break up?" T-Murray asked then answered without giving Will time to answer. "-Because you cheated on her with your now baby-momma, which means you didn't respect her so she don't count."

"I can't believe you niggas is keepin' secrets from the clique. I know you wouldn't do no shit like that to me would you MJ?"

MJ replied with dragging words. "You my dawg and all but if I'm really feelin' her, I wouldn't tell."

"Ahw naw, not you too, but you told me about damn near every girl that done gave you head. What about that cute ass quiet girl that was in private school."

"Aquinas."

"Yea that's it, what's her name?"

"Vanessa and it's a Catholic school not private."

"Same difference, what about her, you went wit' her longer than any other girl."

"Because she was the most submissive and she would do anythang I ask her to do."

"Anythang?" Larry asked amazed.

"Anythang."

"Damn where she at now?" Will asked.

"Oh shawty in da 'A' (Atlanta) turnin' tricks for a dike pimp name Panty Line."

"See, there you go LL she can be the one to turn you out." Will said.

"I got Panty Line's number when you ready LL."

Larry smacked his teeth. "I done told yall I gets mine, I don't need to buy mine."

"That's good LL 'cause payin' for it would take the thrill out of it." Tracy said.

Shawn nodded his head as he accepted the blunt pass from Corey. "Yea I feel ya' on that too T-Murray. She don't like you and she's just tryin' to get paid."

"And I'm just tryin' to get laid." Will replied.

"That's sad cuz."

"What?"

"Nothin' animal."

"That's like runnin' a train on a girl." Shawn said after exhaling. "I ain't wit' that cause one, it's nasty as hell, going in behind another dick, might be bigger than yours." Corey laughed. "Two, 'cause shawty ain't there just fa you, she's fa everybody else."

"A lot of folks don't know that about me, I don't fucka' around wit' trains either." Corey said.

"Fuck that, if shawty freakin' I'm beatin', and it ain't like she ain't gettin' nothin' out of it, she gettin' a nut too, it probably take two or three niggas to please 'er. She ain't doin' it fa no reason, she like it too."

"It ain't the right reason." Tracy argued. "Ninety percent of them girls is scared; they probably been molested, abused, abandon, abducted, and all kinds of shit. So that leaves the other ten percent that you say like it, the freaks. I say personally only five percent are freaks, the other five percent ya'll niggas peer-pressure, intimidate, and scare her legs open. You just nasty. Where the blunt at?"

The blunt was in its fifth rotation when Tracy's words set a thick silence amongst them. They all stared straight ahead through and past Corey as if a television was on the wall behind him playing the most amazing show on the planet, their eyes red and half closed and their mouths gaped open as if they could only breathe orally. Their silence lasted for almost three minutes until Shawn finally broke it.

"A Larry, where Kev at, the blunt almost gone?" It took almost twenty-five seconds for Shawn's voice to register through the thick blanket of THC that covered Larry's brain before he answered.

"Huh?"

"I said where Kev at man, did you tell 'em we was gettin' up in the garage?"

"Yeah I told 'em, me and Will." Larry said then passed the two-inch blunt to Tracy.

"Shhiiitt, he'll be alright." Will dragged out and caused a wave of paranoia to move through Shawn.

"Man I hope yo' cousin ain't out there startin' no shit."

"Hell yea, them mothafuckas is starin' at me." Kevin said in the open instead of in his cup as he stared at the three thuggish teens with an almost devious grin.

One was tall and slim about 6'5, 160lbs, a dirty-light-skinned complexion with sleepy eyes and a face that revealed a rough life. He sat on the left. The one in the middle was almost Kevin's size except his 180lbs was mostly fat while Kevin's was solid. He was 5'8 as too Kevin's 5'9, dark-skin with short braids that looked as if they hadn't been touched in three months. The one on Kevin's right was the smallest, 5'5, 140lbs. but his face displayed an even rougher life than his boys. He bobbed his head to the music pretending not to notice Kevin staring back. Kevin recognized them and could even recall seeing them rumble at a football game last year, he quickly read and sized them up.

The tall light-skinned one depended on his long arms to keep distance from his opponents and it was obvious that he won more than he'd lost, which meant in Kevin's book, he was over confident. The one in the middle is the strongest and the most solid of the three, he'll be depending on wild haymakers and slamming his opponent to dominate his fights. He looked slow. The smaller one is quick, wild, fast, and he looked sneaky so he probably would not attack until one of his lackeys would first. He would be easy.

Kevin was good at sizing up adversaries and it always worked for him, he had even calculated when a foe was too much for him and out matched however, that would not stop him from trying, he believed the best doesn't always win. The possibility of being beaten gave it more thrill and excitement.

"Fuck this shit I'm 'bout to straighten these niggas." It seemed as if DJ C-Los had read Kevin's mind, he mixed in a popular fight song by Crime Mob: 'Knuck if you Buck' while Kevin maneuvered through the crowd. As he approached, he noticed that the smaller one and the biggest one was no longer staring at him however, the tall one was staring with his war face on, obviously ready. Kevin stood in front of them.

"Yall gotta problem or somethin'?"

"What!" The tall one said with anticipated hostility.

"Nigga yall know what I'm talkin' 'bout, starin' at me and shit."

"Naw man we wasn't starin' at chew, ain't no fagots over here, we was lookin' at big-girl." The sneaky short one said.

"Man fuck this nigga man you 'on't need to be explainin' shit to this fuck-boy!"

"Fuck-boy, well what's up then pussy-ass-nigga put cha' hands up!" The smallest reached across the biggest one's chest to calm down his hostile friend.

"Hold on-hold on fellas ain't no need to be fighting over a misunderstandin'."

"Man fuck all that this nigga came over here all crunk and shit, let's fuck this nigga up!"

"Naw Red, chill this Chris' party he my nigga, I ain't finna disrespect his shit. Look man it ain't no beef."

Kevin still sizing up the tall one thought to himself. "This lil nigga thank he slick, talkin' that peace shit, it ain't him, I ain't stupid. He waitin' on me to turn my back, I'ma' give it to 'em."

"Alright then." Kevin turned his back with his senses on high alert. He waited for a shadow of movement in his peripheral or a slight sound of a coward's attack from behind, but instead he heard 'shit talking'.

"Man what kinda punk shit was dat Dre!" Red argued.

"Just chill Red we'll get 'em outside."

"Fuck Chris, I been wantin' to get in dat nigga's ass."

"You know 'em?" Dre ask.

"Yea I know dat nigga, and I 'on't like punkin' out to a crack-baby."

The words were worst than being spat in his face. He turned and walked back over to Red. "You say somethin', I couldn't here ya'?" Kevin said in arm's reach of Red.

Still sitting like a fool, Red stuck his finger in Kevin's face. "You heard me nigga I don't bow down fa' no crack…" Before Red could finish his insult Kevin tossed his cup of gin in his face and when the cup made contact a right hook landed clean and solid. *WHOOP!* This sent Red on a hard and quick trip to the floor. Without hesitation Kevin threw a stiff left-cross followed by a right-hook to the stockier one that was rising from his seat. Big boy stumbled back giving Kevin time to prepare for the right-hook Dre launched, Kevin ducked and came up with a solid right upper cut followed by a strong push that sent him falling two feet into a couple sharing a seat. Cell-phones were pulled. Kevin put his attention back on big boy and delivered a right and left jab then followed with a right-hook that dropped big boy down to one knee. He then grabbed the back of big boy's head and pulled forward as he drove his knee into his face. Big boy goes down on his back and Kevin mounts him by using his knees to pin down his arms and unleashed hard and unrestricted punches to his face.

The crowd of dancers were now focused and encircling the action, more than eighty percent of them held up their camera phones. One shouted. "YouTube baby!" Some fought their way from the back of the crowd to get a better view.

Kevin's punches were relentless and powerful, flowing behind each other left, right, left, right, left. A right broke his nose, then a left knocked out a top front tooth and two concurrent rights in the same spot opened a gash over big boy's eye.

A spectator shouted. "Watch out cuz!" Red was on his feet behind Kevin and had just released a hard right hook, Kev turned just in time for the punch to connect with his jaw, *whoop*. This knocked him off big boy into the wall under a bay window. Red ran over and kicked Kev in his ribs as he was getting up knocking him back down. Red kicked again which Kev expected and blocked it with his left forearm. Kevin threw a jab into Red's stomach knocking the wind out of him bellowing him over. With a quick two steps, Kevin maneuvered behind Red, dropped and had his right arm between his legs. Kevin lift and took three power steps and tossed Red out the bay window, the shattering of the window competed with the oh's and woo's from the crowd. Kevin watched as Red hit the ground, which was a mistake because Dre was on his feet. He jumped and wrapped his arms around Kev's neck and squeezed.

"Take a nap nigga!" Dre grunted in Kev's ear.

"Damn, did ya'll hear that?" Will said in a sluggish tone.

"Naw, heard what?" Michael said as he dropped the roach in a corner of liquor left in his cup.

"A noise, sounded like…" Will had to lick his lips because of cottonmouth. "…a window breakin'."

"Yeah I thank I heard it too." Shawn slouched down in the sofa.

"Them fools in there crunk as hell, we missin' the whole party." Tracy said also slouched into the sofa as if the couch was slowly swallowing them. "Fuck it I'm too high to get up."

"Me too." Shawn agreed.

"I might spend the night right here." MJ added.

"Yeah, I'm 'bout skint too." Will said as he was about to take a sip until his attention was snatched. "Is Corey over there sleep?"

Corey had his head down on the table that displayed his merchandise. "Naw, I ain't sleep I just gotta put my head down for a minute, that's some good ass weed."

Larry slowly sat up, then stood to his feet. "Shhhhit I gotta piss…" He said silenced by a blissful stretch. "…they crunk in there. I need to be out there gettin' wit' them whoes."

Michael looked up at Larry with a slight smile. "Hell yea you better go out there and get them numbers, I ain't forgot."

"I know you ain't forgot, 'cause you worried, my game is tight, and my pockets finna be tight after I win yo' money."

"A Larry." Will said. "While you in there pissin' take a quick shower, wit'-cha' stankin' ass."

"Hater." Larry labeled everyone before he walked into the house. He saw that everyone was in the living-room packed in a huddle. He knew this sight, It's a fight going on. He ran to the crowd and struggled through to get a view of the action. He broke through to find Kevin struggling to get a guy off his back that was choking him. Larry ran back into the crowd to tell his comrades.

"What kinda bet ya'll got goin'?" Corey asked now with his head up.

"Oh he bet that he can get mo' numbers than me." MJ said.

Corey laughed. "Damn I know it's too late to get in on that bet, especially smellin like that."

"I wonder who threw up on 'em, we would have had to fight about that, no matter who he was." MJ said. Shawn woke from a high's gaze by MJ's words.

"Larry told yall a dude threw up on him?" Shawn shook his head and chuckled. "That boy can tell 'em, hell naw it was a female that threw up on 'em while he was tryin to holla at 'er."

"Hell naw." Will and Tracy said together and laughed.

"Lyin' Ass Larry." Just as Will said that Larry bolted through the door into the garage.

"A ya'll some niggas out here jumpin' on Kev!" All the boys on the couch sat up except Will, who was now standing.

"No bullshittin'!" Big Will stressed.

"He's out here fightin'-come on!"

Will hurried to the door followed by his comrades.

They mowed and stamped their way through the crowd and saw Kevin just as he dropped a knee into the abdomen of big boy that was laying on his back. That with the combined weight of him and Dre on his back cracked two ribs creating a snapping sound that could be heard by onlookers closest to the action. Will ran up to Dre with a right cocked back.

"Get da fuck off my cousin!" He punched Dre in the back of his neck causing him to release his grip and fall to the floor barely conscious. Will showing no pity kicked him on the side of his face snapping him to alertness. William stood over him and gripped a hand full of Dre's shirt, with his left hand and began pounding him in the face, chastising him between each blow. *Thack!* "You punk mothafucka!" *Thack!* "You done fucked wit' the wrong one!" *Thack!* "Fuckin' wit' my cousin!" *Thack!*

Larry began kicking Dre's thighs and side while Tracy and Shawn began stomping the big boy that was bald up in the fetal position. Michael grabbed a lawn chair and signal to Shawn and Tracy to move. He held it by its front legs and began beating big boy. Kevin holding his throat and coughing noticed his comrades had everything under control. He then thought of Red, he looked out the shattered bay window to see Red struggling to his feet, bloody from lacerations on his back and left side. Kevin climbed out the broken window and rushed him. He scooped Red up and dumped him on his head and shoulders.

"Oooohhh Shhiiiit!" Jeff and the other dice shooters shouted as Red's top portion made solid contact with the lawn. The impact almost knocked him out, he laid still on his back. Kevin began to stomp his face, Red covered up, but was a second too slow and caught the first stomp on the right side of his face, the other hit his head, shoulders, and chest along with a few kicks.

"What's up now ole bitch-ass nigga!" Kevin shouted with eyes full of fury, alcohol, and rage. "I 'on't hear no shit talkin' now, huh! I can't hear ya' fuck-boy speak up! Crack baby that's what chew called me, yea you right I'ma' crack-baby and I finna crack yo' mothafuckin' skull!"

Jeff overwhelmed by the vicious beating shouted. "Kev stop man you gonna kill 'em!" Jeff and the others ran over and pulled him off Red. "You got it-you got it, you gonna kill 'em man you don't want no murder charge!" Jeff said as he and the others held Kevin back.

Back in the house, the others were still beating up on big boy and Dre. Other fights had started as well; two girls double-teamed a boy in a corner and by the DJ table, two boys were fighting two other boys. The scuffles sent *thumps* and *bangs* throughout the house, down the hall to Chris' room. Chris ran out with his shirt off holding up his shorts and sweating.

"What in da fuck is going on!" He shouted as he ran down the hall. He saw the fights and a huge hole in the wall over where the girls were beating up a boy, then he saw the shattered bay window. "Oh what da fuck, these niggas done broke out my momma…A a a yall niggas chill, mothafuckas stop!" He yelled but no one paid him any attention due to all of the chaos. "That's it get the fuck out of my house! The party is over got-damn it get the hell out! Oh, yall mothafuckas can't hear me, alright hold up." Chris ran back down the hall to his room. "Baby get up for a minute." He asked in a sweet but stressed and humble way to Courtney sitting on his bed in her panties with a blanket wrapped around her.

"What's up baby?" She asked as she got off the bed.

"Them niggas is fuckin' up my momma's house, fightin' and

shit." Chris lifted his mattress and retrieved a blue steel, black rubber grip .38 snub nose and ran back to the living room, he went over to the broken window, stuck the gun out pointing at the ground, and let off two rounds. *POW-POW.* Everyone stopped moving, he ran over to the DJ table and kicked it over stopping the music. "Now that I got chall's mothafuckin' attention I would just like to say, get the fuck out of my house the shit is over!"

Chris stood at his front door boiling over with anger as he's last few guest left.

"Well it was crunk Chris." One boy said as he walked out the door.

"Yea whatever man."

Corey exited holding up Kelly T. with a book bag on his back. "Sorry fa what happened cuz."

"Yea but not as sorry as I'ma' be when my momma get home."

Kelly lifted her head and slurred out. "Sheee-nihhggahs always fuuhckin' uhp shit. I ain't even finish ghettin' my drank on."

"Don't worry baby I got plenty of liquor at my house." Corey said.

"Oohhwee thatss what I'm tawlkin' 'bout leehts go."

Shawn was the last one out, he tried apologizing for the behavior of his thuggish comrades as they waited in the SUV. "Man, Chris I'm sorry folk, my-bad man I ain't mean for it to go down like this."

"Your bad, your bad!" Chris had to mumble to muzzle his anger. He then walked to the window and stuck his arm out. "Look Shawn, look at my window, what in the hell I'ma' tell my momma?"

"I 'on't know man." Shawn replied in a humble tone.

"Look at this shit I got AC for days 'round this mothafucka, and look at that big ass hole in the wall over there, that's a whole-other damn room!"

"I'm sorry cuz."

"You owe me Shawn, you know that right, you owe me big time. I had my lady Courtney in my bed in her panties about to slide in 'til yo' monkeys started actin' up, scared her damn clothes back on. You owe me big Shawn."

"I know man, whatever it is I got-cha', just let me know cuz."

A look emerged from his blanket of anger, gleaming hope. "First of all forget about thankin' 'bout it, I'm takin' you to talk to my recruiter, no bull-shittin'." Shawn dropped his head in regret for making such an offer in such haste.

"Alright man, you got it. When?"

"I'll call and let-chew know."

Chris and Shawn gave each other dap and a shoulder to shoulder. Shawn started down the steps when Chris stopped him. "A Shawn, remember what I said, them cat's you hangin' wit' ain't nothin' but trouble, watch ya'-self and don't let them get you into no shit."

"Alright man."

Little did they know that Chris' statement was going to be the opposite of the events that would occur the summer ahead.

Chapter 2

Kevin gave a vivid and detailed description of the fight before they had arrived and help.

Shawn sat in silence as he stared out of the Explorer's window contemplating on what Chris said about his comrades. At first he was offended on Chris' views of his friends but now hearing Kevin brag about his glory in defeating the three 'AVP' (Apple Valley Posse), William had told them who they were fighting, he started to consider Chris' views of them. Kevin did mess up the party just as he knew he would, Shawn shook his head. He listened to how MJ bragged about all the numbers he got and how many females he'd grind with at the party, he listened to Big Will complain about not getting as 'fucked up', and even with the windows down he could still smell Larry. Tracy had sprayed Larry with William's vanilla scented car freshener but he could still smell the pathetic-ness of Larry and it competed with the ignorant babbles of a thugged-out Kevin. It was too much negativity, he needed to escape from the 'bullshit'.

He started thinking about his girl Tekela, and was now feeling guilty because he was hanging out with these knucklehead-ass-fools instead of being cuddled up with her and her subtle round belly, that contained his growing child. She knew his friends all too well and she didn't like Shawn hanging with them, except Tracy, he was decent to her. This was one of those times that he regretted hanging with his boys instead of his 'baby gurl'.

"A Will you can go-'head and drop me off at the crib man. I got some thangs I gotta do in the mornin', momma gotta list of shit."

"I feel ya' on that house-work tip, I run through whatever my folks give me, then I can chill fa' da whole weekend." Will said.

Shawn's lie was necessary to get away from his comrades, he knew Kevin, Will, MJ, and Larry would stay out all night and after their inconsiderate acts, he was not up for an 'all nighter' with them. He understood why Larry, Kevin, and MJ didn't like to go home, their situation at home wasn't too pleasant. However, Will had a year-old son and Kevin had a two-year-old son with another baby on the way, by another female. He should be at least spending time with his son or the girl that's pregnant by him, he don't have to be around his mother. Shawn was determined not to be like that he was going to be there for his son or daughter. Thank God he had a good girl, maybe it was the type of female Kevin and Will had children with, Shawn felt slight guilt for not remembering what type of girls his comrades dealt with. Nothing like his lady.

"A Will what-chew doin' man?" Larry asked. "Why we in Garden Brook?"

"You live out here don't chew, I'm takin' yo' ass home what it look like."

"Why you droppin' me off first I ain't ready to go home yet."

"Cause you and T-Murray live the closest and I won't have to double back to Meadowbrooke, common sense nigga. And anyway I'm ready to get-cho' stankin' ass out my ride, you smell like baboon balls." Everyone laughed even Shawn managed to crack a smile despite his mood.

"Yea-well how you know how baboon balls smell, you been sniffin' monkey nuts or somethin'?" Larry tried to redeem himself with a comeback.

"Naw but you smell so bad that that's the first thang I thank of when I smell you."

"That's alright though, I'm still a playa'." Larry said as they pulled up to his house. Larry got out and Tracy moved over in the spot.

"Thank God, I can breathe." Tracy joked.

"A Will yall goin' pick me up tomorrow?"

"Yea just hit me up."

Kevin leaned out of the window to get a better view of Larry and said. "A Larry you'll do me a favor cuz?"

"Yea what's up?"

"Go in da house, boil a big ass pot of water and dive in da mothafucka."

Everyone in the Explorer laughed, Larry attempted to deliver a snappy come back. "Oh I know you ain't talkin'…" But William sped off.

Larry watched as they drove off and with a grin of pride he thought of how happy and proud to have them as friends. Up to the sixth-grade, Larry never had any friends, he was quite small for his age, funny looking by normal standards, and smart, which was considered 'lame' by his peers. He struggled to be notice, liked, and developed a habit of exaggerating his life. He would lie about money he never had nor have, girls he been with, cars, and things he saw and done, anything that made him look interesting or favorable to others. Not being very good at lying at the time made him a target for bullying, that changed when he met Kevin in the sixth-grade.

Larry was being assaulted in the bathroom at school by twin

brothers when Kevin Jones walked in and said. "Why ya'll messin' wit' somebody who can't fight, I bet chall won't mess wit' me."

The twins accepted his challenge and one ended up with a bloody nose and the other with a black eye and busted lip. Larry tagged along behind Kevin every since, the others came later and since the ninth grade, the six have been inseparable. Though Larry gaining friends was good, it created a somewhat negative change in him. To fit and blend in more with his new friends he purposely slacked off in school, became loud, obnoxious, and aggravating and his lying grew worse, it evolved. He became good at it and developed a skill, able to lie his way out of many situations, fooling a lot of people except his comrades. It wasn't necessary for Larry to lie to fit in with them, they accepted him the way he was, for who he was. He just felt that it was his 'thang' his place to provide entertainment and life to the clique, everybody had their 'thang' lying was his.

He walked up his drive way still buzzing from the weed and alcohol and was relieved to see his father's 1989 blue Thunderbird gone. "Good that bitch ain't home."

It is logical to say that Larry's father, Jimmy Watkins was the cause of his son's insecurity, low self-esteem, and why he made up stories about a life he wished he had. Jimmy was an abusive drunk that would knock around his wife (Larry's mother) over any small issue. Some beatings were worse than others, the worst happened three years ago. The summer before his freshman-year, when he beat Yolanda so bad that she had to be hospitalized. She was treated for a mild concussion, two cracked ribs, and a broken arm. The story was that a burglar attacked her. He had not beaten her up as bad since then.

"Momma." Larry shouted as he closed the front door.

"I'm in the back." She responded with a calm tone. Larry walked down the hall of his clean and well kept home to his parent's room to find his mother sitting up in her bed; back against the headboard, remote in hand flipping through the channels trying to find something to watch. "You had fun?"

"Yea, it was alright, until Kevin started fightin'."

"What's wrong wit' that boy he always rasin' hell." She said with a slight confused look on her face. "He reminds me of this boy I went to school with name Minus, always fightin'. He got in a fight wit' his girl friend's brother and was stabbed in the neck."

"Did he die?"

"Naw but he gotta talk through one of those voice box things."

"Damn!" Larry accidently uttered. He had an expression of exposed guilt and tried to recover. "I mean dawg!"

"I heard you." She said giving a suspicious stare. "You been drankin'?"

"No ma'am!" He quickly lied. She gave him another suspicious look then said.

"Come and give yo' momma a hug."

"Ahh ma'." Larry complained.

"Ahh ma' hell, come here boy."

He walked over to his mother's bedside with open arms and right before they made contact she uttered. "Eeww child you stank, what did you do through up on yo'-self!"

"Naw ma' somebody threw up on me, I ain't drank that much… Damn." He thought after realizing what he just said.

"Um-hum I knew you was drankin'. I don't want you drankin' Larry it's bad enough that I let you smoke."

Yolanda didn't object to letting her son smoke marijuana, besides she had been smoking since high school and she figured by being hypocritical in telling her son not to smoke when she indulged in it, would cause friction and troubles between her and her son. It also made her feel somewhat relieved to know he's home and safe getting high instead of sneaking and smoking around people that didn't care about his wellbeing and amongst the elements of the streets.

Yolanda was a heavy weed smoker, a joint in the morning before breakfast, one in the afternoon, and one or two before she goes to bed depending on the quality of the marijuana. Her habit was more than twice as intense as it was in her high school years because dealing with the abuse from her husband was easier to deal with when she got high afterwards. After he would beat her or curse her out, like clockwork he would leave in anger and go get drunk at a bar or a friend's house, or another woman's house for all she knew, this would give her plenty hours of freedom and relaxation. When Jimmy was gone she would turn up her radio and blast her favorite CDs like; Marvin Gaye, Al Green, Patti Labelle, Aretha Franklin, Clarence Carter, and The Temptations. Depending on her mood she would jam to something more up-tempo like; James Brown, Parliament Funkadelics, Africa Bambatta or even some eighties hip-hop. She would dance as if she had no worries as she smoked joints and cleaned the house, this would help her escape from the abuse and terror she lived in. She rarely went anywhere because soon as a bruise on her face would heal, Jimmy would replenish her face with another. This was one of his ways of keeping her in the house, something he learned from his buddy. See Jimmy was a paranoid, insecure, and jealous husband, especially with such an attractive wife.

Yolanda was a pretty caramel completion woman with long, wavy, and shiny black hair that extended just past her shoulders.

People would ask her if she was mixed with something, though she is but didn't know because she didn't know her father, she would always reply. "Nope I'm an all natural negro." She was 5'5, 125lbs. supple barely B cup breast that hadn't dropped after having two kids and one miscarriage (thanks to Jimmy), and a cuffed apple-bottom. Her face displayed the years of abuse like ghostly scares from stitches over her left eyebrow and through her top lip on the right side. However, through the tattered roughness a blurry-eyed person could still see her beauty and easily mistake her for twenty-seven instead of thirty-seven.

"I don't want chew to end up like yo' stupid ass daddy."

"Alright ma', it ain't finna be nothin' like that, I promise you that." Larry followed it up with a son to mother kiss on the cheek.

"Ouch." She uttered with a grimmest face and withdrawing a little. Larry studied her then noticed the dark bruise on the left side of her face, that extended from her earlobe to the corner of her cheek, it was new. The sight of the bruise brought a mixture of anger, sadness, and hate a combination of feelings he had grown to learn how to hide well, however sips of the liquor still coursing through him pushed out the feelings one at a time, the sadness first.

"It hurt momma?"

"Not really, just when I touch it." She said nonchalantly.

The anger inched out while he shook his head. "Ain't chew tired of this shit momma!" Larry's conviction penetrated her chest and gripped her heart, she held back her tears and masked her pain with her strong womanhood.

"Yes, I am tired of it what chew thank child." Some anger in her reply competed with Larry's.

"Well why don't you leave him then?"

"How, with what money? You got some money? Cause if you do I would love to borrow a couple of thousand so I can buy us a house. If I had the money Larry believe me I'll pack our stuff right now me, you, and ya' sister and run off somewhere he can't find us, but right now I'm just not able." The issue brought sadness to their hearts.

"I know ma'." Larry said with humble understanding.

"Don't worry about me baby, I'll be alright, as long as my child-wen got clothes on their backs, food in their bellies, a nice place to sleep, and a roof over yalls head I'll be just fine."

Now feeling guilty for not being able to help he said. "I swear to God momma, one day and some-day soon I'ma' get the money we need to get the hell away from him." The conviction in his voice somewhat troubled Yolanda.

"That don't mean go out there and do somethin' illegal and stupid. You hear me?" Larry nodded reluctantly. "I rather deal with this fool than visiting my son in a cage or puttin' flowers on your grave. You hear me?" Larry nodded as both of their eyes welled up, they fought to keep the tears from escaping. To overcome the thick emotional atmosphere surrounding her and her son, she said. "I don't feel like talkin' about this right now, I'm relaxin'. You wanna smoke?"

"Where it's at?" Larry quickly responded.

"In my jewelry box." This was one of the many spots she hid her stash and the spot where Larry first found one of her stashes. Before she found out that Larry was getting high, he use to steal pinches from her bag just enough for a blunt or three, she thought she was going crazy every time she went to her stash she found it lighter than it was supposed to be. When she finally found out that Larry smoked, he became the number one and only suspect because Jimmy only drink, he stopped smoking a few years after high school, coincidently the same time he started hitting her. She then started hiding her stash in many different spots such as; the tape slot on the barely used VCR, in her pillowcase, between her mattresses, in the mattress, in old purses, and shoeboxes. No matter where she hid it Larry would eventually find her new spot. "It should be two of 'em already rolled up." She said soon as he opened the first of three small drawers on her jewelry box.

Larry sat on Jimmy's forest green recliner next to the three-foot mahogany nightstand that sat between the bed and the recliner and lit one of the joints. Yolanda flipped through the channels when she passed the Dave Chappell Show, Larry inhaled smoke and quickly uttered. "Go back two momma."

She turned back two and replied. "Oh yea, this is a fool here." She put down the remote, accepted the pass from her son, and sat up.

At first she use to feel bad, dirty, and guilty about smoking marijuana with her son, the notion of partaking in illegal mind altering substances with her teenage child in a society such as America, was looked at as shameful, irresponsible, and even criminal. However, America didn't know nor understand what she and her kids faced day to day, it was a different world where she came from, different rules and ways of life. In her home she was enjoying happiness and freedom from a possessive and abusive alcoholic husband that not only beat on her, but would also take his anger out on her sixteen year-old son and twelve year-old daughter. She was also bonding with her teenage son more successfully than most parents with troubled teenage sons, this made her feel joy in a void life filled with only misery. Larry also felt something special when he smoked with his mother it was like something sacred to him. He didn't have to share his mother with his litter sister or his mean ass pops and he didn't have to pretend to be somebody he wasn't. He was her son and she made him forget about his low self-esteem and limited social status, he was happy in this moment, little did he know that the promise he made to his mother to escape their nightmare would come true, but with a price.

"Alright fellas yall be safe." Tracy said as he closed the back passenger door. He walked to his front door buzz almost completely gone thanks to Kevin's altercation. He entered his home to find his father in his usual seat in his usual state, relaxed. He sat in a huge brown leather recliner, his shoes off and shirt off exposing his hairy pop-belly, work pants unbutton as well as his unbuckled belt for comfort, and laid back. He had a twenty-four ounce can of Schlitz Malt liquor Bull in his right hand and next to him on a small fold out table sat the remote to his forty-inch Magnavox. A short glass of brown colored liquor sat by the remote, which was either brandy or cognac depending on what kind of mood he was in or if his ten, twelve, or sixteen hour shift went by smooth or rough.

Mr. Murray was a hard working forty-two year-old welder at a downtown steel mill, Augusta Irion and Bearing Works, he did everything that his boss requested which was a lot more than his job required despite the fact that he was three dollars an hour underpaid than what his skill level's worth. However, Mr. Murray was still able to put one son through college, one in but did not complete college, and buy his pride and joy, his forty-inch Magnavox that mostly displayed sporting events and action packed movies, at the moment he was watching ESPN highlights.

"Hey pops, I'm home." Tracy said standing in the living room entrance.

"Hey son, you home early tonight, it must of been a dead party." He said as he retrieved his glass, took a sip and chased it down with a gulp of his Schlitz.

"Oh naw the party was cool, it was that fool Kevin, he started fightin' and Chris had to shut the party down early."

"That boy is a nut in a half shell."

"Dawg pops, why you still got on yo' work pants?" Tracy asked as he sat on the couch next to the recliner.

"I pulled a sixteen and when I got home I hurried to see who won between the Braves and Phillies."

"Did you win?"

"Oh yeah, I got them fools at the job for sixty dollars, them Braves bad, I'm pullin' for 'em but I know they ain't gonna do it this year." Mr. Murray sipped his Schlitz.

"Yea me too. How momma doin'?" Tracy said with some worry in his question.

"Well she was doin' real good when I went to work this morning, she was gettin' around good, even fixed her some soup. She looked strong, she was sleep when I got home. A little rumbling in her chest, but she look good."

"Yea she looked good when I left earlier, might be a good sign pop, she might beat it."

"I wanna hope so son but I don't want no false hope. We'll just take it one day at a time. A few mo' dollars and I can get 'er that treatment, then I can get some solid hope."

Not only was Mr. Murray taking care of the household and backed his son through college, but he also was taking care of his sick wife.

Tina Murray's doctors diagnosed her with lung cancer and it had progressed to stage four before Jonnie Murray could afford to have her treated properly. Just the staging alone bankrupted Mr. Murray, lab and blood work, X-rays, CT scans, and MRIs were picked up by his job's insurance but radiation, chemotherapy, and medicine had to come out of his pocket. Loans and fifteen years of savings depleted and by that time it had spread to her stomach. His weak insurance only provided Erlotinib, which the doctors told Mr. Murray that her cancer cells were SCLC and not the NSCLC type condition. However, Jonnie wanted to do whatever he could and cover all bases. He didn't know anything about SCLC or NSCLC (Non-small cell lung cancer). All he knew was that his wife was dying and he's going to do whatever it takes to help her, he didn't understand den carcinomas nor paraneoplastic symptoms, he only understood that she was sick and he wanted her well. The doctors told him that it had already spreaded and that it was too progressed for the conventional treatment, but they did mention therapies and treatments that were still in experimental stages, and since doctors didn't have enough long term data they didn't recommend them. Certain side effects could evolve into further progression of the cancer or even have an allergic reaction that could be fatal. Jonnie and his sons were facing a serious dilemma but their conclusion was solid. If the money was available then they would go through with the experimental procedures. Jonnie was working twelve, fourteen, and sixteen hour shifts while his college graduate (Tony Murray) gave every extra penny he had to help.

"Pop."

"Yea, what's up?" Mr. Murray asked with most of his focus on ESPN.

"Why you won't let me get a job, so I can help you wit' the bills and wit' momma?"

Mr. Murray inhaled deeply and exhaled heart-felt frustration.

He sensed his son's sincere suffering. "I done already explained to you Tracy, I want you to concentrate on school. I don't want you to be stuck in somebody's kitchen or plant, them jobs are cursed you'll be stuck on them type of jobs for the rest of ya' life, like me. I don't want that for you. Get a good education and excel ya'-self above strugglin' and I'll be happy. Your momma will be happy, that's all we need. Hell maybe you'll get rich and pops won't have to work no mo'." Mr. Murray said with a small chuckle followed by a sip of his liquor. "What-chew thank?"

"Oh yeah, I'ma' do that fa ya' pops."

"You want a beer son?"

The question shocked Tracy like a small current of electricity, he thought to his self. "Is this a trick question, is he tryin' to trick me into tellin' on myself?" Mr. Murray answered Tracy as if he read his mind or was he thinkin' aloud.

"It ain't no trick question son do you want a beer or not? Hell I know you done drunk befo'."

Tracy hesitated then answered. "Yea I'll take one."

"I knew you would, go get the one I got chillin' in the icebox."

Tracy smiled in an amused confusion as he entered the kitchen. "Damn pops is lettin' me drank, he must be in a good-ass mood." He mumbled to himself as he grabbed the twenty-four ounce Schlitz out of the freezer. "It ain't no Bud Ice but it'll do." As Tracy walked down the hall a feeling hit him, he turned around and headed to his parent's room.

Tina was sleep on her side with her back facing the door, he walked in and around the bed to see her face and there he stood holding the cold beer and staring at his invalid mother.

She had lost a lot of weight, almost eighty pounds, her golden complexion was tarnished with a shade of gray and dark circles surrounded her sunken eyes. She wore an old brown and tan bandana that she had before her first-born, to hide her hair loss from the radiation and her lips had a hint of purple from dehydration. Then it was burn scares on her chest right below her throat from the radiation that not only burned the surface of her skin but also the inside her throat that made it painful for her to swallow.

All this brought pain to Tracy as he watched her sleep, but the major pain-causing factor for him was the sound of her breathing. When she inhaled it sounded as if she struggled to take in oxygen with short shallow breaths and when she exhaled a nerve disturbing wheezing sound was produced. This would always pull tears from him but he eventually learned how to lock it inside, which was now festering into resentment towards the one he blamed for his mother's condition, God.

He watched her sleep for a while until his love and imagination pushed memories to the surface. He saw in her face the mother he missed. The mother that took him and his brother Thomas to the movies and park. The mother that dressed them in funny looking tight clothes, the mother that would feel sorry for him and lie to his father for him the time he broke his father's hair clippers. He even missed the whippings he received from her for bad grades, which was crazy because she was a heavy-handed woman that whipped harder than his dad. The thoughts were strong enough to push out a tear from his left eye then seconds later his right. She coughed violently for a few seconds in her sleep, which broke Tracy out of his state of reminiscence, he then leaned over and kissed her on the cheek. The kiss woke her as if it broken a spell and she spoke in a weak, hoarse and groggy voice.

"Hay baby, you had fun at the party?"

"Yes ma'am. How you feel momma?"

"A whole lot better than I did last weekend, a whole lot better."

"That's good."

She closed her eyes and adjusted her head on her pillow and said. "What chew doin' wit'-cha' daddy's beer?"

"Oh he said I can have it."

"Alright, when I get better I'm puttin' a switch to you and ya' daddy."

Normally the threat would have struck fear in him three years ago, but now under the circumstances it made him fight back more tears, tears of happiness to see that she still had her old spirit. Also, tears of sadness from the reality that she wasn't physically strong enough to beat him and the sound of her statement's weakness piercing his heart.

He missed and wanted her beatings he missed his strong beautiful mother that raised him and his knuckle-head brothers. He took a deep breath as if his reminiscing had exhausted him then kissed her on the cheek as she fell back asleep.

He returned back to the living room with a heart so heavy that his knees was weak and he had to concentrate on not falling down as he sat back in his previous seat.

"Damn son, it took you nine days to get the beer."

Tracy gave a slight laugh. "Naw, I looked in on momma to see how she was doin'." Tracy popped open the beer and took a large swig. Mr. Murray noticed his son's troubled state and tried to console him and give him understanding, or some type of clarity.

"Son I know you worried for ya' mother but it's gonna work out."

"I hope so." Tracy said taking another large swig.

"I know you do and I do too, but if it don't and I tell you this to be truthful, I don't want to put no false hope in you. But if it don't and the worst happens, then it's God's will."

His father's words struck a nerve in him, he was tired of hearing that tired excuse, that lame line of weak and now insufficient logic. He was now angry but he buried it, but not deep enough. "Yeah but his will ain't fair." Mr. Murray almost choked on his beer he had to cough to keep it from going down 'the wrong pipe'. "Momma ain't never hurt nobody never done no wrong to nobody, she's a good person, she was going to church she helps people. Like the time she took lil Jason in while his momma was in rehab. I just don't understand, why my momma. I know plenty of people that deserves worse, cats that beat on their girlfriends, cats that sale massive amounts of dope, cats that hit they own momma, abuse lil kids all kinds of stuff Pop. I even know a dude that killed two people and is still walkin' 'round free and healthy, and my momma is laid up suffering. It ain't right."

Mr. Murray sensed the anger and frustration build in his son and tried again to give him clarity, or some type of understanding. "You're right Tracy, it's not fair, to us but God works in his own mysterious ways. It's his will and his plan and he has reason for everything fair or not."

"Yea pops, that's another one that I done heard half a million times and that still don't make it right. Pop, I love and respect you as my father and as my elder and I don't mean no disrespect when I say this. If that's God's will, God's way, and God's plan, I thank God is selfish, conceded, inconsiderate, and don't give a fuck about his own kids."

This time Mr. Murray did choke on his beer. "Woo-woo-woo, hold up son! I thank you need to put that beer down."

"It's me pop it ain't the beer talkin', I been feelin' this way every since we found out what was wrong wit' 'er. I mean what da' hell, momma got lung cancer and ain't never touched a cigarette in her life. Unless it's somethin' you and momma ain't tellin' me."

"No son, yo' mother never smoked."

"And you don't thank that's kind of cruel and plain out wrong."

Mr. Murray sat still then sipped his liquor, he had to calculate his next statement, it was a delicate subject. He could tell his son that he thought and felt the same way he did now, when the doctors told him the diagnoses.

"Lung cancer! Are you sure, but she don't smoke, never smoked, are you sure. This can't be right. One percent of... Naw –naw, I want a second opinion you don't know what the hell you're talkin' about." The other doctor's diagnoses were the same.

"Son I understand your pain I know you're hurtin', I am too but that's no reason to curse God, that's dangerous. Look Tracy, I'm no devoted Christian like I should be or no holy-roller, matter-of-fact I shouldn't even be talkin' about this with alcohol in me, but I'ma' tell you this. Bad folks have their good time but you never know what's going on behind closed doors, or on the inside. All those people you talked about, they got plenty of problems too and I guarantee you theirs a lot worse than yours, and that cat that you said killed some folks, oh he's gonna get his twice as bad as what he did to them. You should know this without reading the bible or even goin' to church, you have sense and you already know what goes around comes around, you do bad thangs something bad will happen to you. I feel I been a pretty decent person to be blessed with Tina a good person like you, now I figure since you're our son I believe you gotta lot of good in your blood. You gonna be a good person so son please don't let your current situation force a hasty decision that can change you for the worse."

His pop's words filled him with pride but did not change his mind. "It already done changed me."

"How you figure Tracy?"

Tracy took an impressive size swig slash guzzle from his beer, not for taste sake but to wash down his forming tears, he swallowed and said firmly. "I decided that if my momma die before I'm ready for it, I'll never pray, worship, or deal wit' God no mo'."

Stunned by another one of his son's revelations, he could feel that it was truly his son's words and not the alcohol, Mr. Murray was filled with mixed emotions and troubled thoughts. "I tell you like this, son you are seventeen and I feel you're old enough to make the decision on your relationship with God. All I ask is that you remain a good person you was raised to be. I feel a man can be a good person without being a Christian. It's kind of like that sayin' yall got, 'do you'." Tracy was surprised at how up-to-date his pop was on the slang. "Don't let your situation do you. I don't agree with your decision but I can give you advice and the advice is don't give up on God so easily. Maybe you'll change your mind when you're older and wiser. Whatever your outcome or decision is I'm your father, I love you, I'm here if you need me, and I'll respect you. I'll be proud of you, hell I'm proud of you now." His father's words touched his heart and snatched out a few tears that he tried to quickly wipe away before his father noticed, but Mr. Murray caught a glimpse of the wipe.

"Why? What have I done for you to be proud of me?"

"What have you done for me to be proud of you?" Mr . Murray replied as if the question was out of place. "Cause you graduated high school."

"Yea but you have a son that graduated college and one that

made it to his second year."

"Yes, but I didn't."

Tracy's attention snapped over to his pop, discovering something new. "What, you ain't graduate pops?"

"Nope, I dropped out in the eleventh grade to take care of ya' mother and Tony. I thought you knew that, it wasn't a secret, ya' brothas knew."

"Naw I just assumed."

"Now Tina went back to school, I didn't. I wish I had, but now I got three sons that passed me in life, I'm happy and proud, lets me know that I did somethin' right. And it's not only that chew graduated, but because you ain't like these knuckle heads in the streets, you made good grades and good decisions somethin' I never did. You've never been locked up, somethin' I can't claim, and you didn't have no babies at an early age or all over the place..." Jonnie's stare at his son changed from father to son, to detective to suspect. "...or do you?"

The statement brought a smile so strong that a miniscule laugh escaped it. "Naw pops, I ain't got no babies. Don't worry pop if I did you'll be the first I'll tell."

"Good." Mr. Murray exhaled in relief. "And see you're a lot smarter than your brothas were when they was seventeen and both of them made it to good colleges, Tony would of graduated but he was in the wrong place at the wrong time, but I'm still proud of 'em. Now call me narrow minded or stereotypical but I judge a man a lot on the success of his children.

You're a man to me now but chew ain't by law so don't be out drankin' in public, only in my house and don't get outta hand with it. You can brang gals over but don't get out of hand wit' it." Tracy smiled so hard that he had to swig his beer to hide his excitement.

"And when I get a chance to get the Cutlass fixed you can have it."

"Oh-thank you sir I been hopin' and waitin' for you to say that!" Tracy couldn't hide this excitement. He had been wanting Tony's old tan '79 Cutlass every since he left for college.

"Damn, calm down boy, you act like somebody gave you to-morrows winnin' numbers, I still gotta get it fix first."

"Pop all you had to say is that I can have it, I'll get the money to get it fix. But only after I get the money to help momma." He kept that thought to himself. Tracy swigged his beer then Jonnie sipped his liquor then chased it with his Schlitz. Tracy then discovered that he never knew why his father did that, let alone when he started. "Pop, why you do that?"

"Do what?"

"Sip yo' liquor then chase it wit' the beer, you tryin' to get messed up quicker or somethin'?"

"No, not mostly. The liquor is hell on my heartburn and the beer cools it down. Naw, I'm not gettin' lit up, I got thangs to do in the morning. I don't need no hangover, hangovers get worse as you get up in age."

Tracy said with a subtle grin. "I know what-cha mean, that old body don't work like it use to huh?"

Mr. Murray focused a rivalry stare at Tracy and said. "What! What chew just said?"

"I said that old…"

"-Body don 't work like it use to." Jonnie finished. "That' what I thought you said, boy I can do whatever you can do three times better."

"I 'on't know about that pops."

"Oh-I know. I may be old school but class is still in session. What chew need a lesson in football, basketball, baseball…"

As Jonnie rambled off the things he would take his son to school in Tracy took a huge guzzle of his beer, sat it on the end table, then stood up. He walked over to his dad and stood next to him as Mr. Murray continued rambling. "…I'll even school you on ice hockey and I ain't never even played it befo'." Tracy held his fist up chest high in a relaxed boxer's stance. "What-chew doin'?" Jonnie said with a grin.

"Well come on pop, let's see what that old body can do." Tracy moved in front of his dad and began swaying from left to right like a boxer feeling out his opponent before the first strike. Tracy then threw a jab with an open hand and slapped his father on his bare chest with the back of his hand, *pap-pap*, hard enough to create a loud smacking sound and an irritating burning sensation. "It sting don't it."

"Alright Tracy don't get a manly ass whippin' on the day you became a man."

Pap-pap. Tracy delivered two more slaps to his father's chest, both harder than the two before. "Come on old man?"

"Alright boy you betta' watch out."

Pap-pap. "Come on Father Time."

"Alright boy I'm warnin' you."

Pap-pap. Tracy delivered two more slaps then followed up with a push-slap on his chin with more push than slap.

"Oh, okay the grits is cookin' now buddy." Jonnie stood up slow and clumsy.

"Look at the old man, you can barely get up." *Pap-pap*.

Finally, to his feet Mr. Murray got into a boxer's stance and said. "Son you know I love you right, so forgive me for this country ass-whippin' you're about to receive."

"Well come on old man let's see what-chew got." Tracy threw a jab but this time Jonnie slapped it down hard. *Smack*. Tracy threw another. *Smack*. Mr. Murray slapped that one down, then another. Again and again Jonnie dodged and blocked every jab Tracy threw. Realizing it was pointless Tracy decided to change his strategy, his focused dropped to his father's waist and thought to himself. "I'll go in and scoop 'em up and slam 'em real quick, he won't be ex-spectin' that."

But he was wrong. Jonnie was from the old school and had plenty tricks. Tracy initiated his attack and Jonnie countered. As Tracy lunged forward, Mr. Murray stepped to his right while push-ing Tracy to his left (one of his old junior high defensive linemen moves). He then spent and wrapped his arms around Tracy's waist, putting Tracy's back to his front and grunted as he lifted him. "Up you go." He then dropped Tracy on the floor onto his stomach hard along with his weight. *Dooomm*. The living room shook. Tracy let out a sound of windless pain. "Ahhauwwwwwhhh!"

Jonnie then put him in a basic police hold he saw on Cops: He bent Tracy's arm around his back and stuck his knee in his lower back. "I told you boy you too young." With no breath Tracy strug-gled to say.

"Hold-pops-hold up!"

"What's wrong young buck?"

"I gotta-I gotta throw up!"

Mr. Murray quickly got up and so followed Tracy. He bolted to the bathroom and as soon as he lifted the toilet seat it came. "Huugghghguuaaah-hughaah-huaagah!"

Jonnie stood in the living-room with a proud smile on his face. He then looked over at his son's beer can on the table, he picked it up and noticed Tracy barely drunk half of it. "Well at least I don't have to worry about him being an alcoholic." Jonnie said unaware of the two cups of Crown Royal and highly potent marijuana Tracy smoked at the party. Mr. Murray returned to his recliner and ESPN after drinking down the rest of his son's beer. "Michael Vick you my man but Payton Mannin' should be gettin' the bigger check. Hell, you just goin' do something to fuck it up."

After about fifteen minutes of silence from the bathroom Jonnie became curious, almost worried. "Let me check on this boy, I hope he ain't in there dead." He walked down the hall and into the bathroom where he found only a toilet full of vomit. "A boy you betta come in here and flush this mess." After thirty seconds of silence he went to Tracy's room where he found his son sleep on his stomach snoring thunderously, fully clothed with one shoe on and one off. Mr. Murray stood in the doorway staring at his son sleeping as if he was a toddler. "That's my lil man right there and damn it I love 'em." He turned off his bedroom light.

"Momma!" Michael shouted as he closed the front door of his home. "Ma'." He heard no reply. "She must be sleep." He mumbled to himself as he walked down the hall and stopped at the guest room where the T.V was on and his mother in her normal state.

She was curled up in a corner of the couch, an empty fifth bottle of Seagram's gin on the floor and a small glass that had about a shot left in it. The television was on the Lifetime channel as always and she barely held on to the 8x10 picture of her family in her hands; her son, husband, and herself. Every night she would stare at the same picture as she drunk herself to sleep. It was like clockwork; she would buy a fifth of gin and two 12oz. cans of grapefruit juice, drink and listen to old R&B favorites, then fall into a pit of depression, take the same 8x10 off the wall and gaze into it until she falls asleep.

But tonight Michael discovered something different. A pint of gin lying halfway under the couch, telling him that her drinking had progressed to another level, she was getting worse.

Though the picture displayed a happy family, it was the memories of a fatal accident that guided her to drink herself into a sobbing depressed state until she passed out.

It was a four year-old memory of her and her husband (Michael Johnston Sr.) leaving a party, they both had been drinking and they were arguing about her catching him staring at another woman. He drove down an empty dim lit street as she fussed, shouted, and yelled. Michael Sr. being his normal passive self ignored her by silence and simple nonchalant sayings like: "I'm sorry baby you right. You right baby I'm wrong. I'm sorry baby I'll make it up to you. I'm sorry." This made her furious because she knew he was just pacifying her to get her to shut up, he wasn't paying her any attention.

"I saw you lookin' at them bitches, if you wanna be wit' them then go 'head, shit!" Mr. Johnston never was a loud argumentative person, he had a smooth demeanor.

"You hear me mothafucka!"

"Yes baby I hear you."

"Then answer me right then!"

"Baby I'm drunk and tryin' to pay attention to the road, it's dark on this street."

"I don't give a damn! You goin' listen to me!" *Smack*. She slapped him hard causing him to lose control for a brief second and a brief second was all it took for him to swerve and hit a huge pine tree. The impact threw Vicki through the windshield and into the woods, she wasn't buckled in. However, Mr. Johnston was in his seat belt but pinned down by the crushed steering wheel by both arms and was suffocated by the air bag. She never told her son exactly what happened only that his daddy lost control of the car, she left out the part about the argument and the slap that caused the wreck, the guilt drove her to alcoholism. She drunk to deal with the past, but the alcohol only increased her depression and heightened her emotions. Though he didn't like it, Michael was use to his mother's daily routine, it caused him to develop a routine as well. He would cover her up if she looked cold, take the picture out of her hand or off the floor, and hang it back on the wall. He would then pick up her empty glass and take it to the sink, if it had a little gin in it like tonight, he would swallow it down and then kiss her on her cheek, and whisper "I love you ma'," then turned off the television.

In his immaculate room, he took off the party clothes, put on a pair of nylon basketball shorts and stared into his dresser's mirror. Studying his well developed physique he flexed his muscles looking for spots he felt needed improvement. "Still need to work on my arms and chest a lil bit mo' and I'll be straight." He mumbled then his attention shifted from his image to the basketball card that was wedged in the upper left hand corner of the mirror.

It was a 1990 Upper Deck of an Atlanta Hawks forward Michael Johnston, his father. Though he was too young to remember his father's basketball career being that he tore an ACL in his fifth year and had to leave the league, Michael Jr. was still proud to say that his dad played in the NBA, and didn't ride the bench. He would study the basketball card of his father driving to the basket with a relentless facial expression of determination, everyday for motivation. A fact he didn't know was that he's a better athlete than his father was at the same age, he was good at every sport accessible at his high school and excelled greatly in basketball, football, and track and field. There was no doubt of him going pro, scouts told him that religiously but it was that huge hurdle in his life. He looked down at his dresser and lost all of his positive self-confidence when he saw the open envelope. He picked it up and sat on the edge of his bed, the senders address read; The University of Connecticut. He pulled out the letter, unfolded it then began reading the all too familiar disappointing words.

To the applicant Michael Johnston Jr., we sincerely regret to inform you that due to low SAT scores your full athletic scholarship has been denied. However, if you enroll under a student payment plan, take the necessary remedial courses, and increase your SAT score, your scholarship shall be reinstated...

He had read this letter more than ten times along with others from varies colleges saying the same thing, beating himself up inside. The letter was more than three months old but his mother knew nothing about it, how could he tell her that he's a failure, that her only son is a 'dumbass'. He couldn't, it would probably make her worse than what she already is, she had enough to deal with. Besides, he figured that he would handle it himself. His plan was to enroll under the student payment plan, take the remedial courses, retake the SAT, and get his scholarship. A solid plan but there was one problem, money. How would he pay for the courses. The money his father left was low after fifteen years of their living expenses and her drinking, besides he didn't have access to it. He folded the letter in frustration with tears in his eyes, put it back in the envelope, tucked it between his mattresses, and said to himself. "If I can just get my pockets right I'll be straight, everythang will be gravy."

"Damn! I forgot my key." Deshawn said patting his pockets. "Well momma finna be mad as hell."

Ding-dong, ding-dong, ding-dong, ding-dong. He relentlessly pressed the button. "Hold-up hold-up-I'm comin' I'm comin'!" His mother shouted from inside. "You forgot your key again didn't you." She fussed as she opened the door.

"Yeah I did, sorry I woke you up ma'."

"I was up, I can't sleep." She yarned as she walked down the hall, Shawn followed until he came to the bathroom.

"You had a good time at the party?" She asked as she climbed back into bed.

"Yeah, it was alright until Kevin started fighting." He replied while flushing the toilet.

"That boy is a hell raiser, nobody got hurt did they?"

"Naw but Chris' momma is gonna hurt him when she see her living room window busted out and a big hole in her wall."

"What! They broke a window and put a whole in the wall. That's ridiculous, ya'll youngens is too wild these days. See that's why I'm not lettin' you have no party up in here, yall don't know how to act. You ain't brangin' them animals up in here."

"Where Taishell at?" He asked standing at his mother's bedroom door.

"Oh she spent the night at Kenya's house. Oh and Tekela called."

"What time?"

"Well I got home around ten o'clock, she called five minutes after I got here then she called every thirty-minutes after that up to twelve-thirty, and she would of probably kept callin' if I wouldn't of told her I'll tell him to call you as soon as he got home. You didn't tell her you was going to a party?"

"Yeah I told 'er, but…"

"But what, she didn't want you to go?"

"Yep."

"And you went anyway."

"Yea, shoot, I wanna have some fun befo' the baby come 'cause I know I ain't goin' be able to when it's time."

"You got that right, because it ain't about you and her no mo' it's about the youngen. But if you plannin' on marryin' her you need to be there wit' 'er and respect her wishes."

"You right ma'." Shawn said with heavy guilt in his tone.

"I'm not fussin'. Let me lay down and try to go to sleep, I gotta long day tomorrow."

"You workin' both jobs tomorrow?"

"Yep."

"Alright, good night ma'." He walked across the hall to his bedroom, closed the door, flicked on the light, and headed straight for the black cordless Panasonic. It was still on the bed where he left it earlier when he called up his comrades about the party.

He had a typical teenage boy's room; semi-junky with a few pieces of clothes scattered on the light brown-carpeted floor and chair he had for company. He had a full size bed that needed to be made with dark blue covers and two pillows one with a pillowcase and one without. His walls were covered with posters mostly of southern rappers and female actresses. Artist posters of Outkast, Ludacris, Tip, Goodie Mob, Field Mob, Scarface, and The Nappy Roots. He also had posters of rappers from other regions such as; Nas, Krs-One, Twista, Ice Cube, Mos Def and Bob Marley. Above the headboard of his bed were posters of beautiful famous women actresses, rappers, R&B singers, and a few Jet beauties of the week. There was Angela Basset, Nia Long, Jada Picket, Tisha Camble, and Regina King, other desirable woman such as Lali Ali, Marion Jones, Missy Elliot, and a large poster of Angela Davis. On his ceiling directly above his bed was a collage of more than thirty pictures of Da Brat and Alisha Keys. He was fascinated by them.

He laid in his bed still in his clothes and dialed Tekela's number, while the phone rang he stared up at his fantasy, grabbed his crotch and began rubbing and massaging. He blew a kiss at them and said. "If I could have a threesome wit' you two fine a… I wouldn't need another piece of pus…"

"Hello?" Tekela's voice interrupted his brief fantasy.

"Oh hey-hey, what's up baby?" He said surprised.

"So did you have fun at the party?" She said full of attitude.

"Yea it was alright?"

"So how many of dem whoes you danced wit'?"

"See there you go. I ain't dance wit' nobody, anyway you know I 'on't dance."

"Yea whatever, you know I'm goin' find out what went down at that party cause I do have people watchin' yo' ass."

"Good. Cause when ya' lil snitches report back to you I want a big ass apology and you know what I talkin' 'bout cause I ain't do shit but smoke and drank a lil bit and holla at Chris and Corey. Anyway we wasn't there but an hour and half 'cause that fool Kevin started fightin'."

"Uuuuummm-huumm." She mumbled in disbelief. "I'll see. You said Kevin was fightin'. Who he was fightin'?" She asked with a lot less attitude.

"Some fools from Apple Valley, I forgot they names."

"Apple Valley? Is it Red, Dre, and Tim?"

"Yea, that's them."

"Oohh you better tell Kevin to watch his back…Was you fightin'?"

"What chew thank I'ma' sit back and let three niggas jump on Kev."

"He probably started it."

"Yea but it don't matter I gotta ride wit' my dawgs."

"Well know I gotta worry 'bout you."

"Why you say that?"

"Cause I heard them niggas is crazy, they carry guns?"

"You know Kevin ain't worried 'bout no nigga."

"Well he needs to be and you do too, them some fools out there in Apple Valley."

"Believe me baby Kevin is more of a crazy fool than any whole neighborhood in Augusta. Anyway, I 'on't wanna talk about that, let's talk about somethin' else. How you doin' baby?"

She smiled and the residue of attitude completely vanished. "I'm doin' alright, now that chew home, finally."

"How 'bout the baby?"

"Oh she's fine, been squirmin' 'round a lot lately, which is a good thang."

"You eatin' right?"

"Yea I'm eatin'."

"I know you eatin' but are you eatin' right. Fruits, vegetables, not no Mickey D's or Krystal's, fast food, shit like that. Some real food collard greens, black-eyed peas and rice, corn bread, and butter beans. Stuff like that."

"Yes, I have been eatin' right." She firmly insisted.

"Alright now my baby better come out healthy or I'm puttin' my foot in yo' ass." Tekela laughed. "I'm serious. If somethin' is wrong wit' my baby cause of lack of vitamins and a proper diet on your part. I'm foot printin' that cute ass of yours."

"Anyway if you would brang yo' ass over mo' often you would of noticed my momma and aunt cookin' different meals every day for me for the past six months!"

"Alright, I'm sorry calm down, I believe you, oh and eat a lot of seafood shrimp, fish, all other ocean foods."

"Why what's up with seafood?"

"I heard somewhere it helps make the baby smarter, or helps with brain development, or make 'em more intelligent, or somethin' like that."

Tekela gave a slight laugh. "Where did you hear that mess from?"

"I can't remember but just eat it anyway just in case it's true, it can't hurt. Asians been eatin' it since they been here on earth and they some of the smartest folks on the planet, and their race lives the longest, so they must be doin' somethin' right. It's worth tryin'."

"I guess so, I mean I do like shrimp anyway..."

"Ahaawwwwahh." Shawn yarned, Tekela quickly took it as an insult.

"I know you ain't sleepy all that partyin' you been doin' but now you wanna get sleepy with me on the phone. If I was Alisha Keys or Da Brat you wouldn't be sleepy."

"Girl, if you was one of them you would be tired, worn out, and pregnant on top of pregnant with about our sixth or seventh child!"

"What!" Tekela hung up the phone.

"Ole silly ass girl." Shawn said smilin' and began counting. "One, two,..." The phone barely completed the first ring before he pressed the flash button. "You know I'm bullshittin' baby."

"You better be."

"And you betta get use to gettin' off the phone wit' me early cause when I start this job Monday, it's nine to twelve hour days, five sometimes six days a week."

"Yea you right but that's different that's a job not a party. Why you leavin' Captain D's I thought chew said you get your way up there."

"Because it's two mo' dollars an hour, twice as many hours and the raises come quicker. I'm gonna need all the money I can get, 'cause I know hard times is comin'. Shit I might have to get a second job."

"See now there you go, worryin' talkin' like it's the end of your life, I told you it ain't gonna be that bad. I got my granny, yo' granny, my momma, yo' momma, my aunt, us, even Taishell. Stop worryin' so much, it's gonna be alright."

"We'll see."

"Now what I'm worried about is when we goin' do da' damn thang."

"There you go with that again."

"That's right there I go with that again I don't wanna be waitin' fa'-ever."

"What-chew mean forever, we just graduated."

"You know what I mean, don't string me along. Reggie and Patrice got married befo' they graduated."

"Yea and they ain't goin' last a year."

"How you now?"

"Well fa' one Reggie be cheatin' on Patrice, have been since they started talkin'. Two, that fool don't like to work, and three, Patrice don't give head."

"How you know all this?" Tekela said envious that he had gossip that she didn't have.

"Because, you know fellas talk just like yall females. Anyway I told you we goin' do it when my money get right, I 'on't wanna marry you broke."

"All that don't matter to me, do what-chew can, just don't ever cheat or beat on me and everythang is gonna be straight."

"You definitely don't have to worry about that but chew gotta eat, we gotta feed and clothed a child, not to even mention our own crib. I wanna be financially straight."

"Baby we'll make it."

"Okay since you wanna be in such a hurry how 'bout I rob a bank or credit union or somethin' like that, then we can get married the next day."

"Then be on the run fa' the rest of our lives oh that's just pure genius. Then I definitely don't have to worry about chew cheatin' on me 'cause you'll be locked up. Oh, wait a minute, they're fuckin' in prison and as cute as you is they'll be fightin' over yo' booty."

"Hell naw, funny real funny. Well, how 'bout I rob a dope boy or a easy brand new baller 'round here. I 'on't have to worry 'bout the police then."

"Nope 'cause I'll be visitin' your head stone, they'll kill you."

"Well how 'bout I start trapin' hustle that green and that hard white."

"Okay now let's examine this dumbass decision. You can get robbed and hurt, snitched on or hooked on ya own shit. Hell naw!"

Shawn smiled so hard that Tekela could hear the humor he received from messing with her. "Well it looks like we're gonna be waiting baby because I can't be penniless, I won't marry you if I can't take care of you...Hold up, I know what I can do. I can start messin' wit' voodoo, black magic, castin' spells, and shit like that. Maybe I could find a get rich quick spell and come up real quick like. Yea wasn't you around that when you lived in Louisiana?"

"Look Baby." Tekela's tone changed to a more serious, concerned, and firm one. "You need to get that thought out of yo' head, that's some serious and dangerous stuff you talkin' 'bout. Forget about it."

Her grave tone shocked Shawn. "Damn baby you make it seem like it's real, I'm just bullshittin'."

"Cause it is real and you shouldn't joke around with that mess."

Her words made him sit up in excited confusion. "Come on Tee-Tee, I know you don't really believe in that, do you?" He fought back his minuscule curiosity building in his much-opened mind.

"Believe me baby I done seen it work wit' my own eyes."

"I can't believe this I gotta crazy girlfriend." He said with a chuckle, which produced a little more emotion from her next conclusion.

"Good I'm glad you don't believe me and you don't believe in it, that way I know you'll stay away from it. Now let's talk about somethin' else." Her tone surprised him because this time it carried a sound of relief. His curiosity was fueled and now growing as he sat in a wondrous silence that lasted a few seconds.

"All right, all right-all right, you know I gotta know what you saw."

"No, I 'ont wanna talk about it."

"Come on baby please, see that ain't even right, build me up then renege."

"Let's leave it alone now."

"Ahhaawwhh!" Shawn gave a fake yarn and said. "Well, looks like I'll let chew go baby I'm feelin' kind of sleepy."

"Oh see now that ain't right."

"How that ain't right, you ain't right. You wanna get married don't chew?"

"Yes."

"Well how are we suppose to last as a good strong couple if we can't talk and share thangs wit' each other. You should be open wit' me and tell me anythang and I tell you anythang."

Tekela exhaled as if she let down a heavy emotional barrier she held up all her life, or ready to reveal a lifelong secret. "Alright, I guess I'll tell you."

"Okay see that is what I am talking about we makin' progress." He said imitating a fiftyish, white beard and mustache, black framed glasses, in a grayish coat with an unlit tobacco pipe, and yellow notepad-wielding psychiatrist.

"Yea and I better get a ring at the conclusion of the progress. On the correct finger."

"I got-chew baby, come on wit'-it." He said rushing her and switching the phone to his right ear.

"Boy you better calm down."

"My-bad baby I'm sorry. Go 'head."

"Okay. You remember when you asked about my cousin Steven you saw in some of our family pictures?"

"Yea the one that got hit by a car."

"Yea, that's him. I'm sorry I lied to you but he ain't get hit by no car, we just tell people that. Something else happened to 'em."

"Like what?"

"Can I talk please." She said somewhat flustered.

"I'm sorry baby my-bad, go-'head."

"Thank you. I was a freshmen and my cousin Steven was a senior, a very popular senior. He played every sport, he was in good shape, and on top of that he had good grades. All kinds of colleges was lookin' at 'em and he even had the coach from the Saints come and watch 'em play. Now not only was colleges lookin' at 'em but every girl in the school was too. I mean my cousin had it all and just like a doggish male he tried to do it with every girl that spoke to him our smiled at 'em. I mean from cheerleaders to band members, to the goofy and lame ones, to the rich and snobby ones, and the female athletes, plus some dikes. I even heard rumors of him hittin' a few teachers."

"Damn."

"I know, that was Steven. It worked out for me because every girl that liked 'em went out of their way to try and be all buddy-buddy wit' me. I had juniors and senior girls askin' me to kick it wit' them. Some of 'em even ask to carry my books, I was like naw that's a lil too much. I was the safest freshman in there, you know how juniors and seniors are, I didn't have to worry 'bout that. They use to steal freshmen's lunches but they was buying mine for me."

"That cat had it goin' on, playa-playa."

"Yea , playa-playa is what got 'em messed up. It was the middle of the school year and this new girl transferred from Baton Rouge named Dezaray, she was a junior. Now I give it to 'er the girl was pretty, kinda looked like Titiana Ali but she didn't dress like it, she dressed like… like a virgin, like she was tryin' to hide herself. She was quiet and nice but you know how it is wit' a new girl."

"Fresh meat, all the boys tried to holla."

"Yep and you know who got 'er."

"Steven, the mack."

"Yea, but it wasn't easy like usual she gave him a run, she played hard to get and then when he finally did start seein' her he couldn't hit right away. He had to work and wait on that cochie."

"Oh I know how that is." Shawn said smiling loudly trough the phone.

"Anyway." Tekela said pushing his comment aside. "He did it all, dates, holdin' hands down the hall, talkin' on the phone all night until one of 'em would fall asleep, the whole nine yards. I ain't never seen my cousin like that with any other girl, I mean he actually treated her special. Then he started hittin' it, that's when she really got deep in 'em, she opened her heart right along with her legs. She was doin' everythang for him buyin' him clothes, jewelry, givin' him money, she even gotta big tattoo of a heart with his name in the middle.

Then prom rolled around and two weeks before, he stopped callin' her, going out with her, takin' her calls, I guess the 'brand new wore off, the shit he always did when he was tired of a girl and was kickin' 'em to the curb. Two days befo' the prom he tells her he's sick and that he ain't gonna be able to take 'er. She believed it and started brangin' over bowls of gumbo for 'em, while he was out wit' his friends he had his sistas and me lie for 'em, tellin' her he was sleep.

The night of the prom Steven took some college girl he meet a couple of weeks befo', all that day that girl called every five minutes and every time I would lie to her, tell her that he was sleep. Then around eight o'clock the phone calls stopped and a hour later I hear a knock at the do', I'm so into my videos I didn't answer it, my little cousin Quentin answered it. I thought I heard a female's voice so I turned the TV down and heard it was Dezaray. I got up as quick as I could to get to her befo' Quentin open his big mouth but I was too late. 'Steven went to a dance'." Tekela imitated a little boy's voice. "As soon as he said that Dezaray's face dropped, Shawn I saw all the hurt that girl felt, but she didn't cry she held it in. Then for some reason she looked into the house and stared at me, dead in my eyes and then nodded her head like she was thinkin'. Yea you had somethin' to do wit' it too. Then she left. A couple of days later I found out that she went to the prom and watched Steven and the girl all night.

The next day Steven came home about two o'clock that

evening and I told 'em that Quentin had told her where he was and that Dezaray looked mad. He didn't care, like always when he got caught. 'I aint worried about it she'll be alright.' And as soon as he said that the phone rung, he answered it and with the short conversation they had I knew it was Dezaray. He hung up and said. I told you she'll be alright, that was a bootie-call, I'll holla at-cha'.' Then he left. About seven-thirty he came back home with that same look on his face he always would have after he just got some. He went to the kitchen fixed him somethin' to eat and sat on the couch in the living room.

It was my little sister, me, Quentin, Steven, and his two little sistas on the flo' watchin' a movie. After a while I started to notice that Steven was doin' a lot of scratchin'. First he'll scratch his face then eat a lil, then scratch his arms and chest then eat a lil mo'. I finally said somethin'.

Boy what's wrong wit'-chew, you got crabs or somethin'? He was like.

'Hell naw, I must of walked through them poison ivy vines in da back, I better go take a bath.'

He went up stairs and took a shower and almost an hour later, he comes back down stairs. This time he was scratchin' even worse and he had started coughing a lil. He asked me to look over him and see if he was breakin' out. I did and sure enough, he had a whole bunch of little red bumps all over his body."

"So it was poison ivy?" Shawn eager to ask.

"Well that's what we thought it was. He went up stairs and put some Calagel on the rash and went to bed, that was about eleven-thirty, eleven forty-five somethin' like that. I'll say about two o'clock in the mornin' I wakes up to go to the bathroom, I'm walkin' down the hall and I hear Steven in the bathroom with the do' closed coughin' like he was dyin' or somethin'. I knocked on the do' and said. Steven you alright? Then he said cryin'. 'Naw cuz, I'm messed up!' It scared me because I ain't never seen nor heard my cousin cry or even sad. I said what's wrong, then he said. 'Come and see!' I opened the door and I almost passed out when I saw my cousin standing over the sink in his boxers, all I could do was cry. He had these big-ole, bubble like bumps all over his body, from the top of his head to the bottom of his feet. Not no poison ivy rash or no insect bites these bumps was nasty they looked like…" Tekela paused to search her mind for a comparison to what she saw. "You know that bubble plastic wrap that companies use to wrap fragile stuff, that kids like to pop?"

"Yea I know what cha talkin' 'bout."

"They was like that but the size of a quarter and full of some yellowish puss, it looked bad. I looked in the sink and saw blood clumps in it that he had coughed up. Then he looked at me wit' tears in his eyes and said. 'Tee-Tee somethin' wrong!' I started shakin' and cryin' even worse, I never heard Steven sound so helpless in my life. I ran to my momma's room and woke her up and when she saw Steven she nutted-up, she started cryin', panicin', screamin', and shakin' her hands. She woke up everybody else in the house, when she finally calmed down she wrapped Steven up in gauzes and bandages then called a few doctors but it was too late for house calls, they told us to take him to the emergency room but Steven didn't want to go outside like that, he didn't want nobody to see him. So after momma wrapped 'em up she put 'em to bed and watched over him. Me, my sister, Quentin, and Steven's two sistas all slept in the hallway by his room door incase somethin' happened. For the rest of the night he coughed, tossed and turned, and sometimes he coughed up blood clots, it was scary.

The next day the doctor came over and looked at 'em and shit he wasn't no damn help, cause all he said was that it was an allergic reaction to somethin' and gave 'em a shot of somethin' I forgot the name of it. Then he said keep a eye on 'em and in about two days he should be fine. Yea right, two days turned into two weeks and two weeks turned into two months. She called doctor after doctor and all of them said the same thang, It's an allergic reaction.

For months I watched my cousin suffer, I would look after him in the evenings when my momma went to work and she would watch over him in the mornings when I went to school. Everybody at school would ask about 'em, I would lie and tell them he moved out of town, somethin' like that. Then I noticed that girl Dezaray would be starin' at me some times, but I ain't thank nothin' of it. Summer rolled around and thangs got worse. The heat made him itch worse and every time he scratch those bumps they would pop and all that creamy puss would ooze out onto his sheets, we had to change his covers at least three times a day, sometimes more."

Shawn on the other end of the phone had his face bald up in disgust as if he had a detailed image of Steven's grotesque condition in his mind. He wanted to express his disgust verbally but he knew it would have been inappropriate so instead he gave sympathy. "Dang baby."

"And the smell, he would smell so bad that it made my stomach hurt every time I brought him food, water, or had to change his sheets. You know how spoiled raw ground beef and raw iron smell?"

"I guess."

"Well it kind of smelt like that in his room but worse, then on top of that he couldn't hold down any food, more than three bites he'll throw it up. I watched my cousin deteriorate." As she told her story the memories pushed out the same sad feelings she had when she took care of her invalid cousin. Tears built up in her eyes and her voice became oppressed by emotions, which Shawn noticed. He now felt guilty for surfacing such painful memories with his selfish curiosity, she continued.

"Every day I had to watch him suffer, every day I had to listen to him cough and spit up blood, every day I had to watch him look up at me like...like...help me Tee-Tee, help me?" Tekela could no longer hold back her emotions she released some of it with a whimper and though the guilt in Shawn grew, his curiosity over whelmed him, he had to know the whole story. "I... I... didn't know what to do. Every day of going in and out of that room made me start thankin' crazy thoughts. Thoughts that I'm so ashamed of that I never told nobody."

"You can tell me baby." Shawn assured her with a humble tone.

"I, I wished. I wished that...that he would go ahead and get it over wit' and just die!" Speaking those dark secrets and troubling thoughts from her past made her brake down even more, Shawn was shocked by her confession but was understanding and sympathetic. "I know I'ma' fucked up person fa' thankin' like that but I just couldn't take it no mo'."

"Naw baby, you ain't fucked up that's a lot for a teenage girl to handle, for anybody to handle. You're only human baby. And if you don't mine me askin', where Steven's momma was at durin' this time?"

"Oh she died from a heroin overdose when he was like ten my momma and aunties been rasin' 'em."

"Oh I'm sorry to hear that, but you ain't fucked up don't say that."

"I guess, it's just that I loved 'em but I hated that I had to watch him suffer like that. I spent my whole summer in that house, in and out that room. I missed out on all kinds of stuff, I even missed more than half of my tenth grade year, that's why I was kept back, I would of graduated last year. But it was fa' Steven so I guess it's alright." Tekela paused to control her sobs, wiped her tears and continued.

"Well by the beginnin' of the school year people found out that Steven wasn't out of town and that he was at home sick. Rumors started, first it was cancer then it was AIDs, you should of seen the panic, girls he had been wit' was runnin' to get tested. After they realized it wasn't AIDs people started visiting every day bringing gifts and givin' their condolences. Momma and me never let 'em come up stairs, we sat all his flowers, cards, and gifts on his dresser so he could see how folks was thankin' 'bout 'em. Almost everybody came to show their support; neighbors, his friends, girls that liked him and girls he did wrong, coaches and not just from our school but other high schools, even some college coaches came. People he ain't seen since elementary school came through. I remember one man that had came to see 'em, he told me that he played for our rival school and when they played against us his eleventh grade year and Steven's tenth grade year, Steven tackled him and broke his leg. Then he said it healed in a way that it helped his runnin' and helped him to get into the NFL. He gave me the old cast cause he wanted Kevin to have it maybe it'll brang him luck, he said. I told Steven about the man and showed him the cast; Steven smiled because he knew who the man was, since he got sick that was the first and last time I saw my cousin smile. I forgot his name but he plays for one of them NFL teams. Yep, everybody came except that girl Dezaray.

We tried everything lotions, creams, medicines, our church even came to pray over him but he never got better, just worse. Then my momma job changed and she was back on the nightshift, so I was able to go back to school, it was past the middle of the school year and I was already kept back. I just went to keep my mind off Steven but soon as I got to school the questions started: How Steven doin', is he alright, is he comin' back to school, what's really wrong wit' 'em? Stuff like that which just made shit worse. Then one day in the hall somebody bumped into me, I looked and it was Dezaray. She gave me this crazy grin like she was up to somethin' then she said.

'How yo' cousin Steven doin'?' Befo' I could answer she said. 'Don't worry, it'll be all over real soon.' Then she walked off. Shawn, when she said that I got this crazy feelin' somethin' bad was about to happen. I said forget my last class and ran home. I got to the house, ran up stairs and saw Steven sittin' up with his head dropped down and a long bloody strang of slob hangin' from his mouth. I thought he was dead until I tapped 'em on the shoulder. He lift his head and he looked like he was drunk, he said.

'Hey cuz.' I said, you alright Steven, then he said.

'Tee-Tee thank you fa' takin' care of me, I love you.'

I said I love you too, what's wrong wit'-cha'? Then he said.

'I'm thirsty can you get me some water?'

I walked out of his room and got halfway down the hall when I heard him start coughing real bad, it sounded like he was chokin' so I ran back to his room. He was layin' on his back chockin', like somethin' was caught in his throat. I ran over to him and I could see somethin' red and bloody comin' up out of his throat every time he gagged. He couldn't breathe, I ain't know what to do so I ran down stairs to catch my momma befo' she went to work. We ran back to his room and found him on his back, dead with a bloody, slimy thang hangin' out of his mouth. She called the ambulance and later on we found out that, that red thang was a part of his stomach. Then, come to find out that the whole time he was coughin' up those blood clots, he was really coughin' up pieces of his insides like; his stomach, intestines, kidneys, and his liver."

"Baby, fo'real!" Shawn said in shock.

"Yep, and you know what, befo' my cousin got sick he weighed a hundred and seventy five pounds, when we buried him he weighed sixty pounds.

"Damn."

"Yep, they say that they don't know how he lived as long as he did. It was like somethin' was keepin' him alive so he could suffer. Later on after the funeral me and momma started cleanin' up Steven's room. She took his blankets down stairs to burn them and I had pulled his mattress when I found a memo book and some pens. I knew what it was, I just let the book lay in my hands and open to where I needed to start.

"After the prom me and Vanessa got us a room, she was wide open all night. Them college girls is wild I can't wait to step off in there. I spent the night with her and before we left we hooked something up for the weekend. When I got home ole-girl Dezaray called. She said she saw me at the prom and before I could lie she stopped me and said it's all gravy I just want a little something one last time. I felt like I owed her that much.

I got to her house and she came to the door in some lingerie, looking good! I walked in and she had the sexy black and red candles burning and fixed me a fat plate of the best spaghetti I ever tasted. I hope auntie don't find this book because I'm sorry hers was better. I never tasted vinegar in nobody's spaghetti before, different but good.

After I ate she took me up stairs where she had more black and red candles burning then she undressed me. She gave me some head, which was the first time she had done that. Then she climbed on top of me and slow motioned with it. She was wetter than usual. About fifteen minutes into it she started mumbling some words. I thought she was coming until I recognized clear words in order like a poem or something. Then she whispered in my ear. My pain is now your pain, I suffered now you suffer. Then she kissed me then rolled me on top of her. I beat it up, then fell asleep. Thirty minutes later, I wake up in a big spot of blood in the sheets. I woke Dezaray and asked if she was alright. She said, now I am. I told her about the blood and she didn't even look at it, she answered quick. Oh you must of knocked my period on. I left, hungry as hell."

Shawn heard Tekela turn the page.

"He stopped and started back the night I found him messed up in the bathroom." Tekela continued reading.

"God please help me, something is not right, I woke up about 2:45 in the morning, I couldn't breathe I coughed until I felt something coming up. I ran to the bathroom and threw up. Bumps all over me itching and burning. I threw up clumps of blood. It feels like somebody is in my stomach carving off the walls. Tee-Tee saw me and the look in her eyes scared me more than the blood and bumps. Something is wrong.

It's been three days and I'm still sick, my auntie called the doctors but they said it's an allergic reaction. I ain't never been allergic to nothing. The bumps on me feels like something is alive in them and they won't stop squirming. I want to take a razor and scrape them off me.

It's been a week now and I'm still the same. I had a crazy dream last night. First it started with Dezaray opening her front door and letting me in, all I see is her and the candles. She sat me down in a black and chrome casket and feed me that spaghetti, I could really taste it. Then we had sex in the casket and the stuff she whispered in my ear kept echoing. My pain is your pain, I suffered now you suffer.

I've been in this bed almost a month now and I'm going crazy. I know what's happening to me, I don't understand why I didn't recognize it early, like when it took place. I grew up around voodoo and root workers. She got me, she put a curse on me. I wish I could get her ass back but I don't mess with that. I wish what's going to happen will hurry up and happen.

The summer done came and went and I'm still in this bed, my cousin Tee-Tee takes care of me, I know she is tired of being my babysitter. She missed her whole summer because of me. I love her and I'm sorry she's going through this with me I wish I would just die and get this shit over with.

Poor Tee-Tee she missed half of the school year, she's going to get left back. She's a good person, I'm glad she's blood. This is my last time writing, the pen and pad is getting heavy I know it's almost over. I ain't scared. I'm ready to get this over with. I hope my sisters know I love them and auntie thank you for raising me because my momma was too strung out to do it herself. You are my momma. Thank you Tee-Tee for being there for me. I'm sorry for being a burden.

Before I finish writing I want this to be known. This is my last wish, I wish that somebody would get that girl Dezaray make her pay not only for what she did to me, but for going against God and fooling with devilish stuff.

"And that's what happened to my cousin Steven." Shawn sat speechless.

"Damn baby. I don't know what to say about that. So, what happened to that girl Dezaray?" There was no answer and Shawn thought she didn't hear him. "Baby did you hear me? What happened…"

"-I heard you. If I tell you this you promise not to tell nobody else."

"Baby, come on."

"Promise!" She snapped.

"Alright baby, I promise."

"Alright now, I'm trustin' you. Well after I found Steven's notebook I showed it to my momma and watched her read it. She cried and nodded her head then I heard her say, 'I knew it'. Then she asked me did I know where Dezaray lived, I said yes. For four days she bought and filled up four different jugs with gasoline. We then went to the girl's house and my momma parked in the driveway, got two jugs from the trunk and started dousing. I got out and got the other two and helped, we splashed it everywhere the doors, windows, walls, and in their garage. Then momma struck a match and threw it on the front porch, then *whoosh*, the whole house was in flames in like ten seconds."

"Damn, that's right baby burn it down!" Shawn celebrated.

"That's not all baby. While we was watching the house burn, we saw Dezaray and her momma standing behind her, holding her. They was standing in the window watching us watch them burn."

"Whaaaattt!" Shawn uttered in a whisper. "You mean to tell me…"

"-Yes Shawn, me and my momma killed that girl and her momma."

Shawn was struck with silence at his girlfriend's confession, he couldn't believe it, his pretty, sweet, petit girlfriend is a murderer. He thought he knew her, murder, she stood back and watched two people burn. Then he thought about the night he took her virginity. 'If you cheat on me I'll kill you, slow.' He took her warning for granite then, but now the warning seemed to be a possible promise. He was speechless.

"Shawn, Shawn, say somethin'."

"What can I say." He replied with a nervous tone.

"Anythang, don't get quiet on me speak what's on ya' mine."

"I guess you had to do what chew had to do."

"That's right, she killed my cousin so we killed her." Shawn again shocked at his girl's ruthless comment. "And that's why I don't want chew even thankin' about that stuff. It's evil. Now that I gave you my all, deep secrets, virginity, and now yours and my first child, you can give me at least two things. Marriage and monogamy."

"I promise I'll marry you as soon as I'm financially stable. I might have another way."

"Well, tell me."

"The military."

"Yea, that's a possibility. I mean you would be away a lot and you can go to war but at least you ain't in prison. Would we get married?"

"Yep as soon as I did the basic training thang."

"Well let's put that on the list for finance, aahhhhaw." She said followed by a yarn of relief and drowsiness.

"Sounds like you ready to lay it down."

"No I don't wanna get off the phone with you yet, bad enough I ain't gonna get to see you none this weekend, momma makin' me go to Carolina wit'-'er. Shot I wanna stay on the phone until we leave." Tekela complained.

"I hear ya' baby but look, you ain't just sleeping for yo'-self you sleepin'…"

"-For the baby I know, that's a smooth way to get off the phone. I'll give it to you tonight because I am tired, up thankin' 'bout chew at that party."

"I love you Tekela Burnet." Shawn said in a strong whisper.

"I love you too baby."

Shawn waited until she hung up first, he then laid back on his bed too overwhelmed to take off his clothes, only his sneakers, he laid staring up at Da Brat and Alisha Keys but his mind wasn't on them. All he could hear was faint residue of his mother's snoring reverberating off her bedroom walls and his loud thoughts.

"I can't believe this, my girl, my soon to be baby-momma, wife, is a killer. I guess in the right situation it can be brought out of any-body, I guess. And that voodoo-black magic-witchcraft shit is real. I believe her but I still want to see it for myself." He yarned and his eyes closed.

"So what's up cuz-o you going to my crib or you going to the house?" William asked after taking a pull off his Newport.

"Shit it's Friday night and momma done got that check, you know what time it is. She gettin' zooted and booted, I ain't tryin' to be 'round that shit tonight."

"I hear ya'."

"Auntie home?" Kevin asked.

"Naw she went to Florida to a dental convention, she gone fa' two weeks."

"Damn."

"I thank she bullshittin' though."

"What chew mean?"

"I thank she's down there creepin' on pops."

"What, you thank auntie is cheatin' on yo' daddy?"

"Thank, cuz-o I know she is. Hell he cheatin' on her. Talkin' 'bout he's flyin' to New York to meet wit' some cat he went to college wit' to talk about startin' up their own law firm."

"They might be tellin' the truth."

"Some of it's true, they did leave to do all that but two weeks, come on, I'm young but I ain't dumb."

"So they going through wit' da damn thang?"

"What? The divorce? Hell yea."

"How you feel about it." Kevin asked as he licked the small cut on the inner wall of his bottom lip.

"How I feel about it? Nothin'. Don't bother me."

"Oh, I thought chew would be all depressed and sad, ready to run away or shot up a mall or a school like them fragile ass white kids on them after school specials. Mommy and daddy is splitting up and it's all my fault." Kevin performing a bad impression of a young Caucasian child. "Maybe if I run away or kill some people they will stay together boo-whoo!"

Will laughed then pulled his cigarette. "Man that shit don't bother me. Shiiitt they gotta do what they gotta do, it's better than stayin' together and bein' miserable fa'ever. Anyway I'll benefit from them splittin' up, if anything, I'll have two places to choose to live in."

"Who would you pick to live wit' first?"

"Probably pops, cause he movin' to New York and shiiitt I wouldn't mine slangin' this country dick to them city whoes, show 'em how we do. And I wouldn't mine the change in scenery. I mean

I love da AUG and I'm a Georgia boy to da' bone but I would like to get away for a minute, see somethin' different for a change. What chew thank?"

"Shit I say do what chew do cuz-o. If it was me and I had a chance to leave, I'll haul ass and never look back."

"Damn cuz-o it's lilke that?"

"I hate this mothafuckin' place."

"Naw, this ain't the same fool that be in da' club yellin.' AUG! 706! And knockin' niggas out is it?"

"Don't get it twisted, now I'ma' rep my city to da' fullest but I still wanna leave this shithole. I can't stand it here, I done had too much bad luck in this bitch. I done lost a brother here and my momma and everywhere I go I end up fightin'." Kevin said with subtle frustration.

"Shiiitt, you make it seem like you like fightin'."

"While I'm fightin' yea and I 'on't mine lettin' out some anger every now and then, but it's a time and place fa' everythang and these ignorant ass niggas don't know that and that's when murders take place. Like this one time I took this pretty lil thang to Applebee's, you know the date thang, when the waiter brought our food out I noticed fo' niggas from Sunset had walked in. Now two weekends befo' I beat da' brakes off a Sunset nigga and damn shown-nuff he was one of 'em. After 'bout ten minutes into my meal the one I beat up gets up and walked to the bathroom, we made eye contact for a second but he acted like he didn't recognize me, then he gets back to his table he must of told his potnuhs 'cause I heard one of 'em say. 'Well shit let's get that nigga.' And then he stood up. So I stood up and walked over to his table. I said what's up so ya'll boys wanna get some straightnen or somethin'. The one I beat up stood up and said hell yeah. I punched his ass and another one of them fuck niggas. They jumped me. Fo' Sunset niggas and they didn't even leave a scratch on me. I tried callin' shawty after that and she told me she can't mess with me 'cause I'm too thuggish."

"Damn."

"I know she was fine too. Then one time I took this shawty to the movies, we leavin' out and as I'm holdin' the do' fa' shawty, this nigga went out of his way to speed up, walk through the do', step on my foot, and bump me. I looked 'em dead in his eyes and said damn cuz, I can't get no excuse me or somethin'. Then another nigga behind him said. 'Hell naw fuck boy!' I looked and recognized buddy, it was a lame that I slapped at a sto' a couple of days befo'. He was from Allen Homes but he had three of them Underwood niggas wit' 'em. I already knew what time it was so I swung first. Shit like that I gotta deal wit' on a daily bases, you'll get tired of that shit after awhile. I wanna be able to go out and have a good time. And what if I'm wit' my son or lil brother ridin' or at the park or somethin' and a nigga I done put my hands on see me and gets to shootin'. My son or my lil brother could catch one. I 'on't like livin' like this cuz-o. So if I had a chance to get the hell on I'll take it wit' no questions."

"Yea I see where you comin' from." Will said with understanding as he pulled into the driveway of the double garage two-story house.

William Cooper unlike his comrades was considered as being a privilege kid growing up in a financially plentiful home. His father was a new but successful lawyer and his mother was a five-year dentist, successful enough to start her own practice. However, their success came with the neglect of their son and instead of spending quality time with Will they spent money on him and the race for success also fatally damaged their marriage.

"Damn we should of got a blunt from Shawn, I ain't even get to hit it the green."

"Pops got almost a twelve pack of Budweiser in there, you can get a couple of 'em. William said pressing the alarm button on his key chain. And I thank he got a bottle of Hennessy in there too." William unlocked then opened his front door, as he disarmed the alarm Kevin followed in behind him and took a seat on the huge Broyhill couch.

"Damn!" He uttered when he noticed the 64 inch plasma television mounted on the wall. "When ya' pops got that?"

"Got what?" Will said from the kitchen.

"This plasma jank."

"Oh about three weeks ago." Will said returning to the living room with two twelve ounce long necks. "That fool paid almost six stacks for it and only watched the bitch twice."

"That's alright though because I'll watch the hell out of it for 'em."

"I hear ya', here you go." William passed Kevin a beer. "The remote is over there, go ahead and check it out."

Kevin grabbed the remote from off the dark oak and glass top table. He turned on the TV and sunk down into the couch as if he was taking off in a fast car. "Woo! This shit is nice." He said as he opened his beer and surfed through the channels.

"Go 'head and get comfortable cuz-o, you can sleep down here or in the guest bedroom."

"Do the guest room gotta plasma too?"

"Naw." Will said with a chuckle.

"Well, I guess I'll be sleepin' in here."

"You need some shawts or somethin' to sleep in?"

"I'm straight, I can sleep in this, and I 'on't feel comfortable with puttin' my nuts in a pair of shorts yours been in."

"Nigga my nuts is clean, fresh, Mr. Planters 'round this piece. I'll be back." William went up stairs while Kevin kicked off his shoes got up, walked across the deep expensive cream color carpet to the DVD tower against the wall next to the plasma, and immediately found something of favor.

"Constantine, good shot." He loaded the Samsung DVD player and walked around on the soft carpet looking at family pictures positioned around the living room. William, his mother, and father smiled and boasted their family togetherness in his face, it brought on some depression and anger because his home didn't have a smidgen of love and happiness Will's had. Fortunately his anger and depression was quickly smothered with humor when he saw one of Will's pictures of him when he was six. The funny haircut and missing two top front teeth made him laugh. He walked over to an oak Broyhill curio cabinet where he noticed a family photo album, he grabbed it and sat back down on the couch. He opened it and immediately started laughing at the first picture, which was the same picture of William he saw on the curio, he flipped as he sipped.

The first set of pictures was that of his Aunt Victoria and Uncle Raymond in the hospital, Victoria pregnant and about to deliver while Raymond comforted her. The next set of pictures displayed Will's head squeezing out of Victoria. "Damn Grandma' you got it all didn't ya'." The next page of pictures was of William's first birthday party, Will making a mess of a chocolate icing cake with a blue and white number one candle in the middle.

The next page was of William's fifth birthday party, Kevin stopped and gazed at the pictures of Will surrounded by most of their cousins. It was six year old Kevin, Mitchell, Eric, Melissa, and Carlton. They all were smiling and full of innocent happiness. On the opposite page, one of three photos quickly caught his attention that brought a heavy pressure over his chest and stomach. It was a picture of his aunt Victoria and her husband, his grandmother, his uncle James and his wife Pam. Uncle Jessie and his wife Wanda, aunt June, and his mother and father. He took a deep breath as if he was about to confess to a shameful crime, exhaled slowly, and then took a gulp from his beer. He put his eyes back on the photo and shook his head. He had forgotten how beautiful his mother use to be, before the crack addiction.

Healthy, bright-eyed with long lashes, full lips, copper tone, and unblemished skin, a beautiful bright smile, lustrous jet black shoulder length hair, and full cheeks with deep dimples. The image of his mother before him seemed to be a stranger. The depression was kicking him in the stomach and he wanted to snatched the beautiful figure out of the photo and replace the mother he had now with the better one. The image of the man with his arms around her added more stress. He was a tall, solid, smooth dressing man in his late twenties that wore a lot of flashy jewelry, he looked proud with his arm around his lady, his wife, Kevin's father. It's been a while since he died and even though it was a long time since he saw his father, time was not the only factor for forgetting him almost completely. It was the streets, it killed him when Kevin was thirteen. All he knew of him was what stories he heard from his mother and old school drug dealers that use to run with him. However, he did have two fond memories of his own about Lenny that he would play back in his head from time to time when he would forget his face. One was when he was eight and Lenny brought in a pair of boxing gloves. He coached and played with him all evening, then went next-door and got Junior. He was a lot bigger than Kevin plus three years older.

THE 7TH MAN

Junior had beaten Kevin up on numerous occasions in the strip of yard between their houses but he never backed down nor stopped until their parents stopped them. Sometimes Junior would just get tired of beating him up and would stop. He was not then, but is now thankful for his father making him fight, it made him a tough and fearless teenager. He gave more ass whippings than he took and the ones he took he took them well.

The other fond memory he had was when he beat up Junior for the first time. Junior had popped the chain on Kevin's bike, Lenny was in the bathroom smoking 'dragon shit'(marijuana laced with heroin) when he saw out the window, Kevin on top of Junior unleashing a fury of punches. Lenny rewarded him, he took little Kevin to the movies, they ate pizza, Lenny bought him some new clothes, and a better bike and that weekend Lenny took Kevin to Playville, twice. They road go-carts, played video games, and had fun until Playville closed and he was too sleepy to play anymore. Those were the fondest memories of his father but they was not the only memories, just the good ones. He had two others that were just as clear.

Once when he was eleven, he ran into his parent's bedroom with a permission slip from school for a field trip. He found Lenny in the bed in the midst of a heroin ride, belt loose around his arm and needle lying next to him. At eleven Kevin knew what was going on, from movies he'd seen and the company Lenny and his mother kept. He still asked his dad to sign the paper. Lenny seemed so tranquil and nice while signing, that Kevin felt it was the perfect time to ask for some money.

"How much...you need, son?"

"About thirty dollars."

Lenny pulled out a bunch of bald up bills that scattered onto the floor and bed. He rumbled through them and picked out what he thought was three tens but was three hundreds. He handed it to Kevin and laid back to finish enjoying his ride. He later had one of the best time periods of his life with the money however, it was overshadowed by finding his father four years later with a belt tight around his arm, needle hanging from it, he dozed off and never woke up.

He turned the page and gulped his beer just as Will was coming down the stairs. "I see you popped in that Constantine, good cause I still ain't seen the whole thang yet."

"What! This is the shit, I 'on't know what it is but I love this mothafuckin' movie."

"I know, it's just that every time I try and watch it I be so fucked up that I end up passin' out befo' I even get to the middle of it."

"Oh, a cuz-o I can get another beer?"

"Hell yeah help ya'-self, Shiiitt you can have as many as you want."

"So yo' pops let's you drank now?"

"Cuz-o, that fool let's me do anythang I want. Smoke, drank, brang whoes over and beat, whatever. That's another reason I might go and live wit'-'em if they or when they get a divorce."

"Damn. I figure since he a lawyer he'll try to have you on lock down."

"Naw, he told me that I could do whatever as long as if I keep a clean criminal record."

"Damn that's straight, I would never act up."

"He just bribin' me. See I thank he's thankin' about runnin' fa' office or becomin' a judge or some shit one day and you know havin' a child wit' a criminal background will blemish 'em, make 'em look bad." Will explained returning from the kitchen with four more long necks, he handed Kevin two.

"True-true-true. Why you gave me two?"

"We finna run 'em."

"Alright."

"One." Will said then they both twist the tops off. "Two, three." They both turned their bottles up to their lips and began guzzling, eleven seconds later William finished first, only suds slid down the inside of the bottle while Kevin was barely half finished. Kevin could never out drink William nor out smoke him. He would end up either passing out, vomiting, or fighting somebody that he thought looked at him wrong. "I'll teach you how to drank one day. What's that, one of our photo albums?"

"Yea I was just flippin' through it." Kevin said after giving up on their little competition.

"I thank this is the one…" Will mumbled. "Yea this the one."

"The one what?"

"It's a picture in here I want chew to see, I 'on't know if you seen it or not." William said flipping and searching the pages. "Bam here it go right here. You seen this one befo'?"

Kevin studied the picture. "Naw I ain't never seen this one, damn all of 'em in there."

"Yep"

Kevin stared down at the 5x8 photo of three women, sisters holding their toddlers and giving beautiful full smiles. One was William's mother Victoria, she was holding a then, eighteen month old William. Next to her was June, she was holding a fourteen month old baby boy and next to her was Meshell Kevin's mother. Once again he couldn't believe it was his mother, she was the prettiest sister. She was holding a two-year-old Kevin giving a smile of pride. Standing behind the sibling trio was their mother, she looked almost the same age as her daughters just a lot stronger and weathered.

"They look young." Kevin said.

"Hell yea."

"Damn you had a big ass water jug head!"

"Hold up yo' head ain't too small either."

"A cuzo, you might thank ya' cousin kinda sick but, Aunt June is fine as hell."

"Oh don't feel shame, I be thankin' the same shit." Will confessed, both of them gave a slight laugh at the weird thought.

"Look at lil Dominic. When was the last time you heard from him?"

"Last summer."

"What's up wit'-'em?"

"He said he was fuckin' wit' da rap thang, said he just gave Lil Jon and LA Reid his CD and was waitin' to hear back from 'em."

"Oh that's cool, I hope he get on."

"Yea me too. Damn, yo' momma and mine look a lot alike. I ain't really notice that until now."

William's comment created shame in Kevin causing a mumbling response. "Hum, the bitch don't look nothing like that now."

Will felt awkward from the response his comment created. "Damn cuz, that's yo' momma, I know she ain't the best and ain't been doin' right but that's still mom-dukes."

"Fuck that." Kevin almost snapped as he opened his other beer "She ain't none of my momma. If she was any kind of mother she'll put that shit down and raise her damn kids. If not for me at least fa' Kayvion, you know what I'm sayin. He ain't nothin' but eleven years old and gotta watch his momma act like a animal. If it wasn't fa' me and grandma' I 'on't know who would take care of my lil brother. Do you know how many game systems Kayvion done had? Two Playstation twos, a Game Cube, and two X- boxes, the bitch ended up pawnin' all that, just to get high. Me and grandma' went in on another PS2 last month. We keepin' this one at grandma's house, cause I'm tellin' you if my momma steal this one, I'm puttin' my foot in 'er ass."

William was stung by his cousin's hateful words about his mother. "Naw cuz-o, don't do dat, you ain't supposed to hit cha' momma."

"Hell she ain't actin' like a momma."

"Well shit, talk to 'er or somethin', don't put cha' hands on 'er. That's fucked up, I heard that shit take years off yo' life."

"I done the talkin', mo' talkin' than a drunk man at confession, it goes in one ear and she smoke it out. Will, you know how much grandmamma and yo' momma ran they self crazy tryin' to help her." Will nodded slightly then dropped his eyes back to the picture. "Grandma' put 'er in rehab first, she got out and was straight fa' three months befo' she relapsed. Then grandma', wit' yo' momma's money stuck her in there again tryin' to help 'er. She only lasted two months, then she tried to snatch some nigga's dope out there in Meadowbrooke and got jumped on and put in the hospital. Who paid the bill?" Kevin didn't give Will a chance to answer. "Yo' mom-ma. She went back into rehab, came out and lasted nine months surprised everybody but you know how it go, grown folks is goin' do what growin' folks wanna do. So I'm like fuck it, it ain't no savin' her, I'll take care of my own. All I need is some money, a couple of stacks and I'll move my son and lil brother to some off the wall state, haul ass." Kevin sipped his beer and stared at the TV but not watching it instead catching a glimpse of how life could be. "Just let me fuck around and come up you'll see. That's why I wish Markell was still alive, he would of made sure we was straight."

William caught the sadness in his thuggish cousin. He was use to seeing him in an aggressive form, like jumping across the counter at McDonalds and beating down the boy on the grill for a reason William still does not know. He felt it was appropriate to interrupt the flow of tension with a tactical question. "So cuz-o, where would you go if you had the money?"

"To visit or to stay?"

"To stay."

"I'll go live somewhere like Wyoming, Massachusetts, Idaho, Iowa, or Wisconsin some shit like that."

"What!" William responded. "Why places like that, it ain't no niggas there."

"Now you see what I'm sayin', low crime rate, worry free, a good place to raise my seed and my lil brother."

"I wouldn't say all that, you'll have somethin' to worry about, them crackers runnin' yo' black ass from 'round there."

"Naw, 'cause if I had the right kind of money I'll get some land off in the woods, isolated. I ain't botherin' them crackers so they ain't gonna bother me."

"Another thang, it's colder than penguin pussy up there, you know niggas ain't made fa' dat shit. I give you two weeks and you'll be haulin' ass back to Georgia wit' a lynch mob behind you." William said then took a big gulp of beer.

"Hell yea." Kevin laughed. "But all bullshit aside, if I had the money it ain't no tellin' where I would go or what I'll do. But I do know I would leave though, that's real. But, it's about that money, gotta get that befo' I can make any kind of moves."

The rest of Shawn's weekend was a rainy, dreary and isolated one. His mood made him cut himself off from the rest of his social circle, he didn't answer the phone for Tracy, Larry nor Michael and when William and Kevin came by four different times Saturday and Sunday he only peeped out of the window at them. When Tekela called he told her he was sick and that he would call her back, which he never did. It wasn't just the weather that had him down all Saturday but the thought of him becoming a father soon had engulfed him in depression. His remedy was weed and contemplation, he began smoking 5:30 a.m. Saturday morning when his mother left for work and smoked every so often when his high would die down. He stressed about being unprepared to become a father, he wished he had listened to his mother about wearing condoms but it was too late for that now, the baby is on its way and he was scared. He thought of all types of jobs and things he could do to support a family but his conclusions were the same, they were going to struggle for a long time before the good times would come. He was tired of struggling, him, his sister, and his mother struggled their whole lives every since his pops left his mother in forty three thousand dollars worth of debit. He refuse to struggle, he was determined to find a way to get a large amount of money in a short period of time. He tried to come up with something but all Sunday his mind was cluttered with the thought of what his girl did and the story she told: His sweet lady killed two people and Steven and his encounter with witchcraft. He believed his girl but he was still curious, he needed to see it for himself if it work. After hours of contemplation and getting high, he decided that if he had the chance and if the opportunity presented itself, he would try witchcraft.

"I mean, hell it's not an unforgivable sin, I'll just try it once and ask God for forgiveness. Yea, that's what I would do." Deshawn laughed at his thought as he laid in his bed. "But where in the hell would I get the info from on witchcraft, I don't know nobody that mess wit' that shit. Oh well, it's just a bullshit thought. Let me go to sleep so I'll be ready fa' this job tomorrow."

Shawn finally fell asleep unaware that tomorrow he would have an answer to his dilemma.

Chapter 3:
The Curious one

"So how you like it so far?" The skinny light skinned young man asked.

"It's straight, ain't too hard and it ain't slow."

Shawn started a job at Carole Fabrics a textile plant that special in the manufacturing of curtains, blankets, pillows, and other interior fabrics. The owner was a third generation capitalist money hungry narcissistic jerk, that under paid his employees ridiculous rates and couldn't conceive the fact that his workers were, people.

"It's just, the supervisor."

"Yea, Mrs. Debbie Hoy, oh yea she's a bitch. Nobody in this plant can stand 'er, she done had her car keyed up, tires slashed, and her windows bust out on two different times. She gotta real nasty ass attitude and always comin' out the mouth wrong, then ten minutes later she actlike it's all-good like nothin' happened. And she's a snitch, if she see somethin' she don't like she's quick to run and tell it, even on people in other departments. I 'on't know what the hell her problem is, her man ain't fuckin' 'er right or somethin'."

"Damn, I might have a problem wit' her." Shawn said in slight frustration. Deshawn and his partner's job was simple; they were to box up and ship out all they ready shades that were assembled in the department next to theirs. A simple task that Shawn could have easily tackled within the first hour of the shift but being that he was distracted by a peculiar individual, it took him a little longer to catch on.

"A cuz, what cha' name again?"

"Cedric, but everybody just call me C. Yours?"

"Shawn."

"Alright. What hood you from?"

"Da' Ville."

"It's some crazy fools out there."

"Hell yea. So C what's up wit' buddy over there?" Shawn asking about a tall lanky and skinny Caucasian young man about twenty-one or twenty three years of age. He dressed in all black; a black T-shirt that read 'Mayhem: The sickness of order...' in red, black pants with silver buckles on them and that were so baggy that his black steel toe boots were completely covered. Despite the summer weather, he wore a black cloak , similar to what the character Blade wore. He had shoulder length curly hair dyed black and his finger nails were also painted black. The main attraction to the human spectacle that made everyone stare, were the ghost white contacts with a tiny black dot as a pupil that he wore.

"Oh you talkin' 'bout Daniel. I 'on't know cuz, I thank that cat worship the devil or somethin'."

"Why you say that?" Shawn asked with a grin on his face.

"Why I say dat, look at 'em that fool wear black all year round no matter how hot it is, he barely talk to folks, and he be drawin' these crazy ass symbols at his workstation. One time I could of sworn I saw the star of Lucifer drawn on a piece of card board by his workstation."

"You sure it was the star of the devil, cause you could be confusing it with the Star of David."

"The star of who?" Cedric replied with a confused look on his face.

"It's a Jewish thang and it's a lot of star symbols out there that don't got nothin' to do with the devil."

"Oh, well I wouldn't know nothin' 'bout that."

"And the reason why he dresses like that is because he's a goth."

"He's a what?" Cedric said with an even more confusion on his face.

"He's gothic."

"Man I 'on't know what da hell…"

Shawn grinned again. "It's like, a way of life or a class of people." Shawn struggled to explain. "Okay, you know 'bout cha' thugs and what they live by."

"Yea." Cedric replied.

"Okay you got cha' pretty boys."

"Yea ole conceited ass clowns."

"Yep, then you got cha' druggies ."

"Yea cats that base their lives on gettin' high, always gettin' fucked up."

"Yep, then you got cha' hip-hop heads."

"Yea."

"Then you got goths, mostly a white thang you'll find a few gothic niggas out there but that's very rare. All I can tell you about them is what I got from this goth girl I knew in the ninth grade: they believe that you can't have life without death, creation without destruction, light without darkness, sugar without shit. Now it's probably some gothic people out there that do worship the devil but hell I know some gangsta-ass-thugs that worship the devil."

Suddenly Cedric's attention was stolen from Shawn by their supervisor Mrs. Debbie, standing about ten feet away with her hands on her hips and a stern look in her eyes. "Hold up dawg, Cedric warned. The wicked bitch of the south is starin' at us." Shawn turned around.

"Alright gentlemen a lot more work and a lot less talking would be wonderful." She said with a salty attitude.

"I can't stand that bitch." Cedric mumbled as he stapled an order form to a box.

"What's up wit' that broad's hair-do, she looks like Ronald McDonalds' oldest sister."

Cedric let out a loud laugh at the unexpected insult that caused the 'Wicked Bitch of The South' to turn and give them another stare. "Let's get to work befo' I end up cussin' this heifer out." Cedric suggested.

"Fa'-real." Shawn agreed.

The two worked and strategically struck up conversations for half of the day, Cedric mostly doing the talking. He asked questions to get to know him more and to help the day go by quicker. What school he went to, did he know certain people from certain 'hoods' and what he do on the weekends, the ice breaking questions. Shawn only gave short and direct answers not being rude or anti-social, it was because he was distracted by thoughts his open mindedness manifested.

"I wonder what that cat got in his head. I wonder what he know. I bet I can learn a lot from that cat. If anybody know somethin' about witchcraft, I bet he does. A lil bit at least, or know somebody that do. I should ask 'em, but he might be one of them withdrawn isolated depressed and shut-in mothafuckas. All clammy. Mothafucka might pull out a sword or knives on me or some shit. Listen at me, stereotypin' him and shit that ain't me, actin' like the majority of the closed minded folks in here. Maybe he want attention and don't mind conversation. Only one way to find out. I'll holla at 'em on lunch break."

Ms. Debbie called Daniel over to ask him to do another un-necessary task. "Fucking bitch." Shawn read from Daniel's lips, he then slammed down his pen and went to the 'Wicked Bitch of The South'. Shawn noticed she had interrupted Daniel while he was in the middle of writing something, his curiosity pushed him over to Daniel's work station. He read the back of one of the Carole Fabric's address label:

Have you ever went into a fit,

where you vomit your food and later regret it

and cry cause you're so pathetic?

Never mind you don't get it.

You're clouded by the dreams to fit in,

you'll never win,

living a lie is hard

but it's harder to live as you are,

hating what you are

You can't relate, you're below me- I'm elevated by the truth

that to know pain is to be true.

"Oh yea I'm hollin' at this cat on break. All he can do is tell me to get the hell on. I hope, he might snap, go to his car, pop the trunk and pull out swords, big ass daggers and shit. Come back in here and gets to slicin' folks up. I know who he would get first, Ronald McDonald's big sister. I can already tell he can't stand her. He won't get me, I'm too damn quick, unless he pull out a rifle then he might have a..."

"That ass was good wasn't it?" Cedric asked snapping Shawn out of his mental conversation.

"What's that? I ain't even hear ya."

"I said that was some good ass." Shawn looked confused. "I saw you over there day dreamin', deep into it like you was thankin' about some good ass from the past. Believe me, I know how it is, make you wanna go find her number."

"Oh naw, it ain't nothin' like that, thankin' 'bout some ways to get some quick money."

"That would of been my next guess. A Shawn, you blaze man?"

"Yea, why what's up?"

"I got half a blunt in da car, you can come and hit it wit' me on break if you want."

"Naw I'm straight, I 'on't wanna fuck around and staple my hand wit' this big ass staple gun." Shawn held up the yellow and black Bostch 10-50 air pressured staple gun.

"I feel ya', mo' fa' me."

"'Preciate it though. What time is lunch anyway?"

"We got." Cedric said pulling out his cell phone. "Fo' minutes."

The two worked in anticipation for the four longest minutes they could ever recall, Cedric ready to get high and Shawn ready to approach Daniel. Shawn then noticed Daniel retrieving a book from his workstation along with an MP3 player and headphones. He took a few steps in the direction of the cafeteria, then the bell rung, more like a long annoying beep.

Shawn analyzed the lunch line, too long to be waiting in, besides he was broke. He then scanned the cafeteria and saw Daniel sitting at a table alone reading a book with his earphones in. He walked past Daniel's table over to a wall of vending machines, he bought a bag of Doritos, a honey bun, and a Snicker bar. He then walked over to Daniel's table and sat on the opposite side directly in front him. Daniel's eyes rose up from the book just enough to notice Shawn taking a seat.

"You don't mine if I sit here do you?"

"They say it's a free country." Daniel replied in a questionable mumble.

Shawn sat and dropped his head in grace, finished then opened his honey bun while reading the title of the book Daniel was reading. Edward Lee 'City Infernal.' "Is that any good?"

"Of course it's Edward Lee." Daniel said without lifting his eyes from his book.

"So what's ya' name man?"

"Don't you already know?"

"Why you say that?" Shawn gave a slight puzzled look.

"Because when there's a new person in the plant I'm usually the icebreaking topic. You know, who's the freak in black."

Shawn now felt like a suspect that had been just verified as the culprit. That's just what he had done earlier that day. "Well yea, you're right about that. Shawn thought to himself. Damn it's goin' be hard tryin' to get some info from this cat."

"So, go ahead and ask me."

Shawn almost choked on a piece of his honey bun, it was like Daniel had read his mind. "Ask you what?"

"The question that you want to ask me."

"What makes you thank I want to ask you something?"

Daniel flipped to the next page and without lifting his eyes from it he answered. "Because only three people ever sat at the table with me the whole two years I've worked here and they asked me two questions. Where did I get my contacts and two of them ask me do I worship Satan. I figure that's what you want to ask me."

"Oh naw-naw I could care less about that."

Daniel eyes rose from his book and gave Shawn a suspicious stare. "Hold up I'm not no fucking fag if that's what you want to know!"

"Noooo-no-no, hell naw! It ain't nothin' like that either."

"Just checking." Daniel's eyes returned to his book." Well in that case, go ahead and ask."

"Alright, now you might thank I'm crazy or somethin'."

"That'll be a first." Daniel commented on the slight irony.

"Well maybe not. I was wondering, do you know anythang about witchcraft, voodoo, black magic, shit like that?"

The question surprised Daniel something that was almost impossible, he didn't expect that question from this type of person, a black youth. He had actually stopped reading his book and was now studying Shawn. "Witchcraft, why are you asking me about witchcraft?"

"Well I hate to be the stereotypical type but for the same reason why everybody ask if you're a devil worshiper, cause you're a goth.

"No not why you choose to ask me but what's the reason you're curious about witchcraft.

"Oh-okay-okay. Well I'm in a tight situation right now and recently the idea of usin' witchcraft seems like somethin' I need to try. My problem is that I don't know nothin' about it or anybody that does, that's where you come in."

Daniel put down his book and stared at Shawn for thirty seconds. "You have enemies you're tryin' to get revenge on?"

"Naw nothin' like that."

Daniel exhaled in disappointment. "Oh. Hum, it's money,

you're trying to get some quick cash."

"Yep that's it, I need money bad and quick."

"That should have been my first guess it's usually always money, vengeance, lust or power. Are you serious?"

"Hell yea."

"You better be damn sure because the black arts is some serious and dangerous shit."

"I heard. So you do know somethin' about witchcraft?"

"Yea, I know a little, a few spells and incantations, nothin' major." Shawn adjusted himself in his seat with a smile of excitement.

"So you'll look out for me, help me out?"

"I think I can give you a small and weak money spell."

"Yes! I appreciate it and I'll pay you back for this."

"Trust me, keep your thank yous."

"So, what kind of stuff do you know, what can be done?"

"Well a lot can be done, with the right spells and I know enough, as far as I'm willing to go that is."

"Like what can you do, give me an example?"

"Well, I know a few vengeance spells. If it's somebody you feel has crossed you, done you wrong somehow, I know a spell that can cause them to get so sick, they would puke and shit themselves at the same time every hour, every time they eat or every time they think about you until you feel they've suffered enough. Or, I can fix it so that one of your enemies fear you so much that they'll lock themselves in a closet for days without food or water, shaking in their own piss from fear of just your shadow. I even know a spell that will have your enemies in Serenity mental hospital thinking that they're a glass of orange juice and scared that someone is trying to drink them."

"Damn, you can really do all that?"

"Already done it. But that's not a fraction of what I know."

Shawn felt it was too good to be true, too convenient, either he was real lucky or this cat is bullshitting him, delusional or starving for attention. He decided to continue digging to find out.

"But that's not all you know is it, I mean I ain't tryin' to hurt nobody, I'm just tryin' to get some dollars."

"That's not all I know, it's just the stuff I dabble in. I had a few deep rooted issues I hadn't dealt with yet, I had a lot of enemies in high school but, they've been taking care of."

Shawn gave Daniel a suspicious look. "A, I come in peace."

"I know." Daniel said with a ghost of a smile. "Besides I've gotten all my vengeance."

"Good." Shawn replied in relief as he opened his Doritos. "What else can you do, can you like, make a fine ass girl fall in love with the ugliest dude in the state?"

"Now see that's a big misconception people get from TV. See there's limits and rules to the black arts. One, being emotions, good emotions of the heart. Too many limitations on the heart except for hate, but the mind is like open space. No limits. You can make a girl so obsessed with a dude or vice versa that she would think she's in love with him. Those are obsession spells or lust spells, not love spells."

Shawn nodded like a student receiving vital final exam answers. "You ever done it?"

"Nope, I only mess with vengeance spells and a few money spells."

"Okay that's what I'm talkin' about. Shawn replied with eager curiosity. Tell me about the money spells."

"It's not what you think, you don't perform a spell and the next morning you wake up with a bag of money in your room. It's more, watered down than that, at least the ones I've messed with. As a matter of fact that's the last spell I've done."

"How did it work? Tell me about it."

"Well, it was about six months ago and my mom had lost her job and couldn't pay the next two months mortgage, so I did a money spell. It was a Wednesday that Friday I got my check and the company fucked up and over paid me."

"How much?"

"Let's just say they added a one in front of my original three hundred dollars."

"Damn you had a extra thousand dollars on yo' check." Daniel nodded. "That's the spell I want, the one you did."

"Now look it might not work exactly like that, it may come different."

"I don't care just as long as it comes."

"Alright. But before I give you this I have to let you know something."

"Alright."

"You know those sayings, for every action there's a reaction and what goes around comes around."

"Yea."

"Well in witchcraft and black magic the rules apply, worse than what the spell caused, most of the time three times as worse."

"Damn, I didn't know that." Shawn replied with slight disappointment. "What happened to you, after you got the money?"

"I ended up getting pulled over for speeding and the cop found some weed my brother had stashed in my car five months ago and forgot where he put it. I ended up paying six hundred for the speeding ticket, a misdemeanor charge for possession, and about forty seven hundred dollars in fines and probation fees."

"Damn."

"Yea, so do you still want to do it?"

Shawn nodded then replied. "Yea, yea I still wanna fuck wit' it."

"Alright, I warned you."

"Yes you did, so you gonna write it down and give it to me after work?"

"No, what I'll do is give you my number cause I have to look the spell up I can't remember it off hand. And plus it'll give you more time to think about what you are doing before you just jump right into it."

"Oh I don't need to thank about it, I'm ready."

"We'll see." Daniel said and Shawn replied with a thought to himself.

"This cat just don't know how broke I am. I'll try anythang right now, and anyway he might be full of shit and this whole thang might be a waste of time. Only one way to find out." Shawn contemplated while he finished his Doritos conceiving another thought. I wonder what he meant, as far as he was willing to go." The thought irritated him like a gnat buzzing in his ear. He had to ask. "So Daniel, what did you mean by as far as you're willing to go?"

"That there are things I will never do."

"Like?"

"You ever heard of invoking the spirits?"

Shawn looked extremely puzzled. "Vote for what!"

"No." Daniel gave another ghost of a smile. "Invoking, conjuring, calling a spirit or meta-physical being over to our physical world."

"Naw I ain't never heard of that. A spirit, meta-physical?"

"A spirit, an angel, a demon anything from the other side that wants to come over."

"A demon?"

"Yea, you do know what a demon is don't you?"

"I guess, they're like Satan's little helpers or something?"

"Yea something like that. But that's something I wouldn't mess with."

"I 'on't blame you, what would be the purpose for brangin' one over anyway, how would somebody gain from that?"

"Oh a person could gain a lot. See when somebody conjures up a demon, the right kind of demon, it will do anything that person orders it to do, anything."

"How's that I thought demons work for the devil."

"They do it's kind of complicated. Daniel put his book down and exhaled. You have a huge thirst for knowledge I see."

"My momma said that I always been a very curious child."

"That can be good but curiosity can be a curse if you can't control it."

Shawn nodded. "Can you explain how the demon thang work?"

"Do you know the story of Lucifer and how he use to be an angel?"

"Yea, they called him the Morning Star because he was so beautiful that he shined, ole pretty mothafucka." Daniel was somewhat surprised at Shawn's knowledge. "Oh yea I know a lil somethin'."

"Okay, well what else do you know?"

"Uuhm, oh yea, I know he got the big head and thought he was on God's level and that he should be in his place. He started some shit up in heaven so God kicked his ass out and that's when hell came about."

"Closer than I thought. Well, during Lucifer's uprising in heaven he had accumulated a lot of followers, other angles that believed in him and his cause, now right before God put a quick end to Lucifer's plan a lot of those followers turned on him and tried to get God to forgive them."

"What happened?"

"See the rules of God's forgiveness for man are different for angels and the big man wasn't having it because soon after he cast Lucifer out into the bottomless pit, he cast them out as well. When they got to hell, Lucifer captured them and locked them in a prison where they are to be tortured for eternity or until a human releases them. That's where the conjuring and invocating comes in. See when a human performs an invocation ritual they're opening a door between our world and theirs allowing spirits, demons, and other things not of the physical world to pass through. See Satan still feels he's God's equal and to be better he grants them forgiveness and gives them the opportunity to be set free. That is if the demon can get the one that conjured him up, to perform as much evil as possible, when Satan is satisfied he sets them free."

"Damn, that's some other shit there." Shawn replied leaning into the info. So do all of 'em do the same thang or is there certain ones for certain, deeds?"

Daniel smirked strong enough to let out a minuscule laugh then shook his head. "The curious one. He who seeks knowledge must bear the responsibility of truth. Look, like I said, I'm into vengeance and a few money spells, I don't fool with invoking. I only know but so much about demon classification but I do know of one of them. Zeinoch, you use him through your dreams."

"Your dreams?"

"After a person conjures it up, it can only be manifested through that person's dreams. This is the way to maintain control over the demon."

"How can you control a demon in yo' dreams when you can't control your dreams?"

"See that's another complicated situation but I see you still wanna know."

"I'll appreciate it." Shawn said with a grin.

"Okay, during the conjuring a connection is made between you and the demon, or if you and let's say three of your friends call it, then a connection is made between the four of you and the demon. It'll exist until the demon is sent back to hell. The connection between the four of you all will give off like a psychic sense amongst you."

"You mean like, I'll know what they know, and feel what they feel, and vice versa?"

Daniel was impressed by Shawn's understanding. He could also tell that Shawn was intrigued which made him disprove a stereotypical trait of a gothic youth, which was: being closed off, self-isolated, and an outcast from the quote on quote normal way of American life and society. However, Daniel would have shut Shawn down as he did many other people and labeled him as the typical closed minded, brain washed, ignorant, and fearful of the truth human but he noticed Shawn was different. Genuinely he thirst for knowledge, like himself, fool heartedly but passionate and open-minded. He didn't care that Shawn was talking to him to pump information out of him, a favor because it was a different type of favor, one that didn't involve his wallet nor his car. He saw Shawn as a pupil and not as a burden-polluted fake ass friend.

"Yea but just slightly different. It has to be something major, like an extreme fear, a burst of anger, extreme and sudden hate or sudden pain, something like that. Now I'm not sure if you'll be able to see what they see but if it's something seriously wrong with you they'll know and if something is wrong with you..."

"-My potnuhs will know."

"There you go. Now I do know for sure that your dreams will be connected and you all will be able to control it, Zeinoch. For example: after you call on it, go to sleep, it'll appear ready for your command, I think your consciousness enters its body and you control it by thought or emotion. You can dream it walking into a bank kill everybody, or not, break open the safe, and there you go riches."

"Damn, that's some ole X-files shit." Shawn mumbled then kept his next thought in his head. "I should try this conjuring shit, it sounds like it's more fun and more profitable. Naw, I better stick With the simple shit, you gotta crawl befo' you walk Shawn. So," Shawn said aloud, "do you know how to do it?"

"Now how did I know that was coming. Yes, from reading, I never done it and never will."

"Why not?"

"Too dangerous."

"How, if you're the one controlling the demon?"

"It's other factors you have or I have to consider. One is that Zeinoch feeds off your hate, anger, rage, and inner evil deep inside of you. I myself have so much anger, hatred and rage inside of me that he'll have no problem becoming a physical being and there'll be some serious problems. See I forgot to tell you that when the human has done significant amount of evil through Zeinoch, Satan grants him freedom by allowing him to become a physical being making him uncontrollable. I don't want to take that chance."

"Have you ever known somebody that done it?"

There was a pause then Daniel replied. "Yea, my pops." Daniels answer seemed disturbed, he quickly ended the matter. "And I don't want to talk about that, so next question."

Shawn saw the brief presence of pain in his face, he understood and quickly grabbed another question racing through his mind. "So how many people can be involved in a spell or ritual?"

"The amount doesn't really matter it can be from one person to a hundred people participating."

"How do you know all this stuff?"

"Books, the net, and my folks, mostly my folks."

"So yo' peoples was deep into it?"

"It was like an addiction with mom but she doesn't mess with it anymore. In her case though witchcraft helped her."

"How's that?"

"She use to be a bad alcoholic but when she discovered the dark arts she changed, it's been seven years since she had any alcohol."

"I guess… *Buuuzzz!* Shawn was interrupted by the lunch bell. Damn lunch is over already."

"Yep time to go back to work for Carrot Top."

"I can tell you can't stand 'er."

"I despise the bitch. Sometimes I imagine myself trying out different torture techniques on her."

"Damn." Shawn said as they rose from their seats and made their way to their department. He could see and feel people staring at him and he knew why; the new guy is talking to the freak.

"Don't worry, a month into it you'll be feeling the same way too."

"Yea I can see that, she already done started bitchin' at me."

"I saw that, that's not even a fraction of her wrath. The creature fucks with me at least three times a week."

"That's fucked up."

"That's not even the best part, I've been in this hellish place for a little more than two years and I've only gotten two raises."

"What, they told me in the interview they give raises every six months." Shawn said with worry.

"They're suppose to but it's up to the supervisor to give it to you or not. The crone don't like me."

"Now that's wrong. Maybe you should do a vengeance spell on her."

"I have." Daniel said with a grin under his serious face.

"You serious about revenge ain't cha'." Daniel nodded. "Well if you nut up and decide to take revenge out on the plant with an AK47, please let me know ahead of time befo' you go Columbine 'round here."

Daniel grinned. "You don't have to worry about that I hate guns, it's a pussy way of doing things."

"Good." Shawn said in relief.

"If I did it I would use two swords, a few knives, daggers and other types of blades."

Shawn stopped in his place in shock from Daniels comment. "Damn I was thankin' that earlier!" He said in his head. He started back walking to his work area and noticed the rest of the employees in his department gathered around Mrs. Debbie's desk. She was staring at him and Daniel with her arms folded and a look on her face displaying that she was in bitch mode. She looked at her wristwatch then back up at Daniel and Shawn. "This bitch is stupid." Shawn mumbled under his breath.

"You got that right." Daniel turned and said surprising Shawn not knowing he had said it loud enough for Daniel to hear. They joined the eight other employees and was greeted accordingly.

"Lunch is over at twelve-thirty guys, Daniel you already know this, Shawn I know you're new but you still have to get with the program."

"Yes ma'am." Shawn replied then looked over at Daniel who was signaling him to look at the clock on the wall. Shawn read 12:32 (two minutes late) then shook his head. "Yea I'ma' have a problem wit' this bitch."

The quick huddle was a brief meeting to inform employees that the plant would be shut down tomorrow for fabric inventory and possibly Wednesday. After the five minute meeting, they returned to work, Shawn worked the rest of the day with a heavy mind, he couldn't wait to get off, get the info he needed from Daniel, and try it. He debated if he should try it alone or with his comrades and how would he convince them to try it. He already knew that if he smoked the rest of the weed he had left over from the party with Will and give him some alcohol he'll be down. Larry would do it just to fit in and Tracy would do it because it's his idea and he and Tracy are tight. He would have trouble with Kevin and Michael he wasn't too sure about those two but it's worth the try he thought. Besides, if they don't want to do it, he'll do it by himself. He would ponder so hard that he would find himself talking to himself.

"A Shawn, you." Cedric said. "You might wanna move from in front of the door." Shawn moved from in front of the double door entrance, which is the entrance to another department where the women assembled the shades and curtains that he and Cedric boxed up and shipped out.

"Why what's up?"

"You'll see in two minutes."

Two minutes passed and Shawn and Cedric were sweeping up their work area. "Watch this, watch the door." Shawn stared at the door, three seconds later a buzzer sounded throughout the plant and then five seconds after that a swarm of old and young ladies came rushing through the door. Sixty percent of them were of Asian descent; Korean, Japanese, Philippine, and Chinese. A few women from other countries such as; Greenland, Iceland, and Scotland. There were a few African American women and a few Hispanic women. They all stampeded out of the plant.

"Damn!" Shawn uttered.

"Yep them women don't be bullshittin', they'll run yo' ass over quick to get up out of here. They tryin' to beat that line at the traffic light on Bobby Jones expressway."

Shawn and Cedric finally made it out to the parking lot after walking behind a group of old ladies that lipped with bad hips, knees and ankles. Shawn found a spot on the wall, leaned against the wall and lit a cigarette.

"A you need a ride cuz?" Cedric asked.

"Naw I'm straight, my potnuhs pickin' me up, 'preciate it though."

"No problem, I'll holla at cha Wednesday, hold it down."

"Alright, you too man." Shawn watched as Cedric walked over and got into a well kept and clean, blue 1985 Chevy Caprice Classic. He cranked it up and its pipes roared like an angry bear.

"Damn, sound like a monster." Shawn said impressed. "And it's clean." Cedric drove off with a blow of his horn. Shawn then put his attention on the rest of the ladies leaving out of the plant and walking to their cars. "Damn it's a lot of fine ones up in here, look at the ass on her. Now I'll do somethin' different to her." Shawn mumbled to himself. When the parking lot began to get clear, he became worried. "Shit I hope I ain't miss Daniel." Just as he finished his sentence, Daniel walked out of the building with his MP3 and earphones in his left hand. "Good I thought missed you."

"You still want to go through with this?"

"Hell yea, I'm dead-ass serious." Just then Big Will pulled up blasting a song from the Southern based rapper T.I.P. Kevin in the passenger side rapping the lyrics and bouncing around along with MJ and Larry, while Tracy calmly bobbed his head in the back seat behind William. Will blew his horn. *Beep-beep.* Shawn held up his finger signaling to William to give him a minute, Tracy notice Daniel and commented first.

"Who in the hell is that Shawn talkin' to?"

"You mean what, in da hell is that nigga talkin' to." William said then tapped on Kevin's shoulder to get his attention from the musical vibe he was stuck in. "Kev."

"What in da hell is wrong...that white boy, is he stuck in da matrix?" Kevin said.

"Watch me fuck wit' Shawn." William said then began blowing his horn. *Beep-beep-beep-beeeeep.* Shawn was receiving Daniels phone number when he got frustrated with Will's irritating action. He held up his finger again then shouted.

"Hold up man I'm comin'!" Everyone in the Explorer noticed Shawn's frustration and laughed.

"So what time should I call you?"

"Call me any time after seven, I should have the information you need by then."

"Cool, I'll hit-cha' up 'round eight, oh and thank you."

"Hey, don't thank me yet." Daniel said and walked off.

"So what's up Shawn, I ain't know you knew Dracula's lil nephew." Kevin said as they drove off.

"That's Daniel, a cat I work wit', he gettin' somethin' for me, some information."

"Information on what, how to be a day walkin' vampire?"

"Naw man." Shawn said with a chuckle.

"Info on what I'm curious?" Michael said.

"Just a lil somethin', I'm keepin' it on the low fa' right now."

"Oh so you can't tell ya' boys?" Tracy hassled.

"It ain't like that, I'ma' tell yall when the time is right, I wanna make sure everythang is straight first."

"Alright, fuckin' wit' them crazy ass crackas he goin' have you blowin' up government buildings and shit." Kevin said.

"Yea that cat do look like he's one hidden message on a heavy metal album away from killin' his whole family." William added.

"That's fucked up." Tracy laughed.

"Don't that mothafucka get hot wit' all that shit on?" Kevin asked.

"I guess, I 'on't know." Shawn replied with a slight laugh.

"Shawn you still got some mo' of that green left?" Will asked.

"Yes sur, two fat ass blunts but I need some cigars."

Tracy pulled out and counted two dollars and sixty-three cents. "I got-'em."

"What chall boys got on da drank?" Will said grinning into his rearview staring at his comrades in the back.

"I'm broke." Larry answered.

"Yea, we know." Kevin said while digging in his pocket and pulling out three dollars. "I got three."

William added his large contribution. "I got three too."

"I got two." MJ added.

"That's eight, so that's two bottles of dat Mad Dog, what's up?"

"Run it." Shawn agreed with a hidden agenda. "Matter of fact I can pull three mo' dollars and get three of them black cans."

"Okay then." Will said.

MJ pulled out his wallet and began searching and found three dollar bills folded extremely small behind a condom. "I almost forgot, I got three mo'."

"So I'll get T-Murray, Big Will, and mine, you got Larry's, Kev's and yours." Shawn said.

"Naw let me get Will or T-Murray's, I ain't fuckin' wit' Larry." MJ protested.

"Why, that's fucked up!" Larry complained.

"Naw it ain't fucked up, you never finish yo' two-eleven, you always leave it and let it sit and get hot."

"Man I'ma' drank it all, watch."

"Yea that's what you always say and Will always end up finishin' it."

"Hell yea." Will agreed.

"Alright, I'll get Larry and Tracy." Shawn said with a laugh.

"We got eleven dollars, enough fa' two bottles of MD 20/20 and six black cans." Will said as he pulled into the parking lot of the One Stop convenience store.

"Don't get Larry no two-eleven get that fool a Miller High Life or a wine cooler or some shit like that." MJ said.

"Look I'll out drank everybody in this ride, twice, and that's real talk."

"Look-look, look at Hollywood's beggin' ass." Kevin said pointing at a man standing in front of the store engaging in an excited conversation with six older men, all were holding brown paper bag covered beers in their hand, except Hollywood. "Call 'em over here cuz-o and get 'em to get the drank for us."

"A, Hollywood, let me holla at cha' for a minute." William shouted out of his window.

"Heeeyyy young blood!" Hollywood greeted with a groggy voice damaged from cigarette and crack smoking. He was a 5'10, dark skin, badly groomed man that wore dirty denim shorts and a faded black and holey D-A-R-E T-shirt. On his head was a cap that use to be white but was now a dingy reddish-brown that read 'No Problem!' Despite his poor appearance he held his head high and walked with the coolest strut ever seen around south Augusta. "Hey what's goin' on young bloods what chall doin' for it?" He said giving William dap through the window.

"Shiiittt, tryin' to sip on somethin', you know how it is."

"I hear ya' young blood, I'm tryin' to do the samethang. What's up Kevin I ain't see you over there what's goin' on?" Hollywood reached in the driver side window over Will to dap Kevin, Will getting a quick whiff of Hollywood's funk, turned his head, bald up his face and sunk back into his seat as if he was trying to escape some extremely poisonous gas.

"Nothin' much, what's up wit'-chew?"

"Shit I'm alive so I guess I'm doin' alright. Hey fellas what's happenin'?"

"Nothin', chillin'." Tracy and Shawn answered.

"They he go! What's up MJ, boy you cleaner than Skeeter's peter boy look at cha', I know you gettin' all da trim. You remind me of myself when I was out here hittin' these streets. You doin' alright?"

"Yea I'm cool." MJ replied with a slight grin on his face.

"I hear dat, so what can I do fa' you fellas?"

"You'll run in da sto' and get us six two-elevens and two bottles of MD 20/20?"

"Yall young skippers tryin' to drank like men, what chall know 'bout that 20/20, them black cans, yall goin' hurt somethin'. Yea

THE 7TH MAN

I can do dat fa' you fellas. Look here yall thank yall can scrape up another dollar to get a old man a beer?"

"I got-cha' 'Wood." Tracy said as he got out of the back driver side door. "What kind of cigars yall want?"

"It don't matter." Will replied.

"White Owl." Shawn shouted.

"And a Swisher." MJ added.

"Yall see how the game can flip on a nigga." Kevin said as he watched Hollywood follow Tracy into the store.

"You talkin' 'bout Hollywood?" Shawn asked.

"Yea. I mean how can you go from one of the biggest ballers in south Augusta to the biggest baser in the neighborhood."

"That's how it is." MJ said.

"How much did you say the feds caught 'em wit'?" Shawn asked.

"I ain't really sure but I remember three feds carried out two black trash bags a piece full of money and dope."

"Damn!" Larry uttered while shaking his head. "I wonder what make them fools wanna try that shit, I mean they see how it do folks, they should be the wisest."

"It don't always go down like dat." Kevin answered.

"I wonder what made 'Wood wanna try it." Larry said.

"I heard some cat put a gun to his head and made him smoke a gram." William said.

"Naw cuz-o, I thought chew knew." Kevin responded with subtle surprise.

"What that ain't true?"

"Hell naw!" Kevin giving a slight laugh. "He fucked around and met a fine ass crack head, gotta room wit' 'er fa' three days and da nigga ain't been right since."

"How you know that?" Larry asked.

"Cause him and my daddy started sellin' dope together, they was tight."

"What happened?" Shawn asked.

"My daddy stole my momma from 'em and they stopped hangin' together. They ain't turn into enemies or nothin' like that, they just went their separate ways. But ended up in the same place." Kevin mumbled.

"That's fucked up." Larry said.

Tracy exited the store followed by Hollywood. "Here you go fellas, thank you fa' da cold-one." Hollywood passed the bag through the window.

"Shiiittt, you looked out fa' us." William said.

"Alright yall boys be safe now."

"You too." Will said as he backed out. "Damn dat nigga smelt like fungus feet."

"I smelt 'em way back here." MJ said with pity. "He smelt mo' like dolphin piss."

"Damn!" Will laughed out along with the rest.

"Yall get comfortable, I'm finna run up stairs and grab da box." Will said dropping his keys on the coffee table.

"And get a deck of cards too." Kevin said as he took the bag of alcohol from MJ.

"A Will let me check my, My-Space page to see who done hit me up?" Larry said stopping Will mid-way on the stairs.

"Man ain't nobody tryin' to be yo' friend wit'-cho' lame ass."

"You crazy as hell, my page froze up 'cause I had so many whoes tryin' to click on me."

"Man whatever, anyway my computer gotta virus in it, I can't do shit wit' it."

"Damn." Larry uttered in disappointment.

Tracy took a seat on the couch while Shawn along with Larry walked around in fascination like they always do when they visited Will's home.

"Kev, I don't understand why yo' cousin like stayin' in the streets so much, wit' a crib like this," Shawn shouted to Kevin in the kitchen, "I'll stay home." Shawn now talkin' to Larry. "Me and my girl, butt naked on this soft ass carpet."

"Yea this that expensive shit." Larry giving his appraisal. "I done fucked on this kind of carpet befo', it wasn't this color it was..."

"Yea Larry." Shawn cutting Larry's lie short.

"Real talk, me and this girl name Jackie."

"Don't nobody wanna hear dat shit Larry." Michael said.

Larry ceased his lie but only from the sight of something fascinating and new. "Oh shit, look at this TV! That's one of them plasma janks."

Will was descending the stairs with an X-Box and all the trimmings while MJ prepared the card table. Kevin came out of the kitchen with six plastic cups. "So what's up who playin' spades?"

"I'm gettin' on that Madden." Tracy answered.

"Me too." Larry said grabbing a controller.

"I'll run a game of spades." Shawn said as he pulled out a cigar and began splitting it down the middle.

"I'll get in on a game." MJ said as he and Will set up the chairs.

"Okay, me and Kev against you and Shawn to five hunned, we playin' deuce of diamond deuce of spades..."

"Hell naw!" Shawn shouted from the kitchen as he dumped the tobacco out of the cigar.

"What?" Will shouted back with a sneaky grin on his face.

"You Know what." Shawn said walking back into the living room while rolling up the blunt. "You and Kev ain't finna be on the same team, yall niggas be cheatin', usin' codes and shit to tell each other what's in yall's hand. No sur, me and Kev, you and MJ."

Kevin and William always dominated when it came to spades, with all the time they shared together growing up, they developed expert cheating skills in games, especially card games.

Will set up the table, he took out a pen and some paper to take score, then wrote down the names of the teams; 'Playas' and 'Haters'. Shawn rolled up another blunt as fat as a Twix candy bar and the other the size of a pen. "Alright fellas. Will said as he shuffled the cards. We going to five hunned."

"We playin' sand-baggin'?" Michael asked as he poured his cup of MD 20/20.

"Hell naw and first hand bid itself."

"You ready for this ass whippin' Larry?" Tracy asked as his team the New England Patriots kicked off to Larry's Philadelphia Eagles.

"Man you crazy, I'm finna do it the way the Super Bowl should of been done." Larry responded with confidence. Shawn lit the blunt as Will dealt the cards.

"A where my drank at?" Larry asked as his man was tackled soon as he caught the ball.

"You gotta pour yo' own problems, I ain't no bartender." Kevin said. Tracy pressed pause on his controller and got up to fix him a drink while Larry snuck and turned down the volume, un-paused the game, and ran a touchdown. Tracy returned to his seat and realized what Larry had done.

"You cheatin' ass... That's alright I'm still goin' dawg yo' ass out."

Shawn took very light and small puffs from the blunt, cautious and easy, Kevin sitting across from him notice and had to comment. "Damn Shawn, why you smokin' like you scared of it?"

"Oh yea that's right, you ain't smoke none of this at the party? Tell 'em Will."

"Cuz-o, that's that killa, you can't hit that like a grown man." Shawn took a few more pulls and coughed as he passed it to Will on his right. William began taking cautious pulls.

"Not you too cuz-o, you can out smoke and drank all of us and you hittin' the blunt like it's yo' first time smokin'."

"A Kevin, that weed ain't no play toy, that's the shit there." Shawn warned.

"You'll see." William said as he threw out an ace of hearts then passed the blunt to Kevin. Kevin snatched it from him and said.

"I'ma' shame to say you my cousin, smokin' like a lil girl. I ain't scared."

"Please sir, forgive me." William said trying to imitate a British child. Kevin then took a huge pull, Shawn impressed with Kevin's attempt said.

"Look at the big smok..." Before he could finish Kevin let out a huge sick sounding series of coughs.

"Auuuugggghhhawaacacakkk-auuuauufgggh-auuuggahh!" Everyone erupted in laughter.

"I told you-I told you!" Shawn laughed. Kevin was coughing so hard that he had to pass the blunt to MJ, back up from the table and bellow over. Veins bulged all over his forehead and his eyes turned a fire engine red. Their laughter continued as he continued to cough violently like a forty-year three pack a day smoker. Will laughed even harder when he notice a foot long string of drool hanging from the middle of Kevin's bottom lip.

"Hell naw, that fool slobberin'! We tried to tell you!"

"Damn!" Kevin said after catching his breath, then wiped the drool from his lip. "Where da hell did you say you got this smoke from?"

"Chris sold it to me." Shawn replied with laughter. "It's off da chain ain't it?"

"Hell yea."

Tracy dominated Larry on the X-Box, game after game Tracy won by a blow out and Larry always came with the same excuses. "That wasn't my team, I'm 'bout to pick my real team now. Somethin' wrong wit' my controller. The computer is cheatin' fa' you." Tracy became bored.

"A man, I been whippin' yo' ass fa' over an hour, don't chew wanna play somethin' else. Put that Soul Caliber in."

"Oh yea, Soul Caliber, I got that game on lock." Tracy chuckled at Larry's comment.

The blunt was down to about two inches small when MJ tried to pass it to Shawn. Overwhelmed by his high, Shawn couldn't handle anymore. He held his hand up and said with a sluggish voice. "Naw, I'm straight." Michael then tried to pass it to Kevin, which had his head facing down and taking his cornrows loose.

"Kev, Kev." MJ dragged out. Kevin looked up at the smoking nub, he too overwhelmed by his high, just stared at it for about eight seconds before responding.

"I'm straight."

Michael then looked at William who had his eyes closed and moving in a rhythmic manner as if he's dancing to a tune in his head. "Will, Will. MJ said in a lazy tone with his arm extended with the smoking nub waiting to be taken. Will, Will, Will, Big Will,

Will." Shawn laughed at the dead manner MJ called Will and how Will didn't realize what was going on. "Will, Big Will, Big Will, Will, Will, Will, Will."

Kevin aggravated by the annoying calling interrupted with a loud. "William!"

Will snapped out of his dreamy state and opened his eyes. "What's up?"

"It's on you." Kevin said.

"Oh my bad, here." William threw out a five of clubs.

"Naw nigga, the blunt." Kevin said grinning.

"Oh, damn. Yall lit up another blunt?" He said as he leaned forward and received the pass.

"Naw man it's the same one we been smokin', where the hell you been?" Shawn said.

"Man, I was in Cearia's video that one-two step wit' Missy Elliott. They had me in the sandwich, they was the bread and I was the meat." Will smiled and took a few pulls from the blunt, Kevin shook his head as he stared at his cousin confused.

"Cuz-o, you strange."

Shawn laughed and in a loud whisper with his eyes closed he said. "Hold up-hold up, I'm finna try it watch this-watch this."

Kevin and MJ stared at Shawn with humorous confusion while William watched him as if to be waiting on a spectacular event. Shawn puckered his lips and made smacking sounds. He lift his hands and began to caress the imaginary person he was kissing. Kevin and MJ was now completely confused while William laughed and asked. "Where you at Shawn?"

"I'm in my room, and I got Da Brat on my left and Alisha Keys on my right siting on my lap and I got both of their nipples in my mouth, suckin' on their pretty-ass titties."

Will now excited. "Okay then that's my boy!"

The boys at the table could vaguely hear the sounds of Larry's frustration from being relentlessly dominated by Tracy on the video game. "Shit! Damn! Mothafucka! Oh! Man! Ain't this a bitch!"

Kevin finally notice Larry's grunts. "What's goin' on over there, T-Murray you beatin' the shit out of Larry on the game?"

Weighed down by his high Tracy sat sunk in the couch. His eyes were low and red, and playing the video game with little effort. "Hell yea, tearin' his ass up."

"Hell naw, Larry protested. It's somethin' wrong wit' Will's controller."

"Boy you crazy as hell, I just bought them sticks a few days ago. You just sorry as hell."

"See what it is, I'm too high, I can't play good when I'm high, real talk."

"Whatever man." Tracy said as he got up slow weighed down by THC. "Matter-of-fact, I'm finna turn it off, I'm tired of whippin' yo' ass." He walked over to the game system and turned it off.

"You lucky as hell, I was just about to get serious." Tracy ignored Larry's comment and began channel surfing with the remote. He stopped at an attractive black female newscaster that was giving a local breaking news report.

"If you're just tuning in, I'm standing in front of the Wachovia Bank on Wrightsboro Road where four masked gun men ran in and robbed the bank at gun point. Authorities were alerted at four-fifteen today by a teller's silent alarm. Police arrived just as the gun men were exiting…"

The news snatched the attention of everyone in the house. William, Michael, and Kevin sat up in their seats, while Shawn stood up and walked over to the couch where Larry and Tracy sat focused on the TV.

"...A brief but deadly standoff took place between officers and the gun men which ended with the deaths of two of the suspects and an officer. Two-year officer Troy Hillman was fatally wounded when a bullet struck him in his neck. The name and photos of the two suspects has been released and they are identified as twenty-two year-old Jason Beard and twenty year-old Theodore Harris."

As soon as the names were mentioned and the photos of the two men appeared on the screen Kevin, William, and Michael stood up and ran over to the television. "Oh Shit!" Will shouted.

"Hell naw!" Kevin said.

"Damn." Tracy said shaking his head in disappointment.

"JB and Theo done got killed tryin' to rob a bank!" Larry said almost shouting.

"Shhhhhh!" Shawn hissed holding up his index finger to hear the rest of the broadcast. They got quiet and listened.

"Three other officers were also wounded two only suffered minor injuries while the third officer, Leroy Hearns' injuries are considered serious but not life threatening. The other two gun-men, which are unknown at this time escaped on foot and was last seen entering the Wyld Woods apartment complex where police has been searching for over an hour, there is no word on the capture of the individuals and are describe to be wearing masks of the characters Shrek and Donkey. One of the assailants, Shrek, is about six foot one and weighs between a hundred and fifty to a hundred and sixty pounds. The other is about five eight, medium build between a hundred and sixty-five to seventy-five pounds. They are considered armed and extremely dangerous. If you have any information about this crime or the individuals involved, you are ask to call the Richmond County Sheriff's department at 706-711-0279..."

"I just saw JB and Theo at the sto' about a week ago." Will talking over the newscaster.

"A week ago, me and Shawn smoked a blunt wit' them cats two days befo' Chris' party, last…Wednesday." Kevin mentioned.

"Yea and I remember we was all bullshittin' about pullin' a lic and comin' up real quick."

"Well I guess they wasn't bullshittin', they was real about that shit."

"Yea but now they're real dead." Tracy said in a parental manner. Shawn nodded agreeing.

"I wonder who the other two was?" Larry questioned.

"Tall, one-sixty, one-fifty. That sounds like JB's cousin Slim." Will giving his theory.

"Yep. Shawn agreed. And who Slim always hangin' wit'?"

William and Kevin looked at each other while Tracy and MJ looked at Shawn, they all answered together. "Shitty D!"

"Them boys is off da chain." Will said.

"Naw them boys is crazy." Tracy corrected. "And stupid."

Kevin walked off and into the kitchen shaking his head and smiling still in disbelief of the news he'd just witness. He opened the refrigerator and grabbed his can of 211 Steel Reserve and opened it. "Why you say that T-Murray they was just tryin' to get paid just like everybody else, shit my nigga maybe we should try some shit like that." Kevin leaned on the kitchen doorway as he took a large sip.

"Why, so we can be on the run like Slim and Shitty D, or dead like JB and Theo. Hell naw."

"See that's the problem, yall niggas ain't got no heart." MJ, Larry, and Will all displayed expression of offense. "Yea you too cuz-o, I love ya', you my blood and all but chew scary, all of yall. I'm just being real, yall scary. Stop thankin' 'bout gettin' caught, if you got a good solid plan, follow it and willin' to go all out, then shit you straight. The other two Slim and Shitty D they good as gone, you heard da news. Police been searchin' over ah hour, you know how small Wyld Woods is. The police searched that whole complex in the first twenty minutes, them boys is gone and if they do get caught, then they're stupid. Other than that they paid."

"Yea they might get away, they might be paid, but Slim's lil cousin is dead and now Slim gotta live wit' that for the rest of his life." Tracy said. MJ, Shawn, and Will looked at Kevin waiting for a response, Kevin simply shrugged his shoulders and took a sip of his beer.

"A, that's part of da deal, them boys knew what they was gettin' they self into, they knew what could go down."

"Yea you right but what if that was you and Big Will and Big Will got killed?"

Kevin nodded. "Oh yea, I'll be fucked up, hurt but I'll buy the tightest suit I can buy to wear to his funeral." William chuckled and shook his head, Tracy also shook his head as he stood up.

"That's cold Kev." He said heading to the kitchen to get his beer.

"How is that cold, I know cuz would do the same thang, wouldn't you Will?"

"Yea-yea I would." Will agreed.

"See, I mean what I'm supposed to do turn myself in, that'll be crazy and stupid, hell he'll probably be mad at me fa' that, I'll see 'em in the afterlife."

"Hell yea." Will agreed with a grin.

"Naw I ain't sayin' turn yo'self in, I'm sayin' I wouldn't rob no bank in the first place but if, I mean a big if, if I was to try somethin' like that, I'll do it wit' some cats I don't give a damn about, not wit' my folks. That way if one of 'em get burnt, then oh well, you know what I'm sayin?"

"Yea, that make since." MJ said.

"I feel ya'-I feel ya'. Kevin agreed. Well forget about robbin' a bank, it's other kinds of lics out there, we could do some shit like…"

Kevin paused and sipped his beer, which helped bring up his idea. "Like rob the dope man or somethin', I mean at least he can't call the police. Six niggas in his face wit' pistols and choppers, easy lic." Kevin walked back to his seat at the card table.

"Okay then, see I'm wit' that." William agreed as he walked to the kitchen for his beer.

"But once again yall niggas ain't got the heart."

"Shit I ain't scared on that tip, I'll hit a dope boy up." MJ said.

"Me either, I ain't scared. Real talk." Larry said.

Kevin shook his head at Larry's response. "How 'bout chew Shawn?" Kevin sipped his beer. "Would you be down wit' somethin' like that?"

"Yea I'll be down wit' it. But who you know 'round here ballin' enough that's worth, buyin' the pistols, takin' the risk, then splittin' the money six ways. It ain't that many niggas 'round here, I know of that got enough paper to even take that chance, it'll be a waste of time and energy."

"T-Money." Kevin replied. "He got plenty of bread."

"Yea but he'll be hard to hit wit' all them niggas out in front of his buildin' shootin' dice and they all be heated." Will informed Kevin as he sat in his seat at the card table.

"Shit, burn them niggas then run up in T-money's shit."

Tracy now walkin' back from the kitchen. "See that's easy fa' you, you're crazy but see I ain't no killer, I can't just pop somebody that easy. How 'bout you Shawn, can you just kill somebody for money?"

"Naw, I 'on't thank I could."

"Could you MJ?"

"Nope."

"How 'bout you Big Will?"

"I 'on't know depends on how much money I'm gettin'."

Tracy then looked at Larry. "I know yo' ass ain't finna kill nothin'."

"Hell naw." Kevin agreed.

"What chall fools talkin' 'bout, yall don't know me, I'll burn somebody. Matter-fact I done already killed somebody." Larry's tone was strong and boastful everyone else looked at each other with sarcastic expressions, another one of Larry's lies however, they all had to hear his story.

"When you killed somebody Mr. Gangster?" Will asked.

"Man I burnt this cat last summer, see I ain't wanna tell yall 'cause I ain't know how yall would respond knowin' that cha' boy is a killa'."

Shawn shook his head with a smurk on his face. "So what happen why you had to do buddy in?"

Larry had no problem rolling right into a well constructed fable. "See this what happen right, real talk. This cat tried me 'cause I fucked his sister in da ass and you know me I'ma' playa."

"Um-hum." Shawn sarcastically agreed.

"And I was like don't front me, yo' sista is old enough to make her own decisions, any way you don't want it wit' me, 'cause I don't play da radio. And so..."

"Larry don't nobody wanna hear dat shit man. Kevin interrupted. Back to what we was talkin' 'bout. What about Gunswanga?"

"What about 'em?" Shawn asked.

"We could rob him, he da biggest dope man in Augusta, he gots to be sittin' on about twenty mill'."

"Listen at what chew just said, the biggest dope boy in Augusta, now if we can't hit T-Money half hustlin' ass what makes you thank we can hit a nigga like Gunswanga?" Tracy said.

"Yea cuz-o you know that nobody knows who he is or what he look like, I ain't never seen 'em befo'."

"Me neither." Shawn said.

"That nigga is like a ghost, a… Gangsta ghost." MJ said after sipping his MD 20/20.

"I ain't never seen 'em either but it's ways to find out who a nigga is, Augusta ain't that big. Yall niggas just scared, scared to get money."

"I ain't scared." Will quickly objected.

"I ain't never scared." MJ said.

"Me neither." Followed Larry.

"I ain't sayin' I'm scared of gettin' money." Tracy replied. "I'm scared of gettin' locked up fa' some bullshit or gettin' shot up over nothin'. I'm down wit' gettin' paid, I'm just not down wit' caged up fa' da rest of my life tryin' to get it. I ain't built fa' that shit and I ain't ready to die yet. That'll be too much fa' my momma and pops to deal wit'."

Kevin took in Tracy's words and understood his position. "You know what, I feel ya' I forgot all about that. How ya' momma doin' folk?"

"Oh, it ain't no change, I mean she have her good days she have her bad days. Just a lil mo' bad ones lately." Kevin noticed Tracy's emotions change by his facial expression after he sipped his beer.

"What the doctors sayin'?" William asked with concern in his voice.

"The same thang they been sayin', that if she don't get that surgery and treatment soon it ain't goin' be nothin' they'll be able to do for 'er." Tracy sipped his beer again to hide his building depression however unsuccessful, it filled the room and caused a moment of silence that could only be broken by the person who caused it. "See Kev, I need some quick money just as bad as you do but it's only so far I'm willin' to go, you know what I'm sayin."

"I see what chew mean. But me personally I'll do anything fa' money."

"Anythang?" Will quickly asked.

"Anythang...Hold up, except some gay shit, I ain't fuckin' 'round wit' no shit like that."

"Would you jack yo' dick in front of da whole school, durin' a assembly, in the gym while a preacher talk about celibacy?" Will asked.

"Fa' how much?" Kevin asked.

"Two G's."

"Where's da lotion." Kevin replied. Michael laughed along with Will and Tracy.

"Would you slap the president for five stacks?" MJ asked.

"Twice."

"Shiiittt you're a bad man. Would you fuck a handicap girl fa' ten stacks?"

"Mentally or physically handicap?"

"Physically."

"I'll hit it raw."

"You's a nasty nigga." MJ replied shaking his head with a smile.

The conversation put Shawn into deep thought to the point of talking to himself in his head. "This is a good time to hit them wit' it, yea I should bring it up now while they're talkin' about money. Hell yeah I'll..."

"I got one." Larry said disturbing Shawn's thoughts. "Fa' fifty G's would you fuck a dead girl?"

Everyone stared at Kevin anticipating his answer. "As long as If da bitch ain't decomposin' and stankin', I'll beat it up."

"Ahh shit you nasty mothafucka!" Tracy said in disgust.

"Ahh naw, I can't believe you Kev." MJ replied with his face bald up.

"Damn cuz-o, I can't believe we related."

"What?" Kevin said with a cynical grin on his face.

"You sick that's what." Tracy said then took a sip from his beer.

Shawn looked at the mahogany trimmed, gold numbered, glass face clock above the couch Tracy, Larry, and MJ were sitting on. It read eight-twenty three. He decided to ask. "Would you try witchcraft?" The question was too low for anyone to hear. He tried another approach. "What if I said," he said louder and getting their attention, "I might know a way you can get money, well we can get money without the risk of gettin' killed, locked up', or bein' on the run."

"I'll say you was full of shit cause if you knew somethin' like that we wouldn't be here talkin' 'bout gettin' money, we'll be countin' money instead." Kevin replied.

"I just found out today."

"Well, how?" Kevin asked.

"Yea spit it out." Will said.

"How? I'm curious." Tracy said.

"Witchcraft."

"Witchcraft?" Kevin said with a look of confusion.

"Yea witchcraft, black magic, voodoo spells and shit like that."

Kevin looked over at Will in confusion and Will returned the expression. "What da hell is David Copperfield talkin' 'bout?"

"I-'on't know cuz-o, I thank the liquor or weed done went to his head, maybe both of 'em mixed together done messed 'em up."

"Naw I'm straight, and I'm dead-ass serious. You said you would try and do almost anythang to get paid right?"

"Yea, almost anythang."

"Well if you could do magic to get money, would you do it?"

Kevin looked around at all his comrades that looked just as confused as he did and gave a slight laugh. "Yea, I would, who wouldn't it's too easy but that shit ain't real and ain't no hunned dollar bill just finna magically appear out of nowhere."

"But what if it was real, would you try it?"

"Yea I would."

"Well what's up, let's try it." Shawn said with a cynical look on his face.

"What? You need to put that drank down, did you lace that weed. Kevin chuckled. What chew know about witchcraft?"

"I 'on't know shit about it but I know somebody that do." The confusion amongst everyone was immeasurable especially with Tracy, being that he knew Shawn the longest and had a closer bond with him than anyone else in the crew.

"What you been hangin' wit' Harry Potter and nem?" Kevin joked causing everyone to laugh, even Shawn.

"Naw man, the white boy at my job."

"Oh you talkin' 'bout the white Blade." Will commented.

"Oh yea Dracula's lil nephew. Yea he do look like he got somethin' twisted in his brain." Kevin said.

"See me and the white boy gots to talkin' on our lunch break and I found out that his momma and daddy use to mess wit' it and he picked up a few thangs. He told me one time he did a spell and a couple of days later when he got his paycheck the company fucked up, and over paid him by a stack."

"Damn!" William said impressed as he looked around at the others.

"Same thang I was thankin', so I asked him could he put me down wit' some of that, he gave me his number and told me to call 'em if I was serious. That's what we was talkin' 'bout when Will pulled up and started blowin' his horn all crazy." Shawn gave Will an accusing stare and Will gave a marijuana giggle.

"Shawn, that cracka is full of shit, he just fuckin' wit'-cha' head. That shit ain't real." Kevin said then guzzled his beer.

"I wouldn't say that Kev." MJ surprising his comrades, especially Kevin and Shawn.

"What! I know you don't believe in that hocus pocus shit too MJ?"

"Believe it, shit I done seen some thangs happen."

"Here you go." Kevin said shaking his head in disbelief.

"I'm fo'real Kev, I done seen some crazy shit happen befo'." The subtle conviction in his voice was noticed by Tracy and Shawn.

"You serious MJ?" Tracy asked.

"Dead-ass."

"What chew saw?" Shawn asked.

"Yea I gotta hear this, tell us and Willow Offgood what chew saw." Kevin said in a chuckle. Michael shook his head then began.

"When I lived in da A in da sixth-grade it was this cat name P-Nut, big ass nigga, almost yo' size Will and thugged out and wild like you Kev, head bussa, hard core-ass nigga, I mean he was in the eighth-grade knockin' grown ass men out."

"Okay then." Kevin said in admiration.

"Then it was this lil cat name Emmanuel, everybody called 'em E-man, weird lil cat stayed to 'emself, didn't talk to many people. He was into video games and that Dungeon and Dragons type shit and read a lot of books. Anyway P-Nut use to always fuck wit' E-man, jive on 'em, un-tuck his shirt, push 'em around, knock his hat off his head if he had one on, you know lil shit like that. He never put his hands on 'em or hurt 'em physically, just embarrassed 'em shit like that.

Then one day I'm playin' ball at my house in the circle wit' some other cats, E-man lived across the street. After hoopin' on them clowns for a couple of games, E-man comes out his house wit' a cute lil shawty, I mean she was dressed real goofy and fucked up but she had potential, surprised the hell out of us because nobody knew E-man had friends let alone a girlfriend, so we just figured it was his cousin or somethin'. Then about ten minutes later P-Nut walks around the corner wit' two of his homeboys, he saw E-man first and by the time E-Man saw him and tried to avoid-'em by going in da house, it was too late. P-Nut said.

'A what's up E-man.' Like Emmanuelle was his homeboy. For a minute that's all we heard from across the street, then we saw P-Nut push E-man into the girl sittin' on his steps, E-man got up wit' both fist up wit' a mean look on his face, ready. Then yelled out.

'I'm tired of you always fuckin' wit' me!' Then he threw a wild-ass-slow-ass right hook at P-Nut, it was so slow that P-Nut saw it comin' and dogged it. We all ran over to see what was about to go down 'cause we just knew P-Nut was finna get in his ass but P-nut wasn't mad, matter-fact he started laughin' and said.

'Uh-oh E-man got some nuts but that's too bad 'cause this finna hurt like a bitch!' He turned E-man around, reached in his pants, and gave him the worst wedgy in history. He pulled E-man's underwear so hard that it lifted him off his feet."

"Damn!" Will uttered.

"He was in da air hurtin' until his draws finally ripped and he fell on the steps next to the girl. Then P-Nut told the girl.

'You might wanna put some ice on that.' Then he walked off and everybody went back across the street and started back ballin'. The whole time we was ballin' E-man sat on his porch starin' acoss the street over at P-nut wit' tears in his eyes, rockin' back and forth. The girl had her arms around him tryin' to make 'em fell better I guess, but that nigga P-Nut just made it worse by yellin' shit at 'em every ten minutes. 'You better get some pliers and get them draws out cho' ass boy! What da hell you lookin' at, I know yo' punk ass ain't cryin'!' Stuff like that, 'til E-man and that girl finally went in da house. I'll say about ah hour and a half later he came back outside wit' ah red plastic cup, one of them party cups. He walks over and stands right behind P-Nut. P-Nut turned around got up in his face and said.

What, you need to borrow a pair of draws or somethin'? E-Man said.

'Nope, I just want to tell you this...' Then he started sayin' some ole crazy shit, like he was speakin' another language, some shit I ain't never heard. Then he hocked up a big ass lump of cold and spit it in the cup. P-Nut said.

'You thirsty or something?' E-man didn't say nothin' he just took the cup and splash the shit that was in it all over P-Nut's chest, see he had took off his shirt earlier while we was ballin'."

Shawn captivated by MJ's story asked. "Well what was in the cup?"

"It looked and smelled like piss, so we believe it was piss."

"Ahh naw!" William said with an expression of disgust.

"So what did P-Nut do?" Kevin asked.

"What you would of done?" MJ answered with a question.

"I would of beat his mothafuckin' ass."

"That's what he did, he beat E-man up so bad it didn't make no since, I mean I ain't never seen nobody get beat up that bad. P-Nut was slamin' 'em, puchin' 'em, he was kickin' 'em all in his head, ribs and stomach it was crucial, he did da mothafucka to 'em. But the crazy thang about it, the whole time the beatin' was takin' place I could of sworn I saw E-man on the ground smilin'. Eventually we had to pull dat nigga off of him befo' he ended up killin' 'em. Then everybody left except me, I felt sorry for E-man seein' 'em on the ground laid out bleeding and barely movin', I helped 'em up and damn near carried him to his house. I got to the steps and that's when the girl opened the doo' for us. I helped 'em in and over to his couch and said. What da hell was you thankin' man you know that boy is crazy. Then he said. 'I have to stick up for myself some-time.' I told 'em. You sure did pick a fucked up way of doin' it. I looked at the girl and told her. And why you didn't call the police or somethin', she said. 'Why didn't you do somethin'. I got quiet then cause I started feelin' bad. Then she said. 'Besides outsiders can't interfere or else it wouldn't work right.' I was confused, I was like for what to work right, what is she talkin' 'bout? E-man said. 'Nothin'-nothin', it's nothin'.' It was gettin' late so I told 'em. Well anyway I gotta go, you goin' be alright? He said. 'I'm alright now everythang is alright now.' I walked to the doo' and told 'em. You might wanna get checked up just in case somethin' is fucked up. He was like. 'Naw I'm okay but I appreciate the help.' Then I left."

Michael took a huge sip from his beer then continued. "About a week go by and nobody seen nor heard from P-Nut, he didn't come to the basketball court, the parks, he wasn't on the block or in school, well he barely came to school anyway so that wasn't strange. But see he sold a lil weed too but he wasn't answerin' his cell or his house phone. So two weeks go by and still no sign of P-nut. I was tryin' to get a sack one day and couldn't find none nowhere, I said fuck it, I decided to go to P-nut's house and knocked on his bedroom window. I walked around to his house and knocked on the window, he opened the window and moved the curtains back but just enough to peak out, that's how he talked to me, like he was hidin' somethin'. He was like.

'What's up MJ.' I said nothin' much, what's up wit' chew, where you been folks been tryin' to get at chew fa' the longest. He said. 'Oh, man I been sick and shit but when I get right I'll be back on da block.' Now P-Nut was always crunk, loud, always braggin' and jiven but that day when he was talkin' to me through the window he sounded sad as hell, I said. I hope you be all right man. Oh yea you straight, you got some green? He said. 'Yea what chew want?' I said a dime and he passed two sacks through a hole in the screen, I slid the money through the hole and when he took the money he left the curtain pulled back a little, I guess it got hung on somethin'. I said appreciate it and walked off, while I'm walkin' I takes a look at the sacks and they're fat as hell, instead of him given me two nick sacks he gave me two dimes.

So I figure hell, since he doin' it like that I mine-as-well get two mo' sacks from 'em, so I walked back to his house and befo' I tapped on his window I heard 'em say.

'Damn, I'm fucked up!' So, curious as hell I peeped in where the curtain was pulled back and saw P-Nut lookin' in his mirror with his back facin' me. Then he turns to the side and looked in the mirror and yall niggas wouldn't believe what I saw." Michael took another sip from his beer.

"What, his skin was pealin' off ?" Shawn eagerly asked.

"Nope."

"Then what was it? Will asked impatient.

Michael took a sip from his beer, set up, looked at Shawn, then Tracy, then Kevin and said. "He had titties."

"What!" Kevin said then burst into laughter along with Tracy.

"Damn, fo'real!" Will responded.

Shawn's eyes widen along with his mouth. "Damn!"

Kevin still skeptical argued with laughter. "Man please, you bull shittin'."

"I ain't bullshittin', this thugged out nigga had big, firm, pretty ass titties, wit' da big nipples."

"I 'on't believe that shit, now I expect somethin' like that from Larry's lyin' ass but from you MJ, I'm surprised."

"I 'on't know Kev, you never know, my ole lady told me some thangs. It's a big world out there cuz."

"Whatever man." Kevin said then sipped his beer.

"What about you cuz-o you believe that shit?"

"I 'on't know Kev it's possible."

"Ahhh not my own cousin. Kevin said with disappointment. T-Murray tell me I ain't the only nigga in here wit' some sense. You believe that shit?"

"I'ma' see it to believe it type cat." Tracy answered.

"Well what's up, let's see." Shawn said looking at Tracy then Kevin.

"You's a silly nigga, you need to stop drankin' and smokin'." Kevin said shaking his head.

"What's the matter Kevin, you ain't got no heart."

"Ohh he might of tried you then." Will said laughing.

"Yea he did." MJ said.

"What, you scared?" Shawn continued. "You ain't got shit to lose. You did say you'll try almost anythang then be real about what chew said, don't bitch out."

"Ooohhh!" Will shouted along with Michael both standing and excited by Shawn's words towards Kevin.

"Ooh shit!" Tracy said sitting up along with Larry and watching Kevin's reaction which was him nodding with a sneaky grin on his face as if was thinking, Shawn you know I owe you a ass whippin.

"I mean come on Kev thank about it, if it's fake then what chew lost, time. I mean we just sittin' here getting' fucked up, but it it's real, if witchcraft is real, then that's easy money right there." Kevin folded his arms and sat back in his chair and contemplated, Shawn then looked at T-Murray and said. "T-Murray you did say that chew down wit' gettin' money as long as it don't involve pistols, jail, or gettin' killed, well there you go no guns and no police."

"Run it, I'll try it." Tracy said.

"What about you Big Will?" Shawn asked.

"It don't matter to me, I ain't scared." William answered.

"How 'bout chew MJ, you down?"

"You know what." Michael said looking at Kevin instead of Shawn as if he was challenging Kevin. "I'll try it and hope it works just to prove to you that what I saw was real. MJ then stood up and pointed at Kevin. And I challenge you to try it because you hurt me Kev, puttin' me in the same category as Lyin' Ass Larry." Kevin laughed a little.

"How about chew Larry."

"I ain't scared, let's do it."

Shawn then gave his attention back to Kevin but now his stare was more serious. "So it's on you, what's up?" Kevin looked at each of his comrades, all of them still had grins on their faces from Shawn's bold comments, which echoed in his head. "Don't bitch out." He being the most coward less, wildest and toughest one in the crew, he had no choice but to say.

"Go ahead and call ya' boy Harry Potta' up."

Chapter 4

9:06 pm displayed on a clock in the shape of an eye on the bleeding walls, actually it was the red light of an oddly crafted lamp in the bedroom. Its dim red light gave off a dark eerie atmosphere, its maker was one of the twins that occupied the room. Derrick and Daniel, two personalities of extreme differences in a cramped room but they managed to achieve their privacy with a simple black silk curtain that equally divided the room.

Derrick's side, which a visitor would see first after walking through another black curtain that covered the entrance, was that of a stoner's habitat, which he was. His half of the room's walls were covered with posters, one displayed twenty different types of marijuana plants such as; Purple Haze, Hydro, G-13, Kine bud, Blueberry, Kush, White Willow etc. Another poster was of Bob Marley taking a pull off a huge joint. Another of the rap group Cypress Hill standing in a marijuana field, next to it a poster of purple mushrooms growing upside. The water casted reflections of naked fairies masturbating and staring in waiting at whoever looks at the poster. This was Derrick's favorite poster, he would stare it when he would reach the peak of his high. He was a cocktail druggy, weed, ecstasy, alcohol but his favorite was shrooms freshly cow-shit picked purple top mushrooms. Though acid was a lot stronger, it was too hard to find and sometimes led to bad trips but he could always rely on shrooms. He always kept a sealed stash no matter the season, in fact, that is what he was inebriated on now. A handful of purple tops, with the help of a half of joint of Jamaican Red Hair marijuana soaked in shroom water and partially dried in his dehydrator, and a Percocet that he washed down with vodka and orange juice. He sat on his bed, back wedged between the headboard and the wall with his mouth open in an almost trance like state. He was in his gray Hightimes t-shirt and a pair of blue jogging pants watching his Lords Of The Rings collectable DVD set. His high from his cocktail of drugs made him feel as if he was on the quest himself.

On the other side of the curtain was another world, a world of dark expression. Daniel's walls were covered with over a dozen of black construction paper all baring quotes written in fluorescent active white chalk. The quotes were of Daniel's opinion on life, whenever he would experience a major event such as; love lost, death, a fight, a struggle or something new, he would create a new quote or simply write a word. His walls were covered with sayings such as; Life, Death, Love, Anger etc. Sayings like; destroy to create, pain is eternal, a soul without a spirit, Scream Quietly! Etc. There were a few drawings amongst the statements, like an upside down open hand with a detailed drawing of an eye in the palm and in the back-ground it was raining upward. Another was of a severed head of a man screaming while two snakes slithered out of the mouth on opposite sides positioned ready to strike their host.

His bedspreads were black and his headboard was covered with the darkest red fabric he could steal from work. There were well over fifty horror novels most of them from repeat authors such as; Edward Lee, Stephen King, Ann Rice and Dean Knootz, barely a fraction of literary material he owned. Under his bed were milk crates full of reading material on varies topics like; Demonology, Demonic Possession, Rules and Rituals of Magic, Invoking Lost Spirits, Invocation and Its Procedures, The Holy Bible, Catholicism, the Koran, and dozens of books on spells and incantations.

Daniel laid in his bed on his back with his head at the foot of his bed finishing his Edward Lee novel 'City Infernal' with his headphones on which played Marilyn Manson instrumentals as he read.

Derrick had just put in The Return Of The King disc when the telephone rung, after the fourth ring Derrick finally answered. "Hell, o?" He said in a lazy tone.

"Uh, yea may I speak to Daniel?" The male's voice said on the other end.

"Yea, who is it?"

"Shawn, from work today. Is this Daniel?"

"Nope, I'm his brother Derrick. You said your name is Shawn?"

"Yea."

"So you're the curious one Daniel told me about."

"Yep that's me."

"Well a lot of us drug addicts was curious too and look how we ended up." Shawn had no response for the odd and unexpected advice. "All I can say man is be careful."

"I will."

Derrick removed the phone from his ear and shouted as loud as his high would allow, which to a sober person sounded normal. "A Danyalle the phone." Daniel unable to hear because of his headphones, he just turned a page in his book. "Hey scrotum lips the phone man." Derrick became frustrated realizing that he might have to get up, which he didn't want to do. He finally sat up, moved the curtain back and held the phone out. He calculated the distance then tossed the phone. It floated then landed on Daniel's groins.

"Ahhhaauuu-you motherfucker!" Daniel uttered after the phone made contact, he dropped his book and sat up quick causing his headphones to fly off. He laid back down on his side facing Derrick which was laughing at his pain.

"Somebody's on the phone for you cunt breath."

"You fuckin' penis pimple you could of just told me!" Derrick hunched his shoulders with a grin then closed the curtain. "Hello?" Daniel answered slightly shaken.

"Daniel?" Shawn asked to be sure.

"Yea who is it?"

"It's Shawn from work."

"Hey what's up man?"

"Chillin'-chillin'. I was callin' to see if you was able to do that for me."

"Do what?" Daniel pretended not to remember.

"The spell, the money spell. You said you would look it up for me." Shawn sounded as if all hope he ever had, had vanished, Daniel notice and gave in.

"I'm just messing with you, I remember but I didn't look it up because I didn't think you was serious."

"Oh, I'm serious, I really want to do this."

"Yea, I see. I'll get it for you."

"So, what, do you want me to call you back later while you do that?"

"No need I can do it now." Daniel hung off the side of his bed and pulled out a black milk crate full of books from under his bed and with a brief search, he removed a spiral notebook with black electrical tape covering the front and the back. "You might wanna get something to write this down."

"Okay, hold on a minute." Shawn said walking from the kitchen to the living room where his comrades were in debate.

"We finna see if it's real or not and if it ain't I'm slappin' every-body, twice." Kevin said as Shawn walked over and grabbed the paper that held their spades game score and the pen.

"Okay I'm ready." He said as he walked back into the kitchen and leaned on the gray and white marble counter top.

"All this time I known yall niggas, I ain't know yall believe in that hocus pocus shit." Kevin said.

Michael smacked his teeth. "I seen the shit work, I know it's real."

"All I'm sayin' is be open minded about the shit, you never know." Will said.

"I'm like this, I ain't sayin' it is, I ain't sayin' it ain't, seein' is believin' and it's only one way to find out." Tracy added.

Larry gave his usual false response. "Shit I use to mess around wit' this shawty from Haiti that was into voodoo." Michael had to humor the lie.

"So what happened, why you ain't wit' 'er now?"

"I caught 'er tryin' to nail my draws to the wall above 'er bed."

"What?" Tracy said with the same confusion that was on MJ, Will, and Kevin's faces.

"What in da hell do that suppose to do?" Kevin asked.

Larry got up to turn the video game back on as he explained. "See if a girl know voodoo she can nail yo' draws to the wall over her bed and ya' dick won't get hard fa' no other female but her." Everyone stared at him speechless. "Real talk." He said seeing disbelief on their faces, they then erupted into laughter.

"I 'on't even know why I asked." Kevin said shaking his head.

Tracy stared at Larry and he too was shaking his head. "Man it's amazing how you just come up wit' some bullshit that quick and make it sound so good, LL you are truly talented, you have a gift son, you are the best liar on Earth."

"Fo'real." Michael agreed.

Larry looked at Tracy and MJ then at Will with a straight face and said as only a truly innocent suspect could. "What? Man I ain't...I'm fo'real, if yall don't believe me all you..."

"Larry don't nobody wanna hear dat shit man." Kevin interrupted just as Shawn walked back into the living room staring at the paper he carried. "So what's up Shawn did ya boy Harry Potta' turn you into a Grand Wizard?"

"Naw man he ain't do nothin' like that but he did give me a spell."

Kevin looked at Shawn in an almost shameful way and said. "I can't believe this shit, you really serious."

"Damn real. What, yall done changed yall's minds?"

"Naw we ready, just waitin' on you." Tracy answering for everyone else.

"Yes sur that's what I'm talkin' 'bout." Shawn said as he gave off a look that was part devious and part cynically manipulative. "Alright Big Will we goin' need a few thangs, I hope you got 'em if not, then we'll have to try it later."

"What we need?"

Shawn began reading from his list. "Alright we goin' need some basil, ginger, cinnamon, and some nutmeg."

"We gotta cook somethin'?" Kevin replied in a laugh.

"Naw Kev. So do you thank you got that stuff?"

"Yea we got it, my pops love to cook, he got all kinds of shit in there." Will said as he got up and headed to the kitchen. "You said nutmeg, cinnamon, parsley and what else?" He shouted from the kitchen.

"Naw, basil not parsley, basil and ginger."

"Alright." Will returned with the bottles of spices and sat them on the card table.

"Yall boys some real idiots and I'm even a bigger idiot fa' following along wit' chall dummies." Kevin said then finished off his beer with a long swig and crushing the can.

"Alright I thank this is gonna be a problem. One onyx stone."

"Onyx?" Will questioned.

"Yea, you thank yo' momma gotta ring, necklace, bracelet or anything with a black stone, a onyx stone on it?"

"I 'on't know, I thank…Yea my momma got this bracelet my pops bought 'er when she graduated from dental school. Hold up." Will ran up stairs and was back in less than a minute. Will laid out the bracelet on the table and exhaled some stress. "I thank this is a onyx stone but I do know them six diamonds is real and it's real platinum, so be careful."

"Alright. All we need now is a dollar bill."

"I can't help you wit' that." Will said.

"Me neither." MJ added.

"I'm broke too." Larry added.

"Here you go." Tracy said as he pulled out an old wrinkled and faded dollar bill and laid it on the table.

"Now what, great wizard?" Kevin said as he stood up and headed to the kitchen.

"Well now, since you headed to the kitchen can you grab a bowl."

"Yes your greatness." Kevin gave a bow then returned with a

glass bowl and laid it on the table.

"Now, I hook it up." Shawn grabbed the bowl and the bottle of basil. "Two pinches of basil." He said sprinkling it into the bowl. "One pinch of ginger, three pinches of cinnamon, and now four pinches of nutmeg. Now I take the dollar bill and lay it face down on the spices with the pyramid facin' up. Then I take the stone, well the bracelet and…"

"Be careful Shawn that ain't no bullshit silver, that's platinum."

"Alright cuz, I ain't finna mess up my baby's bracelet, you know I love Mrs. Cooper."

"Yea whatever nigga just don't fuck it up."

Shawn placed the bracelet on top of the dollar. "Now I say the magic words."

Kevin shook his head in shame. "This is some silly shit."

"Alright everybody gotta surround the bowl and hold hands."

"What, hold hands, I know we ain't finna sang Kumbah Yah or no shit like that is we?" Will said.

"Naw man, we gotta create a circle, a connection with everybody that's tryin' to get paid. So come on and quit bullshittin'." Shawn held out his right hand. Everyone complied and formed a circle by taking a hand, Kevin was reluctant but eventually took Shawn's right hand with his left. "Okay now we all bow our heads and close our eyes and repeat after me." They all bowed their heads closed their eyes and waited.

"Hold up!" MJ uttered then snatched his hand from Larry. "Did you jack off today?" MJ rubbed his palm on his pants.

"What! You got me fucked up, I don't need to jack off I gets plenty of ass."

Tracy then snatched his hand from Larry. "Yea, which hand do you touch yo'self wit'?" Tracy's comment added more laughter to what MJ's comment caused. "I'm fuckin' wit'-cha." Tracy took Larry's hand again.

"Well I ain't, when we finish I'm washing my hand in a pot of boiling bleach water."

"Alright fellas come on, chill out, let's get serious and do this." A few seconds passed after the joking atmosphere calmed down and they dropped their heads, closed their eyes, and waited on the magic words to be spoken. He took a breath and began.

"Oh spirits of either side,

Please lead us to fortune under your guide,

Empower this stone with your might,

So that we may be blessed with money tonight.

This is what we faithfully ask,

Please accept this favor as your task."

Everyone repeated the words, except Kevin who was giggling and laughing. Silence followed the words. Shawn lift his head and opened his eyes and said. "Well, that's it."

"That's it." Kevin said with a smirk on his face. "Now that, that was some real bullshit."

"Uuugghh!" Will said with his face bald up. "Which one of you stankin' ass niggas farted in my house?"

"Oohh-wee, one of yall cats is foul as hell." Tracy said fanning away the stench.

"It ain't me." Larry quickly uttered.

"One of yall smell like bat sweat." MJ said putting his shirt collar over his nose.

"One of yall shitted on ya'self." Kevin said holding his hand over his nose.

Shawn also fanned the stench while looking around for the source of the smell when his eyes caught a faint brownish smoke rise from the bowl. The smoke was so faint that Shawn didn't think he really saw it, he looked away rubbed his eyes and stared back at the bowl. He realized that the contents in the bowl was indeed smoking.

"Hey yall look, look at the bowl it's smokin'."

Will leaned in closer to the bowl. "I see it and that's where the smell is comin' from too!"

Kevin smacked his teeth and laughed. "Yall boys is stupid, that shit ain't smokin' and that smell is Larry's stankin' ass he ain't take no bath."

"No it ain't either look at it, it's smokin' fa'real." Michael said leaning in closer to the bowl.

"I see it too." Larry said.

Michael stood next to Kevin and stared at the bowl to see it from Kevin's view. "See Kev, look!"

"Damn it stopped." Shawn said with disappointment. "But it was there, I'm tellin' you."

"I ain't see shit." Kevin said sitting down. "So now what, where da money at Frodo Baggins?"

"Now we take action."

"Take action? What the hell." Kevin said with a smirk of sarcastic confusion.

"We gotta take action, put somethin' in motion, a plan to get money."

"This is stupid, if we knew what to do to get money we'll be doin' it right now instead of standin' here lookin' like jackasses. Yall said yall saw smoke, well I know a way you can see all the smoke you want. Fire up that other beam Shawn rolled up."

"That's what I'm talkin' 'bout." Will agreed. "So what we gotta do stand in front of an ATM machine."

"I 'on't know Will." Shawn said with some worry in his voice.

"I know." MJ said. "Let's go hop in a dice game."

"Wit' a dollar?" Will asked.

"Hell yea. It's been plenty of times I done sent fools home broke wit' one hot ass dollar in a dice game. Don't underestimate the power of a dollar bill."

"That's my last dollar, we need to find a sure way to make it work for us." Tracy said.

Silence covered the living room as Larry walked over to the couch, grabbed a controller and sat down. "Play the lotto." There was no response for about five seconds.

"That's a good idea LL but the numbers already done fell." Will said.

"Oh yea, that's right." Larry said pressing start on the controller. Shawn's eyes widen as an idea entered his head.

"A scratch off! How 'bout we play a scratch off. Will, you too fucked up to drive to One Stop?"

"Naw, I'm straight."

"Then what's up fellas how 'bout that. We go to One Stop, buy a scratch off and see what happens."

"Run it." Will answered.

Kevin shook his head. "I rather let MJ toss some dice."

"You 'on't mine do you?" Shawn asked Tracy.

"Naw, let's do it."

"Alright fellas." Shawn said after Will cut off the engine in the parking lot of One Stop. This what I'm goin' do. I'ma' buy a scratch off and if we win we split it five ways, Kevin don't get shit 'cause he been talkin' shit all day."

"So, yall niggas ain't finna win shit anyway." Kevin said.

"I'm bullshittin' if we do win we split it six ways. So which scratch off yall thank I should buy?"

"Lucky Sevens." Larry suggested.

"Naw get one of them Love Notes." Will said.

"Get a Jumbo Bucks, I won thirty bones on one of them janks one time." Tracy said.

"Yea those Jumbo Bucks pay out, you'll have a better chance wit' one of them." MJ added.

"Alright that's two for Jumbo Bucks. What chew thank Kev?"

"I thank, you really wanna know what I thank?"

"Yea."

"I thank you should go in the sto' and buy ninety-nine cents worth of sense and split it five ways, and that'll be mo' sense than any of you fools already had."

Shawn shook his head. "Alright I'll get a Jumbo Bucks." Shawn exited the Explore with the dollar and the bracelet in his hand, which contained a real onyx stone.

It was a short walk into the store, a walk that Shawn took almost every day, but today it seemed to be the longest one he had ever taken as thoughts raced through his mind. "Boy I hope I did it right. I hope this is a real onyx stone. It got real diamonds in it so it should be a real onyx stone." Shawn rubbed the stone on the bracelet with his thumb. "Please, please let this work." Shawn contemplated as he stood in the line of two people. "Please, whoever...Damn, I never really thought about that, who makes it real, is it God or the devil. Damn I don't know." The thought began to trouble him deeply he was now wondering what he has gotten himself into. "Ahh man what if this shit is evil, that means if it works then I'm damned, that is if it's evil, but if it's something good and from God then I'm straight." He moved forward after the man at the counter left, that's when something looped in his head. 'Oh spirits of either side'. "Oh shit, spirits of either side, either side, either side." He yelled in his head at the revelation. "Shit!" He uttered out loud interrupting the customer and cashier transaction.

The man in front of him turned and asked. "You're alright young blood?"

"I hope so." The man turned back around. "Of either side." Shawn returned to his head. "That means it can come from either one of them cats. I just hope it comes from the right one." He stepped to the counter as the man walked off, when he got to the door he stopped and said.

"Hey young blood. Whatever it is you going through, control it, don't let it control you." He then walked out of the store. The comment sent a chill through Shawn as if the stranger knew what he was embarking on.

"Man I can't wait 'til Shawn come back and scratch that ticket off so I can laugh in all yall faces, hard." Kevin said. "Not just 'cause yall idiots is going through wit' this bullshit but for turnin' me into an idiot for going along wit' it. Not only that but one; Will you my blood and I expect you to have mo' sense than that. Two, to expose MJ's bullshit ass story about the thug wit' titties, some shit I expected from Larry's lyin' ass, like his bullshit story about his ex-girlfriend Trina the teenage witch."

"That wasn't no bullshit." Larry protested.

"Well did you fuck 'er?"

"Hell yea."

"Like I said, bullshit. And three, T-Murray you gave up yo' last dollar fa' some bullshit."

"Hell I done spent more than that on some bullshit, why not spend a dollar for some knowledge."

"Damn Julius Caesar, why you gotta get all deep on ya' folk."

Naw Kev, it ain't nothin' like that, I always wanted to know if witchcraft and black magic was real or not anyway and the best way to find out is to try it and if the answer only cost a dollar, then educate me."

Kevin grinned then bowed and replied. "Ole Bruce Lee spirited ass muhfucka."

Tracy gave a slight chuckle that was interrupted by Will. "What the hell is you talkin' 'bout cuz-o, T-Murray don't know no Kung Fu. Do you?"

"Naw cuz-o, Bruce Lee wasn't just a fighter he was a philosopher too."

Tracy was shocked at Kevin's knowledge. "Damn Kev, I ain't know you knew that, I read the same thang."

"See just 'cause I'm yellin' thug life don't mean I'm stupid, I got a lil bit of brains. And it's not Kung fu, it's Jet Kune-Do."

"Well we about to see who got the most brains." Michael said as Shawn opened the back passenger side door and got in.

"Well here it is, the truth, anybody got a penny, dime, nickel anything to scratch this wit'?"

Everyone began searching for a coin except Kevin, he shook his head and laughed while offering insults instead. "Look at chall dumb asses." They were coming up with nothing then Shawn looked down at the bracelet in his right hand.

"A Will, you don't mind if I use the bracelet to scratch off this ticket do you?" He asked humbly. William gave Shawn an uneasy look and said.

"Don't fuck it up and clean it off when you finish."

"I gotcha-I gotcha." Shawn replied as he began scratching off the ticket. The SUV was silent except for the sound of the bracelet scratching across the ticket. As he scratched and more of the ticket was revealed he became tense and drawn as he sat in his seat, sweating. He blew the residue off the ticket and stared at it.

"So what's up?" Larry asked anxiously. Shawn didn't answer.

"Well?" MJ asked, Shawn still didn't speak he didn't even twitch his blank facial expression.

"So what is it, oh great wizard?" Kevin said. Shawn handed Kevin the ticket and replied.

"Well it ain't just magically appear out of the sky but here it is."

Kevin took the ticket and read it, he abruptly sat up. "Hell naw!"

"What what it say?" Larry asked.

"Hell naw, this mothafucka just won a hunned dollars."

You bullshittin' cuz-o." Will said.

"No bullshit." Kevin passed the ticket to Will.

"Damn there it is a hunned dollars."

"Let me see." Will Larry said reaching for the ticket. "Oh shit this witchcraft shit is real." He uttered forgetting the fable he told about his voodoo princess.

"I told yo' ass, my name is Michael Johnston not no damn Lyin' Ass Larry, you need to apologize."

"Wait a minute-wait a minute, hold up this could be just luck, he got lucky on a scratch off ain't no hocus pocus had nothin' to do wit' it." Kevin still casting subtle doubt.

"What! The proof is right in yo' face you just don't wanna accept it, luck my ass that was the hocus pocus." MJ argued.

"Yea cuz-o, I thank it was the hocus pocus."

Kevin shook his head still in disbelief. "The shit was just luck, now if you go back in there and get another ticket and win some mo' money then maybe I might start thankin' it's real, maybe."

"Well let's try it like that." T-Murray said. "I mean we all said the words so shouldn't we all benefit from it?"

"I ain't say shit, I was too busy laughing at chall dumb asses."

"You know what T-Murray, white boy didn't tell me that part and I ain't thank to ask but it sounds like it makes sense. Let's try it. Alright fellas, I'ma' buy another ticket to see if I can win again, then I'll give yall the bracelet and a dollar. Then we'll see what's up."

Shawn stepped to the counter and handed the middle aged black woman his ticket, sharing an overwhelming anxiousness with his comrades behind him. Except Kevin who was not in line but leaning against an ice cream freezer.

"Let me get five ones please and another Jumbo Bucks." After the transaction he gave William the bracelet and a dollar, he then gave a dollar to Michael, Tracy, Larry, and when he walked over to Kevin he gave him a smirk before handing him the dollar.

"Here Shawn you scratch off yours first." Will said handing Shawn the bracelet.

He scratched. "Damn, nothin' this time." He said with disappointment as he handed the bracelet to Will.

"Told you, luck." Kevin said. As Will began scratching off his ticket the others huddled around him clutching their Jumbo Bucks tickets full of anticipation. The cashier stared at the boys with crushed brows of wonder. Will finished then calmly handed the ticket to Kevin. "Hell naw, another hunned dollars." Kevin's voice was muffled by amazement, Shawn's heart was racing as well as MJ who snatched the bracelet from Will.

"A be careful wit' my momma's bracelet!"

Michael was scratching off his ticket before William finished his sentence. "Hell yeah!" MJ shouted.

"You won?" Shawn asked.

"A hunned dollars." MJ handed Tracy the bracelet and six seconds later.

"There it is, a hunned dollars." Tracy said handing Larry the bracelet. Kevin hurried over to the counter and bought a Jumbo Bucks ticket.

"I wonder why I didn't win nothing on this ticket?" Shawn said.

"Maybe it only works once for each person." Tracy said staring at his ticket.

"And you know what's a trip yall, we winnin' wit' the same number, a one." Shawn said.

"I got it, a hunned dollars!" Larry shouted. Kevin took the bracelet from Larry and began scratching his ticket.

"Fuck naw, that's fucked up!"

"What Kev?" Shawn asked.

"A damn free ticket, I won a free fuckin' ticket!"

"Ahhh-haa that's what cho' ass get fa' not believin' me." MJ boasted as he headed to the counter to retrieve his money.

"Hold up, all yall won?" The cashier said looking confused.

"-Yes ma'am, except the ugly one." MJ said with one of his suave smiles.

"I thought the short one said he won too." She asked

MJ looked back at Larry and laughed. "Oh not that one, the other ugly one."

"Well hold up while I get the owner, 'cause I ain't got enough to cover all of this."

"You know what." Tracy said snapping his fingers as a thought popped in his head. "It's probably because you ain't take it serious and laughed instead of sayin' the words."

"Yea, that's what it was." Will agreed.

"Fuck that I'm gettin' some money." Kevin said as the cashier returned with the Oriental owner. "Let me get another Jumbo Bucks." He said handing her the ticket, after the transaction he hurried over to the freezer and scratched his ticket. "That's fucked up!"

"You lost?" Michael asked with a huge smile on his face.

"Man fuck this I'll be in da car. I ain't finna stand here and watch chall niggas get money." Kevin handed the bracelet to Will then headed out of the store.

"Don't cry when you get out there." Michael said, Kevin stuck up his middle finger on his way out. "Hater."

"I can't believe this shit, that hocus pocus shit really worked." Kevin said in frustration.

The crew exited the store with Michael in front, pointing and laughing at Kevin. "See what happens when you keep a closed mind about shit." Michael said flipping through his tens and twenties as he got into the SUV. "You feel like the idiot now don't chew. I'm fuckin' wit' cha' Kev, here you go." MJ handed Kevin two tens. "Even though you don't believe my story, we still folk."

Kevin smiled and took the money. "Shit, I believe you know dawg, hell I almost believe Larry's witch girlfriend story."

"Ahh hell naw cuz-o even after this I still know not to believe that fool." William said as he passed two tens to Kevin.

Will backed out of the parking spot as they donated money to Kevin and some to Will for gas. They all put up ten dollars for weed and ten for alcohol, which was an ounce, a half gallon of gin, orange juice, two twelve packs of 211 Steele Reserve malt liquor, a couple packs of Newport's and three boxes of cigars. They all returned to

William's house where they partied heavily. They played cards, video games, and had loud alcohol induced conversations. Time crept by like a thief and before Shawn realized, it was 2:00 a.m. he had to be to work at six in the morning.

"Will can you take me home, I gotta go to work in fo' hours man?"

William drove Shawn home, which was a short drive being that he lived only a mile up the street in the neighborhood across from the One Stop convenience store. William returned just as Larry was cleaning up puke from the kitchen floor, he also fell asleep in the same spot right after he cleaned the last drop. Michael was the second to vomit after accepting Big Will's challenge at a drinking contest, he then fell asleep at the card table. Tracy discreetly walked off to the bathroom and puked for about forty-five minutes without Kevin or Will noticing being that they were in a deep conversation about childhood adventures they embarked on together. Tracy was even able to return to the living room, flop down on the couch, and fall asleep before they noticed anything. The cousins conversed until the sun came up and Kevin finally fell asleep.

Chapter 5

The day was ugly, similar to torture, Shawn was written up for being fifteen minutes late, his head was pounding, he was still buzzing from the alcohol and his stomach was uneasy. He felt like shit and he didn't know how he was going to make it through the day. However, he did have one positive thing to motivate him, the spell, it worked and by the way he felt he was thinking witchcraft seemed a lot easier than this nine to five, more like six to three, nine hour bullshit. But, like Daniel had said it can be dangerous.

His work partner Cedric notice Shawn's red eyes, sweaty face and smelled the gin oozing from his pores. "Damn folk, had a long one last night huh?"

"Cuz you don't know the half." Shawn replied which was an understatement, the weed and alcohol was obvious but the witchcraft was something Cedric could never imagine, however Daniel knew. He told Daniel all about it on their lunch break and was surprised it worked with the unbeliever in the crew.

Three o'clock had finally arrived and he still felt residue affects from last night and to top it off the rest he thought he was going to get from the plant closing for inventory was a crushed dream, inventory had been moved to next month. But at least the day was over. He waited twenty minutes before his mother arrived to pick him up.

"Hey baby sorry it took so long." She said as he got into the tan 1996 Chevy Cavalier. "I had to use the bathroom somethin' awful right before I walked out the door to come and get you."

"That's alright ma' I'm cool." He said with a humble tone.

"So how was work today?"

"I was so fucked up that I barely made it through and I got wrote up." He said in his head. "It was alright. How 'bout yours ma'?"

"Oh I was off today, both jobs."

"How you managed that?"

"I went in to Castleberry this morning and it was a big gas leak and they shut the plant down for three days while they fix it. Then later on this girl that work with me at Golden Corral called and asked if she can work my shift so she can get some extra hours. At first I was about to say no because I don't like the girl, she keep up too much gossip but I said to myself, hell why not relax for a whole day. It might be a long time before I get the chance to be off of both jobs like this again. Shoot I think I deserve it, don't you."

"Oh-yea, and I got any bills you need me to get so don't worry."

"Thank you baby but I want you to start saving for that baby."

Shawn nodded. He stared out of his window as they rode listening to the radio, he thought to himself of how good of a mother he had and how bad she could be, like Kevin's mom. "Yea my momma do deserve a day off, I know what I'll do, I'll take this money from last night and take her out to eat. Yea that's what I'll do."

"Oh yea Kevin and William called a couple of times. I thought they knew you worked during the day."

"They do, I don't know what them fools is thankin' 'bout."

"Well Kevin said give him a call at William's house it's real important. Don't chew get mixed up in no crazy mess with that Kevin boy I know how foolish he be actin', I don't want you in no trouble."

"Ma', I ain't finna let nobody get me in trouble, I got my eyes open."

"Alright now I'm trusting you to know right from wrong, I don't want to be visiting you in prison."

"You ain't gotta worry about that ma'."

For the rest of the ride he pondered on what could be so important to Kevin that he had to leave a message to call him back, for the six years he had known him Kevin never left a message. He also thought about what they did last night and if they should do it again but with better results, that's probably what they were calling about. Then he thought of what his mother had just said. "Don't you get caught up in no crazy mess with that Kevin." He laughed to himself at the irony, he was the one that was getting Kevin and his other comrades in some crazy mess.

The phone was ringing when they entered their home, Shawn looked at the caller ID and saw that it was Will's number. "Hello."

"What up folk what chew doin'?" Kevin replied.

"Nothin', just got in the house, what's up man moms told me yall called, so what's the important message?"

"This what it is, me and the fellas been talkin', about this hocus pocus thang. See, since we know it's real and the shit worked for us, we figure we should fuck 'round wit' it until we get straight. We talkin' 'bout some real cheese, a couple of stacks you know what I'm talkin' 'bout, keep us right for a long time."

"I 'on't know man, white boy told me that this shit can be dangerous."

"I ain't scared, is you? I mean you got us to do it for you, you can't do it fa' us, don't bitch out on us now."

"I ain't scared and I ain't bitchin' out." Shawn looked around to see if his mother heard him. "It's just that I gotta thank about the fellas, I mean how would they feel knowin' that this shit could come back on us."

"Shit ask them yo'self they on the line now."

"What up Grand Wizard." Will said.

"The biggest pimp in Augusta is on the line, what's up Shawn." Larry said.

"The lies you tell." Tracy commented to Larry's greeting.

"Damn, what chall fools havin' a party line or somethin'?"

"See everybody's down wit' doin' it again, we just need you to make it happen."

"I 'on't know fellas, Daniel said this shit is dangerous and it'll come back on us."

"We all talked about it and we down fa' whatever." William said.

"Look." Michael said. "We'll just do it like this. You call ya' boy up, get 'em to give you another one of them spells, one a lil bit stronger so we can get paid big and that'll be it, we'll leave it alone."

"Just one mo' time." Larry pleaded.

Shawn was silent for a moment then replied, firmly. "If this shit gets out of hand and bad shit start happenin', it ain't my damn fault, I warning yall, all of yall, don't blame me fa' shit!"

"Alright-alright no problem it's all on us." Kevin answered.

"Hell naw I want everybody to agree. Will?"

"Alright folk I got-cha', it's on me." William said sealing his fate.

"MJ?"

"I feel you it's my own responsibility." MJ sealing his fate.

"Larry?"

I know-I know it's on me."

"You too T-Murray."

"I'ma' grown ass man cuz, I'm doin' this 'cause I want to not because somebody else want me to."

"Alright then, I'll holla at the white boy. Yall give me 'bout forty five minutes to call 'em and get the recipe then hit me back."

"Alright that's my boy." William said.

"Do ya' thang Harry Potta." Kevin said.

"Alright wit' that Harry Potta shit." Shawn was cut off by Kevin hanging up, he pressed the flash button and flopped down on the couch. He was relieved, even though he showed his friends reluctance, he was happy for his comrades request because he wanted to do it again himself but didn't want to bare the whole burden of the possible consequences. Now he felt as if he was in the clear. He dialed Daniel's number.

"Hello." A woman's voice answered.

"Yes may I speak to Daniel please?" Shawn said in his best proper Caucasian tongue.

"Hold on a minute. Daniel!" She shouted. A few seconds passed and a nonchalant Daniel answered the phone.

"And who is this?"

"Hey, what's up Daniel, this Shawn, from work. Sorry to bother you man it's kinda important, kind of."

"I already know, you want to do it again. Well all you have to do is follow the same procedure you did last time but it's gonna take a lot longer to receive results than the first time."

"Well I'm actually callin' because I need something stronger. A spell that will pay out quicker and more than the last one."

"Well the one I gave you was the strongest one for quickies, you did want money fast right?"

"Yea."

"Now there are others that are stronger but they take a lot more faith, work, and time for them to work and the results won't come for months sometimes years. You would have to perform routine rituals, at least twice a week."

"Oh, damn." Shawn mumbled in disappointment as he felt his hopes being crushed. But then he had a thought. "What about that invocating and conjuring of the spirits?"

"Huh!" Daniel was taken by surprise.

"You remember you told me about conjuring up one of Lucifer's snitches. A demon." Daniel was almost speechless being impressed by how Shawn remembered his little lesson. "Is that right, am I close?"

"Oh yea you hit it on the head. But, it's too dangerous and it's gonna be consequences and that's going to outweigh what you want, which you will get. I don't want to be responsible for the end result."

Shawn took in what Daniel said, gave it deep but brief thought. "I understand but I know right from wrong and I can make my own decisions so I have and will take full responsibility for any end result." The conversation sounded too familiar to Shawn. Daniel felt the conviction in his voice through the phone while Shawn felt like his comrades when they requested from him to do it again. Unknowing to him, just as he had a hidden agenda for answering his comrades request, Daniel also had his. He always wanted to see invocations and conjuring in action but was too afraid to do it himself he was too young to know what really happened to his father and all his mother told him was that, "evil took him". But now he had an opportunity to see it work.

"Alright, but I'm warning you, this ain't no pussy-foot beginners magic, this is some pure balls to the wall evil, I'm talkin' the big leagues."

"Evil!" Shawn quickly responded.

"Oh yea, that's right, evil. What did you think, letting loose one of hell's prisoners is some heavenly and righteous act. This is evil at one of its purest forms, so if you have any doubts then you need to hang up now and let me finish doing what I was doing."

"Naw, naw I'm ready I ain't got no doubts." Shawn lied. He had plenty of doubts but he didn't want to lose what little confidence Daniel had in him being that he sounded as if he was growing impatient, not only that he could hear the complaints of his comrades, especially Kevin. "What, you bitched out, I knew you was a ole soft ass pussy-ass nigga!" He didn't want to go through that.

"Okay, well tomorrow after work I'll have all the instructions you'll need."

"Tomorrow?"

"Yea tomorrow, what is that a problem?"

"Naw, no problem it's just that you made it seem like you was gonna give it to me today."

"No, not today. I'm gonna give you some time to sleep on it, besides I need to look up some information because my memory on invocations is rusty. So tomorrow after work I'll give you what you need. That is if you still want to go through with it."

"Believe me, I will."

"We'll see." Daniel replied then hung up.

"Damn, good bye to you too."

Ding-dong. The doorbell rung soon as Shawn pressed the flash button. "I got it ma'." He shouted as he got up and answered the door. "What da hell." He said as he stepped out the door and saw everybody else in the Explorer. "What chall fools doin'," he asked as they walked to the driveway, "I thought I told yall to hit me back in forty-five minutes."

"We was but we got bored and said fuck it we'll just come over and see what's up." Kevin explained. "So what's up, did the white boy come through?"

"Yea. Now let me ask you somethin', why do it seem like yall some fiends tryin' to get a hit?"

"What chew talkin 'bout? Yea we some fiends, fiends for that green. So let's go do da damn thang."

"We can't."

"What chew mean we can't, I thought you just said he came through, let's get this money and quit playin'."

"I ain't playin', he ain't goin' give me the info until tomorrow?"

"Tomorrow, man that's some bullshit, why tomorrow?"

"Because he gotta look up some info. And he want to give me a night to sleep on it and make sure I really want to do this."

"Sleep on it?"

"Yea, this is some other shit, some serious shit, it ain't goin' be like it was yesterday that was weak. This is goin' be on a whole 'nother level."

"Whatever, as long as if we get paid. But he is goin' come through right?" Kevin said with slight desperation.

"Look at this, at first you was talkin' shit about it now you strung out on it."

"A, if it's 'bout money I'm wit' it." Kevin said getting into the Explorer.

"Yall holla at me after work tomorrow, I'll have it then."

"You want me to scoop you up from work?" Big Will asked.

"Yea that'll work. What chall fools finna do now?"

"You know what it is, smoke, probably play some ball at the center. You comin'?" Kevin replied.

"Naw I'm finna take mom-dukes out to eat, you know show 'er I appreciate 'er."

"A Shawn." Will said.

"Yea."

"Don't let 'er eat too much we suppose to be going out to eat later on."

"Whatever Congo. I'll holla at chall fools tomorrow."

"Alright cuz." MJ said.

"Alright folk." Larry said.

As William backed out of the driveway Kevin shouted from the window while pointing at Shawn. "A. Tomorrow, we makin' some major moves. You da man."

Kevin's tone and facial expression troubled Shawn in an unusual way. He knew Kevin as a hard, sometimes cold, tough, thuggish person but for that brief moment he could see innocence in him, the last drop of innocence in him that would be depleted when they embark on a level of evil that none of them could fathom. Shawn began to feel bad, guilty, the most part of him understood what they were going to do. He understood that they were going to be damned and that he would be responsible for it.

It was crowded, Applebee's were having a buy one get one free well drink special. "So how do you feel knowin' you're about to be a father son?" Cynthia asked as she dipped her cheese stick in the marinara sauce. The question was unexpected but Shawn didn't hesitate to answer.

"Scared, real scared." Shawn dipped his chicken tender into the honey mustard.

"Yea, I know baby, I'm scared with you. But once that baby gets here and be here for a while you goin' be proud instead of scared. Trust me, I was probably the scariest pregnant woman on earth but now I'm the proudest and happiest because I got two wonderful children that I love dearly, so don't be scared. You just make sure you stay by that girl's side and help her in any way and as much as you can. And anyway momma's here and I got-cha' back, I'm willin' to do whatever I can to help. I can't wait it's gonna be my first grandchild, now don't give me another one so soon."

His mother's words was relief and comforting. "I know ma' it's just that I want to be able to do it myself, stand on my own two feet and not be a burden on you, you still have Taishell to raise. Matter-of-fact I want to be the one providing for you someday. What chew thank about the military?"

"Why you ask, you thinking about going in?"

"I 'on't know. See Chris made me promise that I'll go and talk to his recruiter, since I brought Kevin to his party and he messed up his house."

"That sounds fair. I thank the military could be a good start, check it out, I mean it's your decision and I'll stand by you whatever you do but you do owe it to Chris to at least go and see what the recruiters is talkin' about."

"I 'on't know. I just wish I had access to a lot of money to take care of everybody, you Taishell, Tekela, and the baby."

"Son, we all need money but money ain't all we need. My grand-momma told me that after your uncle got locked up." Her words made him think but for only a few seconds after being disturbed by the waitress that brought their entrées.

"Here you go ma'am and sir. Would you like anything else?" The young perky blonde asked.

"No thank you we're okay for now." Cynthia replied.

The waitress gave a huge bleached smile. "Okay well enjoy your meal and just let me know if there's anything I can do for you."

"She's working hard for that tip ain't she."

"Oh-yea." Shawn said with a laugh. Cynthia bowed her head to say grace, while Shawn just stared. After she finished she began eating, Shawn didn't start because he pondered a question. "Ma'."

"Um-hum." She answered with a mouthful of chicken parmesan.

"Do you believe witchcraft is real?"

"Witchcraft! Why you ask me that?"

"Cause it's this guy at my job that mess wit' it and I was just wonderin' if it was real or not."

"I 'on't know baby, I never knew nobody that dealt with that stuff. I really don't know what to tell you on that subject. Maybe it's real or maybe it's not, I 'on't know but I can tell you this, if it is real it ain't nothin' good."

"Why you say that?"

"Because if God wanted us to have magic powers he would have given them to us instead of giving his only son." Her maternal philosophy caused him to question his intentions on tomorrow, however his curiosity over powered his reasoning, his mind was made up.

Shawn and his mother enjoyed their meals and the evening. He felt proud to be able to treat his mother and was able to see her relax with two gin and tonics and two margaritas. He was surprised that she let him drink, a gesture of congratulations for getting safely out of high school.

The three o'clock bell sounded and the employees of Carole Fabrics stampeded out of the plant while Shawn looked around for Daniel in almost disappointment. "Damn, he probably already left. But I just saw 'em." He mumbled to himself.

"Who are you looking for?" Daniel asked standing behind Shawn.

"Oh there you go, I thought you had already dipped."

"Nope, I'm still here. So I take it you still want to go through with this."

"Yes sur."

"Well, here you go. Daniel handed Shawn a folded sheet of notebook paper. Everything you need to do is on this paper. Now it's some items on here you're going to need and I'm pretty sure you don't just have them laying around the house." They headed out to the parking lot as Daniel gave details. "There's this store on Broad Street called The Haven you'll find everything you'll need there."

"Thank you." Shawn held his hand out for some dap, Daniel awkwardly answered the gesture. "I really appreciate this."

"Don't thank me, just be careful." Daniel said with a serious tone. "And if you need me for anything call me, I'll be on standby."

"I will." Shawn said walking over to the Explorer full of his comrades. He got in the back and sat next to Tracy against the door. "What's up fellas?" He greeted giving daps and ponds.

"Nothin'." Tracy said.

"You." Kevin said.

"Chillin'." The rest responded, except Kevin he was distracted, fascinated by the weird white boy, he looked at him in another way, he respected him. Daniel could feel someone watching him as he walked to his black Nissan Maximum, he turned and made eye contact with Kevin. The stare was distant and brief but it was if they saw each other's pain and trials of life and telepathically understood each other. He snapped out of his stare when William drove pass Daniel and out of the parking lot.

"So what's up is that the shit in ya' hand?" Kevin said for his greeting.

"Damn ole inconsiderate ass nigga, I can't get no how you doin', no how was your day at work, somethin'?"

"Oh I'm sorry dear." Kevin said imitating a conservative prude white woman. "How are you doing today, how was work dear?"

"My day was fucked up, my damn feet been hurtin' all damn day, you goin' rub 'em fa' me?" Tracy, Will, MJ, and Larry laughed.

"All bullshit aside, is that it or what?"

"Yea man, it is damn." He said somewhat irritated.

"That's my boy, that's what I'm talkin' 'bout it's time to get paid!"

"So what now?" Michael asked Shawn but was answered by Kevin.

"So now we get some weed, some drank then we hit Will's crib and do da damn thang."

"No not really." Shawn corrected Kevin.

"What chew mean not really?"

"Well first we gotta pick up a couple of special items to perform this spell."

"Special items," Will said, "like what?"

Shawn unfolded the paper and read from the list titled *Items Needed*. Alright we need a wooden bowl, six black candles and some white or black powdered chalk."

"Where we goin' get that shit from?" MJ asked.

"Walmart nigga, Walmart got everythang." Kevin answered.

"Naw," Shawn responded with some laughter, "this place down on Broad Street called The Haven."

"Well Broad street it is." William said as he took the exit to Gordon Highway. They rode bobbing their heads to the music of Augusta's underground rapper Black Burd that bumped out of William's custom stereo system that his father had installed on his sixteenth birthday. Though they were into the music they also thought about what they were about to do, William was the first to speak on the mutually shared thought, he turned down the stereo and stared into the rearview mirror at Shawn. "So Shawn, what kind of spell we 'bout to do?"

Shawn had anticipated the question, he even had a well thought out explanation for it but for some reason he couldn't remember it, he plundered around in his head for it but couldn't find it. After a moment he finally gave a simple and straight forward answer. "We finna conjure up a demon." Shawn answered so nonchalantly that he surprised himself. He could not only see but he could feel the stares his comrades gave him, he waited for their confused reaction that quickly followed.

"We finna do what wit' who?" MJ said staring over at him from the other side of the back seat. Kevin turned off the music.

"We finna conjure up a demon."

"Hold up-hold up wait a minute cuz, nobody ain't say nothin' 'bout no demons and shit."

"Fa'real." T-Murray agreed.

"I figured I ain't have to, yall wanted to get paid so bad and yall was so crunk about doin' it again, I felt it didn't matter what we was doin' just that it worked and that we get paid. So what, yall don't wanna do it?"

Hell yea, I'm still wit' it." Kevin said. "How 'bout you cuz-o you still down wit' it ain't cha'?"

"Yea."

Kevin turned around in his seat and looked at Larry in a pressuring manner. "How 'bout chew Larry, you still wit' it?"

"I ain't scared let's do it, shit." Larry answered showing his blind faith like a soldier following his ignorant commander over a cliff.

"It's on yall, MJ, T-Murray, yall don't wanna do it, ya'll scared?" Shawn asked.

"I ain't say I was scared, I just don't know about this fuckin' wit' demons and shit." MJ said.

"Yea me too. That's some ole other shit there, you go to hell fa' shit like that."

"Come on man, yall niggas bitchin' out on us!" Kevin said in frustration. "MJ all them whoes you be fuckin', T-Murray you ain't no damn Christian. If Will crash this mothafucka and kill all of us right now we'll all go to hell, so what fuckin' difference do it make! Weak ass...Shawn can we do this wit' out dem niggas?"

"Yea, we can. But I don't want to, I want all of us to do this, know what I'm sayin, we're a crew, we all ride together on this. If you two ain't down then I ain't down and I'll just toss this paper out the window."

"Aww naw cuz don't do that!" Kevin said frantic. "Don't fuck it up fa everybody 'cause these two sissies is too scared to get paid!"

"So what's up?" Shawn held the paper out of the window.

Kevin's heart pounded as he stared at the paper as it flapped in the wind as if it was his life and it was about to be blown away, he quickly changed his method of persuasion. "Come on T-Murray, MJ, please, come on yall. T-Murray thank about cha' momma cuz do it fa' her man, come on. I mean, that'll be a real bitch move to turn down an opportunity to help 'er 'cause you was scared. That's some selfish ass shit there."

Tracy quickly responded. "Hold up Kev you steppin' out of line now man! Fa'real." His anger was recognized.

"My-bad folk, I apologize, I 'on't mean no disrespect, I'm just sayin' take advantage of the opportunity that's bein' handed to ya', it's knockin', hard. MJ, thank about what chew can do wit' the money, pay for them classes, get that scholarship back and play ball. Hell you might not even have to worry about no scholarship you might get enough money to pay for school wit' cash. Come on fellas please, just thank about it."

Tracy and Michael looked at each other as if they were asking each other for advice. Michael then looked out at the flapping paper and answered first. "Alright, I'm down."

"Yes!" Kevin uttered.

"That leaves you Tracy." Shawn said still holding the paper out of the window.

Tracy shook his head. "I got a bad feelin' about this, but fuck it. I'm wit' it man."

"That's my boy that's what I'm talkin' 'bout!" Kevin celebrated as Shawn brought the paper back in.

"Alright now what we goin' be doin'?" William asked.

"We goin' conjure up a demon."

"What that mean?"

"We gonna call one up."

"Call 'em, well what if it don't answer?" Larry asked.

"Oh trust me, he'll answer."

"Okay, now how is a demon gonna get us paid?" Kevin asked.

"It's goin' do whatever we tell it to do."

"And how is this suppose to work?" Will asked.

Shawn sat up to explain. "Alright yall know that the devil use to be a angel right?"

"Yea I heard about that?" MJ mentioned.

"Well he was the pretty boy angel, he got the big head and thought he should take God's place, so he got a bunch of other angels, cliqued up, and planned a little war too take over, but you know God knows everythang. Now right befo' it went down a lot of them got scared and went to God and snitched on Lucifer but God already knew what was going down. So Lucifer tried 'em and you know nobody can mess wit' God, he tossed Lucifer's ass out of heaven and into hell. Then later on he kicked his homeboys out too, even the ones that turned on Lucifer.

"That's good for 'em, snitchin' ass...Oh go 'head." Kevin said.

"Anyway. When they got to hell Lucifer snatched all they asses up and locked them up in a prison where they get tortured forever."

"Damn, I ain't know all that." Tracy said.

"Me neither." Larry said.

"But wait this where it twist up at. The devil, still tryin' to play God was like I ain't all bad, I'm better than God I'll prove it to you, I'll show you forgiveness by givin' yall a chance to be free. If a human calls on one of you to do my will to my satisfaction, I'll set you free."

"Let me guess, that's where we come in at." Tracy said.

"Yep that's us."

"So we can get it to walk in a bank and snatch up the money?" Will asked.

"Yep."

"Or we can have it rob one of them Wells Fargo trucks." Larry added.

"Yep."

"Okay-okay I'm feelin' this." Kevin said pleased.

"Alright Shawn we on Broad street, what's the name of this place?"

"The Haven."

"The Haven, the haven, the haven." Will repeated as he looked out of his window at the stores, bars, clubs, restaurants, and vendors that lined the strip. "Oh shit!" He uttered then beeped his horn. *Beep-beep*. He swerved when his focus locked on three females in skimpy outfits walking the sidewalk. "Hey, what's up ladies?" He shouted, they turned with smiles on their faces and waved. "Yall saw them whoes?"

"Hell yea I saw 'em, turn around and let's go holla at 'em." Michael suggested.

"Man fuck dem whoes, let's get this money," Kevin said, "stay focused."

"Hey yea stay focused Will that's a red light!" Shawn shouted pointing at the traffic light up ahead.

"Oh shit!" Will stomped on the brakes bringing the SUV to a tire skidding stop. The abrupt stop almost pushed everyone out of their seat. William chuckled. "Oh my-bad."

"You real focused there Willy boy." Kevin said with sarcasm.

"Look-look, there it is right over there." Larry said pointing across the street to their left.

"Okay Willy Boy you got us right to it, good job cuz-o." William made an illegal u-turn after the light turned green, then parallel parked in front of the building. The sign was a crude and simple sign painted dark purple with black lettering. *The Haven.*

"A yall look at this." Larry said pointing at one of the odd displays in the shop's display window. "Look at this big ass knife."

"Ain't that's one of them crystal balls that them fortune tellers be usin'?" Will asked in subtle amazement.

"This place is somewhere else." Shawn said as he opened the door. They entered an enchanted vibe, soft tribal music played throughout the store and the aroma of foreign incense filled the air. To their left the store's wall were covered with varies types of books such as; Spells for Beginners, How to Talk to the Gods, Rituals and Rites, The Necronomicon, The Grimore, Incantations and Spells etc… Next to the books were shelves of CDs with titles such as; The Sounds of Nature, Songs Of The Wind and Rain Dancing etc… On the back wall were statues of Buddha, The Sphinx, dragons, demi-gods, mythological creatures, skulls, and other beings they never seen before. Next to the statues were incense from Coconut to Baby's Breath. Next to the incense were oils, spices and candles and on the other wall were clothes but not like the clothes found in a common department store. Ceremonial clothing hung from the hangers cloaks, capes, and varies types of headdresses. Shawn now knew were Daniel did his shopping. The store was an outlet of supernatural items, it had everything and exactly what the boys needed.

"Look at this place cuz. I ain't never seen no shit like this befo'." William said.

"I know, much as I been down here on Broad Street, I ain't never seen this sto'." Kevin said.

"I ain't thank it was a place like this in Augusta." Shawn said staring at the wall of books.

"Welcome, may I help you friends?" Said the man behind a counter that sat in the middle of the store. They were so taken by the store that they didn't notice the man watching since they had entered. He was a slim, thirtyish, balding, five-eight, white man with a five inch goatee. All of his fingers had rings on them of different types of shapes and significant symbols. Both of his wrists had more than enough silver bracelets as well as his neck, that was cluttered with silver necklaces. He wore an off white and cream trimmed shirt that was wrinkled and so thin that it was vaguely transparent. His hands was together as if he was preparing to pray and he wore a weird smile as if he was drugged. They immediately classed him as a homosexual.

"Oh naw, we alright, we got it." Kevin replied. The clerk bowed his head, they dispersed, and Shawn pulled out the paper to commence the shopping.

"Alright, first we need a wooden bowl." He said to himself but loud enough for Kevin to hear.

"Here you go." Kevin said as he grabbed a small bowl from a small stack of varies types of ritual dishes. "Nine dollars, shit!" He almost shouted. "This ain't no damn Ramen Noodle bowl."

"Alright, now we need six black candles."

"Here go the candles over here." William said as he gathered six black candles. "Any size?"

"I guess, just make sure they're black."

"What else?" Kevin eagerly asked.

"Now all we need is some powdered chalk."

"What color?" Tracy said standing in front of a shelf of several jars containing different colors of powdered chalk.

"Black or white, either one."

Tracy grabbed a jar of black powdered chalk then followed Shawn to the counter.

"Will this be all you will be needing friend?"

"Yea this it?"

"That will be twenty-nine seventeen."

Shawn looked back at his comrades. "What's up, ain't nobody

gonna help me pay for this?"

"I ain't got but a ten and that's to put on the green." Kevin answered.

"I ain't got but ten and that's fa' gas." Will said.

"I'm broke too." Tracy said.

"What! Yall ain't got nothin' left from last night?"

"Nope." Kevin and Will answered together.

"Maaannn…Yall nig…MJ, you got some change on you?"

"Nope, I'm hurtin'." Michael said patting his pockets as he skimmed through a book titled; Mind Manipulation Techniques: "Natural and Supernatural.

"Damn!" Shawn uttered then looked over at Larry that was reading a small hand book titled; Make her Lust For You: Potions and Spells For The Lonely. "I know not to ask you." Shawn pulled out a twenty and a ten then handed it to the clerk, after the transaction the crew headed to the door when the clerk stopped them.

"Hey friends. May the journey you all are about to take lead you to knowledge and peace at mind, and I hope it be a safe one." His statement took them by surprise, they looked at each other in dismay for about fifteen seconds then left the store speechless.

"Is it me or was that man a sweet-butty-ass-boy?" Will said stopping at a traffic light.

"Oh yea, he was sweeter than a sugar cube alright." Kevin said.

"What was up wit' his hands, I thought he was finna start prayin' or somethin'." Michael added causing everyone to laugh, except Tracy that was gazing out of his window drowning in worry.

"A fellas." Tracy said in a firm tone that calmed the laughter. "Yall ain't feel that?"

"Feel what?" MJ asked.

"That strange shit wit' buddy. That cat know we 'bout to do some hell-a-fied shit. He caught a vibe."

"A vibe?" Kevin questioned.

"Yea a vide. He probably one of them type of people that can feel vides and read auras and shit."

"Ahh man he ain't read shit, he probably say that shit to everybody that leaves the sto'." Kevin concluded. "I wish you a safe journey. Kevin imitating the clerk. He talkin' 'bout the journey you finna take home when you leave the sto'. Hell, that shit fit wit' what kinda sto' it is, make it sound all mystical and shit. It ain't nothin'."

"He probably noticed the stuff we buyin' and know what it's fa' and is wishin' us a safe journey on..."

"-Some hellish shit." Tracy finishing Shawn's sentence, a few seconds of contemplating silence struck them but was ended by Big Will.

"Shhiitt I hope we have a safe journey to get this green, Shitty D and Slim got it hot as hell."

"Especially on our side and Wrightsboro Road way, who we goin' holla at?" MJ asked.

"T-Money is the closest, holla at him." Larry suggested.

"Damn, stuck wit' spendin' my few dollars wit' a nigga I 'on't like." Kevin mumbled just enough for Will to hear.

"I know you don't like-'em cuz-o but you ain't gotta like-'em to like his green, and he right 'round the corner and it shouldn't be hot 'round this way right now. Holla at him our risk seachin' for it in da fryin' pan. Let's get it quick and get home to do da damn thang."

"Yea-yea I know." Kevin agreed leaking with an uncomfortable hate. "Yall know he the one that shot up C-Los."

"Huh, I heard he got shot breakin' in somebody's crib." Tracy said.

"Hell naw that's a rumor he made up to keep folks out his business. He told me how it really went down. He was droppin' off some dope fa' T-Money to some ATL niggas that paid 'em wit that funny money. T-Money found it while countin' it and started bussin' at 'em."

"Damn, C-Los is a decent cat too. But that's just how it is." Will said turning into the Southside projects, he parallel parked along the curb disturbing a four-thug dice game. So who going in?"

"I got it."

"You was just cryin' cuz-o about hollin' at 'em cause you don't like 'em but you wanna go in and get it?"

"I don't, even though he hooks me up better than anybody I know that holla at 'em."

"Here Kev." Tracy said handing Kevin his ten dollars."

"Hey cuz-o maybe he should be the one we get if this thang work."

Will's words snatched Kevin's attention. "Cuz-o you's a fuckin' genius boy. Hold that thought." He said as he got out and shut the door.

"Oh what's up Killer Kev, thought chew was somebody else." A thug said releasing the handle of a Glock .45.

"Oh naw don't do it like that." He greeted with daps and pounds. "T-Money in there?"

"Yea that fat ass nigga in there."

"Is he straight on the green?"

"Kev, you know dat nigga is always straight, he got that good today to, goin' in there and holla at 'em."

"Alright." Kevin walked up the three steps then knocked on the thin metal brown screen door. Seconds later a tall, half-dressed, light skin female answered the door. "Damn. Is T-Money here?"

The girl pushed the screen door open wider and Kevin walked in.

"Killer Kev what's up cuz?" T-Money greeted from a forest green couch, sitting between two females sharing a blunt. Long time no see, What's up wit' cha'?" The dark skinned, fat, bowlegged T-Money said as he struggled to get up from his seat.

"Shit, nothin' much tryin' to smoke good."

"I hear that, what chew need?"

"A dub."

"A dub, cuz I 'on't sale nothin' but weight now, QPs and better."

"Damn I ain't know that shit."

"It's cool I'll look out fa' ya' this time but spread the word, I only fuck wit' weight, no mo' small change comin' through my doo'."

"That's what's up."

"Come on to da back. How ya' crew?"

"Oh dem niggas straight, they out there waitin' on me now." Kevin replied as he followed T-Money down a hall.

"Oh shit I almost forgot. I like how you and ya' boys was knuckin' at that lil party."

"Oh you heard about that."

"Heard, nigga I saw it. That shit is all on YouTube, yall nigga's ghetto famous. I like how you young niggas look out fa each other, I can use some loyal cats like yall on my team. Especially you Kev, you treal as hell."

"I 'on't know T-Money." Kevin said after stoppin' at the end of the hallway at a closet door. "That's a lot of responsibility."

"Yea you right my nigga, it is a lot of responsibility but believe me folk, I'll keep ya' pockets fat, I ain't sayin' give me a answer right now, thank about it and get back at me. And while you thank about it, thank about this." T-Money opened the closet door.

"Daaannnmmmm!" Kevin said into his left fist while his right gripped his crotch in amazement. The closet contained four shelves, the first top three shelves were stocked with stacks of money while the last one was stocked with bricks of compressed marijuana. On the floor was also a black fifty-gallon plastic bag full of loose marijuana from which T-Money retrieved half of his handful and handed it to Kevin. Kevin gave T-Money the two tens and followed him back to the living room. "Damn T-Money I'ma' be real wit'-cha', I ain't never seen no shit like that befo'. That much cheese, shhhiit."

"Oh that ain't shit, that's just a week of weed work. You can do the samethang if you fuck wit' me."

"Hell, I might just do that, I'll get back wit'-cha' on dat."

"Do that, I'm here."

"Alright you hold it down T-Money."

"Oh you know I will." T-Money said as the same girl that answered the door walked Kevin out. "I'm goin' fuck wit' chew alright, you just don't know." Kevin mumbled to himself as he walked over to the Explorer. "A cuz-o you got somethin' I can put this in?"

"It should be some napkins in the glove compartment." Kevin opened the compartment, pulled out a Church's chicken napkin and dumped the weed in it, William noticed the amount he had. "Damn cuz-o he hooked you up didn't he."

"Yea but that ain't shit compared to what I just saw, this nigga just showed me a closet full of money cuz."

"What, fa'real" Will replied.

"Hell yea, three shelves stacked wit' money from bottom to top, then another one at the bottom with pounds of weed and then on the flo' he had a big ass trash bag full of weed."

"Damn!" MJ said.

"Why he showed you all that?" Tracy asked.

"To talk me into workin' for 'em, all of us. He saw how we wrecked shop and bust them nigga's heads at Chris' party."

"He was there?" MJ asked.

"He said the shit is all on YouTube, nigga we famous."

"Okay then. So what did you say?" William asked.

"I shot 'em some bullshit, told 'em I'll thank about it. I ain't fuckin' wit' that shady ass nigga, I'll have to end up whippin' his ass and he got too many guns to be tryin' to go to war wit', that's how C-Los got fucked up. But I'll tell you this, cuz-o that's why you had the best idea in history, gettin' his fat ass. Fa' one he got the stacks on deck, two I don't like that nigga, three he shot C-Los and C-Los is cool folk, and fo' I don't like that nigga."

"You said that already." MJ said.

"Yea I know, that's how much I don't like 'em."

"Why you hate T-Money so much?" Larry asked. "What he do to you?"

"He ain't do shit to me, it's just somethin' about 'em, I 'on't know what it is, but it is what it is and I can't stand it. I ain't never hated on another man but this nigga done turned me into a pure hater."

"How many cigars yall want me to get?" Tracy asked as Will parked at the B.C. gas station.

"Get two boxes of whatever." Kevin answered as Tracy got out of the SUV. "So what's up fellas we goin' use the shit on T-Money right?"

"If it works, then yea." Shawn answered.

"I hope it do, naw fuck dat I know it's goin' work and when it do, damn, it's goin' be off da chain. A whole new way of robbin' a mothafucka. Damn I can't wait." Kevin's hopeful enthusiasm was strong, Shawn hated to have to tame it.

"Sorry to disappoint chew Kev but chew goin' have to wait a lil bit longer."

"What, why?"

"We can't do it 'til midnight."

"Midnight, why midnight?"

"I 'on't know but that's what Daniel wrote on this paper. We don't start sayin' the words until midnight."

"Oh well, that's alright well just smoke out until then."

"Alright fellas we goin' have to smoke outside in the back because my momma comin' home the day after tomorrow and I 'on't want this place smellin' like weed when she get back."

"That's right my baby is comin' home soon." Shawn joked as he put the plastic bag of items on the card table that was still in the same spot from the other night. Larry and Michael sat on the couch and grabbed a controller getting prepared to play a game while Tracy walked to the kitchen behind William after getting the napkin of weed from Kevin.

"A Kev you want me to roll all this up or what?"

"Hell yea go ahead and roll it all up." Kevin shouted back as he sat at the head of the card table starin' at the items Shawn unpacked.

"A Will help me roll all this shit up."

"I got cha'." William answered as they sat at the glass marble trimmed table, Tracy handed William a box of cigars.

"You roll them Swishers, I roll these Phillies them Swishers is too damn sensitive fa' me, I be tearin' them up."

"Don't worry 'bout it, I got it, I can roll up everythang from tree leaves to phone-book paper, just call me Mr. Rollup." William bragged as he opened the box of Swishers.

"A Will, on the real tip, between you and me, what chew really thank about what we finna do tonight?"

"Shhiitt, to tell you the truth I don't thank it's goin' work, even wit what happened last night, raisin' up demons and controlin' it, that sounds a lil off da wall."

"So why did you agree to it?"

"Cause, it's somethin' to do and I'm doin' it with my homeboys, I like kickin' it wit' chall and the curiosity of what if."

"That's what I mean. What if, what if this shit is real, what if we really do call up a demon. You ain't worried about the consequences?"

"What, you mean like going to hell." Tracy nodded. "It's like this, if I died right now I'm going to hell, so why not enjoy life while I can befo' I go. I mean it's a million mothafuckas out there drivin' they self crazy tryin' to find the truth, tryin' to walk that straight and righteous path, but then it be some small reason they be off track, die, and end up going to hell anyway. So I feel like this, why spend my life worryin', why live in two hells, hell on earth and hell after death. I'm gonna have fun while I can and I'm glad I'm doin' it wit' my niggas, I feel damn good to be a part of somethin', it's like a secret nobody else knows about but me, us above every-body else. A secret society, you feel me?" Tracy nodded his head.

"What's the chalk fa'?" Kevin asked as he held up the jar. Shawn pulled out the paper from his pocket.

"Okay, we goin' use the chalk to draw a doorway between the two worlds, his and ours, and also to draw the sign of the demon we goin' call. This right here." He held up the paper for Kevin to see.

Kevin nodded. "Okay what's the candles fa'?"

"The candles is to light the pathway to get to us. Street lights."

Kevin nodded. "Okay, now what's the bowl fa'?"

Shawn's facial expression was now cynical with a huge sneaky grin. "Oh now that's the fun part. I ain't goin' tell you that until the last minute."

"What. Come on man tell me."

"Nope I'll tell you when it's time, chill out."

"That's fucked up but it's cool I can wait." Kevin could barely contain himself, he was excited and anxious. "So what's the demon's name we finna holla at?"

Shawn looked at the paper then struggled to pronounce the name. "Ze, Zee, Zeinu, Zeinoch. Zeinoch, yea that's it Zeinoch, I thank I'm sayin' it right."

"I hope you sayin' it right, I want this shit to work." Kevin stressed. "Cause if you called my house askin' fa' Kalvin I'm hangin' up."

Shawn chuckled. "This is a lot different than a phone call, the pronunciation ain't all that important."

"I hope..."

"What's up yall ready to smoke?" William asked as he entered the living room.

They all followed William through the kitchen and out to his back yard. They all sat on the lawn furniture that was neatly arranged on the huge patio deck that Will's father just recently had built. Michael however, did his usual routine, he went out on William's double court, grabbed the Wilson basketball and began dribbling. "Come on Larry, let me school you real quick in a game of Twenty-one." He said then shot a clean all net basket.

"Hell naw, you be tryin' to show off and shit, dunkin' on people and shit, I ain't fuckin' wit' chew."

"Ahh man I ain't goin' show out, Shawn what's up let's run a game."

"Naw I'm finna fire up this blunt."

"How 'bout chew Kev?"

"Hell naw nigga you ain't finna shine on me."

"What's up Big Will I know you ain't scared."

"Ain't nothin', what's up run it." Will said as he began walking down his patio stairs but was interrupted by his neighbor that was watering his grass.

"Hey Will what's up?" He shouted then turned off the water and walked over.

"Hey what's going on Mr. Stamps?" Will greeted with some dap.

"Nothin' much, just doin' a little yard work. Hey fellas." Mr. Stamps greeted the rest of the crew.

"Hey." Shawn replied as he passed Kevin the blunt with a mouthful of smoke.

"I just came over to say thank you, I appreciate what you did for my daughter, good lookin' out."

"Oh no problem Mr. Stamps, I do whatever I can."

Kevin walked down the stairs then passed William the blunt. "What the hell you did, I know you ain't tried to be no good Samaritan." Kevin's voice and face struck Mr. Stamps as someone familiar to him and he began studying him to recall the memory.

William took the blunt. "Somethin' like that. Mr. Stamps' lil girl goes to Glenn Hills middle, she was gettin' off the bus one day and these three lil knuckle heads was messin' wit'-'er, you know tryin' to feel on 'er and stuff. I ran out and flexed on the lil niggas. I was like what da fuck yall doin' fuckin' wit' my lil sista. Then I jacked the biggest one up and pushed 'em a lil bit just enough to make him trip over the curb. Then the rest of 'em dropped their heads and humbled they asses home."

"Aww, look at 'em tryin to be a big brother, now it would have been funny if them lil niggas would of jumped on you and banged yo' ass up."

"Man you crazy as hell, ain't no lil middle school boys finna bang me up, I 'on't care how many it is. Mr. Stamps this is my cousin Kevin."

"Hey what's up Kevin." Mr. Stamps said staring at Kevin as if he knew him from a long time ago but just couldn't recall where from.

"Damn cuz-o, just tell everybody my real name." He complained.

"Man, he's cool."

"I 'on't know that, fa' all I know he might be the police."

"I'm tellin' you he's cool."

"Believe me young-blood I'm far from being the police." Mr. Stamps was a brown skinned, six-foot-two man that looked as if he use to work out but stopped a few years ago and collected a little family-man fat. He was cleaned cut, moderately handsome, with the face of an experienced man not that of an old one. He wore the age of thirty-four well. "Your name is Kevin?"

"Yea why?" Kevin said with an attitude and a look of suspicion. "Oh that wasn't even me, I wasn't even there."

"Oh naw it's nothin' like that."

"I 'on't care what it was, that wasn't me." Kevin began to walk off and up the stairs as Will began to explain the reason for Kevin's rudeness.

"Mr. Stamps don't pay him no attention his momma dropped 'em on his head about fo' times when he was a baby."

Mr. Stamps was unable to pay attention to William's words being that he was trying to put together in his head on why Kevin seemed so familiar to him. He repeated his name in his head.

"Kevin, Kevin, Kevin." Then it revealed itself causing him to blurt out a name. "Scooter Bug!"

The name stopped Kevin in his tracks, he turned around and said. "What the hell did you just call me?"

"Scooter Bug." Mr. Stamps repeated.

"Scooter Bug, how in da hell do you know that nickname?" Kevin's comrades were speechless except William.

"Damn I'm yo' cousin and I didn't know that one."

Kevin answered Will while still looking at Mr. Stamps with even more suspicion in his stare. "Cause only two people called me that, my brother and his homeboy. Mr. Stamps nodded. "Lance?"

"That's right it's me, what's up Scooter Bug! I Knew you looked familiar." Kevin walked back down the steps and gave Mr. Stamps a proper greeting with some dap and a shoulder to shoulder. "How you doing man?"

"I'm doin'. How thangs wit' chew?"

"Oh I'm blessed, real blessed. I can't believe it's you, little Scooter Bug, I ain't seen you since, since you was thigh high."

"Scooter Bug." Shawn laughed along with Tacy and Larry.

"Why you call 'em Scooter Bug?" William asked.

"Because every time he saw a Volkswagen he always said he was going to get one of them bugs, so me and Markell started calling him Scooter Bug. It's been a long time, the last time I saw you was, Markell's funeral eight years ago. Man me and yo' brother use to do everythang together, slang, get high, get girls, rob, steal, everything. We even went to jail together a couple of times. That was my partner, man I miss him."

"Yea me too."

"Now he was what yall young cats these days call a real nigga, he was as real as they come. He ain't take no mess and he ain't start no mess. He looked out for his people, he was straight up, and you can always depend on him. He was good people, it's messed up how his life ended, he didn't deserve that." Emotions almost surfaced as Lance spoke on his fallen comrade, Kevin as well as his partners could tell that Lance was still hurting from the lost.

"Yea I know but that's how the game go, and that's one of the reasons I don't sale dope. Them crack-heads go crazy fa' that rock no matter who you is." Kevin said as he sat back down in his chair. Lance was now looking at him with a new face of confusion.

"Crack-head, what crack-head?"

"The crack-head that shot my brother. What, you didn't know how he died?"

"Yea I know, I was there, I saw it. Who told you that it was a crack-head that shot him?"

"My momma, why?" Kevin now had a face of confusion and sitting up on the edge of his seat.

"Oh, okay, well, I gotta let that go."

"Hold up." Kevin now standing. "What chew know about what happened to my brother?"

"Look Kevin, I see that this is a family matter and I ain't got no business being in the middle of it. Your mother probably told you that for a reason, I don't want to get in the middle."

Kevin got up and approached Lance in an almost threatening manner. "Look here man, I feel ya' on how you tryin' to respect the whole family thang but fuck that, I'm grown and if you know the truth about what happened to my brother, yo' homeboy, then you need to tell me." Shawn, Tracy, and Larry knew what was on the verge of happening, they've seen it too often and knew Kevin too well. They hurried over and stood behind him ready to grab him when he swing. William put his hand on Kevin's right shoulder in an attempt to calm him down.

"Chill out Kevin, you ain't gotta do it like that Cuz-o." Kevin abruptly pushed his hand aside, Michael walked over to see what was happening.

"Fuck that, he finna tell me somethin' or it's going down right here." Lance gave a slight laugh. "What you thank it's a joke, you thank it's funny."

"Naw I'm not laughing at you. Naw I take that back I am laughing at you because you remind me of him so much, and no disrespect, your brother couldn't kick my ass so I know for sure that you can't kick my ass. But you know what, out of respect for your brother I'm going to tell you what really went down. Now are you sure you want me to tell you in front of your partners. It's going to air some dirty laundry."

"Man these my niggas, I ain't got nothin' to hide from them."

"Alright, then here it is. Your pops Lenny, he use to sale heroin for this big time dealer name Jimmy Cain, I don't know if yall heard of him or not."

"Yea I heard of Jimmy Cain." Tracy said along with Will, Kevin, and Larry.

"Yea I figured yall probably have. Well he had it all from heroin to whoes, from weed to rocks, from coke to counterfeit cash, from chopped cars to choppers. If you need anything just holla out his name, Jimmy Cain, Jimmy Cain. That's what people use to say." The short rap caught Tracy's attention.

"I remember that, my oldest brother had a old ass tape wit' a song on it that had that hook."

"Yea The MTDs, The Mighty Three DJs, from right here in Augusta. Well your pops was selling for him, then he started using, money started coming up short. Jimmy gave him chance after chance to pay him back something he ain't never done for anybody, then he gave Lenny a deadline, pay up or face the consequences. Now Jimmy Cain was a little different than a lot of other drug dealers, he handled shit differently. If you didn't pay him his money he wouldn't kill you, see he figured a dead man couldn't pay up, he'll never get his money. So what he would do is kill somebody close to you, your grandmother, your momma, your wife, husband, kids, daddy. He'll kill one love one every time you was late on a deadline. That's where you're brother Markell came in." Lance's statement touched Kevin just enough to make him inhale some stress.

"The day it happened I was with him the whole day, see like I said before we was slangin' together making a lot of money, we was doing it all with weed, we never touched no crack, coke, heroin, nothing but weed. And on this day we had sold sixteen pounds in four hours."

"Damn." William uttered.

"That's what I'm talkin' 'bout." Shawn said.

"Yall must sold nothing but weight?" MJ inquired.

"Nope, we sold everythang from nickel bags to pounds, whatever they wanted. We was even selling three dollar joints. Broke smokers gotta smoke too. It was a Friday and I was sitting on the most money I ever had in my life, everything was good. I had about eleven thousand to play with and I know Markell had way more than that because he was putting me in the game, he was looking out for me. We was on the way home from the liquor store when we met these white girls at a red light, we exchanged numbers and they was going to call us up in an hour to meet them at the mall. We got to your house and it was just you and your momma home. You remember that day?"

"Yea I remember."

"We chilled on the porch and waited for the girls to call, we had came up with a plan. We decided that he was going to go in one end of the mall and I was going to go to one end and we was going to walk through it and hit every store buying whatever, and when we finished we was going to meet up in the middle and see who had the flyest clothes. You know see who had the better taste in style. You had came outside with a basketball and Markell took it from you and started dribbling it and you got mad 'cause you couldn't steal it back."

"Yep, I remember, the last thang I remember about 'em."

"We chilled for about twenty minutes when somebody pulled up and dropped your pops off. He walked in the house fast didn't pay us no attention, didn't even look at us. Then about thirty minutes later Lenny comes out the house geeked up, I mean he looked like he had snorted a whole eight ball of pure uncut. His eyes bucked, he was sniffling, he had coke crumbs in his nostrils. And the crazy thing about it was that he stopped doing cocaine three years before then, all he did was shoot up but for some reason he was snorting that day. He walked up to Markell and said.

'We need to talk-we need to ride-we-we need to talk-we need to ride and talk.'

Markell said. 'Man I'm waitin' on a phone call can it wait?'

Lenny said. 'Naw-naw it's important it ain't goin' take long.'

So we getting ready to get in the car, Markell in the driver seat, Lenny in the front passenger seat, and I was about to get in the back when Lenny stops me and say.

'This a family matter he'll holla at cha' later.' I was like damn. So I look at Markell to see what he had to say about it, he said.

'I'll hit chew on the cell in a minute.' So they pulled off and I started walking home, I stayed right up the street, when something hit me, it didn't feel right, something told me to run home get in my car and follow them. So that's what I did, soon as I got out of the neighborhood I hit him up and asked him was he alright, he said.

'Yea I'm straight'." I told him, I'm on my way to catch up with you where you at now? He said. 'I'm at the Deans Bridge and Gordon Highway light on the way down town.' I told him to call me and let me know where yall stop at so I can watch his back. He said, 'alright cool,' and hung up. Then about ten minutes later he called me back and said he was at the Gurley's grocery store on Laney Walker Boulevard across the street from Mr. J's, Lenny had went in the store and he was waiting on him in the parking lot. By this time I had just pulled up at the light on James Brown Boulevard getting ready to make that right turn onto Laney Walker. I'm sittin' at the red light and I can see Gurley's parking lot from where I'm at and I can see Markell's car. I said, I can see you, I'm finna park over there in a minute, soon as the light change. Soon as I hung up the phone an old raggedy white and blue '79 Bonneville pulled into the parkin' lot in a space in front of Markell. A short bowlegged chubby dude jumped out with a pistol in his hand, I hit the gas and turned the wheel. I hit the car in front of me at the light and pushed it out onto Laney Walker Boulevard and it got hit by another car. I went up on the curb and that's when he started shootin'. *Pow-pow-pow-pow-pow-pow*, he fired six shots from a .357 into Markell's windshield. By the time I got into Gurley's parkin' lot, the dude had jumped back in the car and was pulling out. I stuck my nine out of the window and let all seventeen go. I hit the grocery store, other cars, and even the Bonneville, I shot the back window out, I'm surprise I didn't hit nobody. I should of followed them and finished the job but I had to check on Markell. I rushed over to his car opened the door and he was leaned over reaching for his pistol under the seat. I stared at my boy for a couple of seconds, he was gone. I heard the police comin' so I grabbed his gun, jumped in my car and drove off. Now as I was drivin' off I saw your pops coming out of Gurleys, he looked dead in my face as I rode pass him.

Now later on that day after the police investigated they said that they found Markell with no money in his pockets and ruled it as a robbery. Everybody that knew Markell knew that he always kept money in his pocket, and that boy that shot him didn't take nothin'. And Earlier that day on the porch when we was talkin' about what we was goin' do at the mall, he pulled out eight thousand just out of his left pocket and he said he wouldn't even spend what was in his right. By them not findin' any money on him and the police sayin' that it was a robbery, I guess that's where the crack-head story came from, maybe that's what your mother believed. Or maybe she knew the truth and didn't want to tell you, who knows. But Scooter Bug that's the truth, your pops set him up."

The revelation burned inside of Kevin, he stood up from the bottom step he sat on during the conversation and walked up the stairs overwhelmed by emotion. Anger, hatred, confusion, frustration, and pain boiled inside of him. His heart pounded, his stomach turned, and his mind became cluttered with thoughts. He wanted to cry but his tough, hard, thuggish mentality wouldn't allow it. He leaned against the handrail by the glass slide door with his back towards his comrades and Lance. He stared down at the grass, surrounded by an uneasy silence that struck them all. Then he broke it. "Did you ever find out who the nigga was that pulled the trigger?"

"Yea, I went lookin' around to find out who it was, I found out some young boy about fifteen or sixteen was earning some stripes from Jimmy. Some cat name Terrell, his people called him 'Rell." The name shocked the crew, they all stared at each other as if they were waiting for the other to speak. "I can't remember his last name."

"What did you say he looked like?" Shawn asked.

"He was dark skin, chubby, and real bowlegged. Why, you know him?"

"I thank so." Shawn answered.

"When I was lookin' for him I heard he skipped town, then about a year and a half later I heard he came back and was making moves in the dope game, with the help of ole Jimmy Cain." The expressions on their faces intensified, then Lance added the finale piece of the puzzle that answered their suspicions. "I heard he was like a small kingpin down there in Southside, I forgot what they call him." The info hit them as if the meaning of life was revealed to them. But before any of them could respond Kevin uttered in anger.

"T-Money!"

"Yea-yea that's it." Lance said nodding.

"T-Money!" Kevin said through clenched teeth. "T-Money shot my fuckin' brother! I can't believe this shit! All this mothafuckin' time I been buyin' weed from this nigga, he been smilin' in my mothafuckin' face, asked me to come and work for 'em! And my, my momma! My bitch-ass momma been buyin' crack from this nigga fa'years and he killed 'er son, my brother!" Hate and anger combined in him, he searched for something to destroy and release the madness, he turned around and his rant was disturbed by his reflection in the sliding glass door. His anger was so strong that for a second his reflection was not his but that of T-Money's staring back at him laughing. The slight hallucination set off his next reaction. He drew back and released a solid right jab to the center of the glass door. *Squiuaacckk.* The glass cracked creating an almost artistic statement of Kevin's anger throughout the door. From top to bottom, from side to side an array of intersecting cracks formed highways, shapes, and even letters and numbers could be seen. William quickly responded.

"What the fuck Cuz!" He ran up the steps and stood in front of the shattered glass in shock. "What the hell is wrong wit' chew!"

"Oh shit." Michael and Tracy mumbled almost in synch, followed by Shawn's.

"Ah naw!"

"Damn!" Larry uttered.

William now mad began to chastise Kevin as he stared at the damage. "Look at this, look at this shit! What the fuck am I goin' tell my folks man!"

Kevin now slightly calm, hunched his shoulder and mumbled . "I 'on't know."

"You don't know! You don't know! Kevin that's fucked up!"

Lance now felt guilty and somewhat responsible for the situation. "Ahh man, William I'm sorry about that lil bruh, I ain't mean to cause no harm, but he told me to tell him." William was unable to hear the apology over his fussing at Kevin, Lance then apologized to Kevin. "I ain't mean to hurt you Kevin but you told me to tell you and I told you nothing but the truth."

There was a break in William's rant long enough for Kevin to reply to Lance's apology. "Don't worry you ain't hurt me, I need to thank you because you just helped us make a decision we was tryin' to make." Lance face displayed confusion as he looked at each one of the boys as if he searched for clarity. Shawn clarified.

"It's a lil inside thang."

"And if the shit work like I know it will, I'll have ya' shit fixed befo' Auntie comes home."

Will shook his head as he walked over then flopped down in a lawn chair. "Man fuck that it's the principle of the shit…"

Michael tapped Will on the shoulder to pass him the blunt. "Here, smoke that shit off ya' chest."

"-Man. That nigga there! He just don't give a damn about nobody else shit." William had to finalize before taking a pull from the blunt.

"We goin' straighten it out." MJ said to console and calm his comrade.

Shawn then walked over to Lance with a humble demeanor. "Excuse me uhm…Mr. Stamps."

"Yea."

"Can you excuse us, it's some issues we gotta work out, a homeboy thang you know, between the fellas."

"Oh yea, I understand. Let me holla at Kevin real quick." Lance walked up the stairs and over to Kevin that leaned with his back against the rail, arms folded. "A Kevin, your brother was like my brother, he looked out for me and I looked out for him. He was my family so you are my family, so if you ever need anything, cash or conversation, food or what little wisdom and advice I can give, I got-cha', if I got it you got it." They gave each other some dap and a shoulder to shoulder hug then Lance headed over to his yard but stopped halfway, turned and said. "I can tell yall boys got a tight bond, don't let nothin' come between that, nothin' not money, girls, nothin'. Yall stay in touch and don't forget each other. And Kevin take it easy man."

Kevin gave Lance an unexpected cynical grin and said. "Oh yea we all goin' take it, real easy."

Chapter 6:
Do da Damn Thang!

It was 10:16 p.m. and the crew had just finished their third blunt. Michael, Tracy, and Shawn was lounged on the biggest sofa while William and Larry shared the smaller one. Kevin was impatiently pacing the den and constantly staring at the clock waiting on twelve. The boys with the exception of Kevin and Will generating tension in the air from anger, were watching episodes of CSI. The three on the lager couch and Larry on the other were enjoying their high while Will's anger for his mother's shattered sliding door and Kevin's new revelation, killed what little buzz they did have.

"A, you know them cats really be solvin' them cases like that too." Michael said with a sluggish and dry mouth.

"Yea, but they don't do it that quick." Tracy said. "It take weeks, months, sometimes years to solve them cases. They be doin' the shit in one shift. What they work eight, twelve hour shifts?"

"Whatever they work I bet-chew they get paid good." Shawn added.

"Hell yea them cats be gettin' paid good." Larry joined in. "I got a cousin that do that shit in Chicago he got plenty cheese. I mean he got a big ass house, real talk, cars..."

Michael looked over at Kevin to see if he was going to put a halt to another one of Larry's notorious lies however, Kevin so impatient and engulfed in anger, didn't hear Larry so Michael did it instead.

"Larry, don't nobody wanna hear that shit man." Tracy and Shawn laughed.

"A Will I can use your bathroom man?" Shawn asked.

Will looked up from a deep thought and answered with an almost depressing tone. "You ain't gotta ask."

Shawn slowly rose from his lazy lounge then Tracy suddenly sprung from his seat and raced up stairs to beat Shawn to the bathroom. "Oh that's fucked up." Shawn said walking up the stairs. "You lucky I'm too high to run up these stairs.

A Tracy, you feel bad about smokin' that weed after what Mr. Stamps told Kevin?" He asked leaning against the wall in the hall.

"Why, because we bought it from T-Money?" Tracy asked while he urinated.

"Yea."

"Yea it crossed my mind but after I saw Kevin keep hittin' the blunt I was like oh-well, he ain't seem to mine so why should I."

"I was thankin' the same thang."

"Anyway we already paid for it, it ain't like we can go get a refund." Tracy said while flushing then washed his hands, he exited and Shawn entered.

"Well I guess that makes it official." Shawn said as he began urinating.

"What's that?" Tracy said from the hallway.

"That we goin' use Zeinoch on T-Money."

"You talkin' like its goin' work for sure."

"I mean, I 'on't know if it's goin' work or not but let's just say it does. Do you thank we should put it on T-Money?"

"I don't see why not, he is a murderer, he do sell dope it ain't like he's a priest, or good Samaritan, it ain't like he marched wit' Doctor King." Tracy giving his logic.

"Yea you right about that but what if we fuck around and kill 'em?"

Tracy pondered on the question for a moment then gave a somewhat honest answer. "I thought chew thought about that already."

"I Did. I Don't want it to go down like that but if it do, as long as if the shit can't trace back to us, then I guess I'm straight wit' it. Tracy you already know we finna do some hell-a-fied shit, and I 'on't know where it's goin' take us or what's goin' happen, so…"

"Don't worry about it, I'm ridin' wit' cha', you watch my back I'll watch yours." They gave each other a pound as if to finalize their already established alliance then made their way back down stairs where they found the others staring at the TV, Kevin standing the closest.

"I told yall I told yall them niggas was goin' get away!" Kevin said slightly out of his angry mode.

"What's up?" Tracy asked.

"Them niggas Shitty D and Slim got away."

"Fa'real?" Shawn replied.

"Hell yea, police ain't got no clues." Kevin said. "A, ain't it's about time for us to get started man?"

"What time is it?" Shawn asked.

"Eleven o'clock." Kevin answered without looking at the clock.

"Let's smoke the rest of this first." Tracy said holding less than a half of a blunt that he put out earlier.

"Yea let's do that first." Will said.

They eased through the halfway open shattered sliding glass

door careful not to finish it off by knocking the glass out of the frame onto the floor, Tracy lit up the stub and began smoking. He took his pulls then passed it to Shawn. He took a pull then had a revelation. "Damn!"

"What?" Tracy asked.

"I gotta go to work tomorrow."

"You'll be alright, just call in." Kevin suggested.

"I already been wrote up for being late and it's just the first week. They goin' end up firin' my ass."

"After tonight you won't need that job." Kevin said as he took the roach from Shawn. It went into rotation three times until an impatient Kevin thumped the roach into the yard. "Alright yall let's do da damn thang."

They all followed Kevin back into the house, Larry for some unknown reason; mainly being that he was high and not thinking clearly, decided to close the shattered sliding door. Will quickly took notice and said with a nervous tone. "Larry what chew doin' man." Larry looked back at William while sliding the door close and said with confidence.

"Oh don't worry Big Will, I got it-I got it." Everyone watched as Larry carefully closed the fragile door and with every inch he pulled the glass would crackle, and with every crackle the boys would tense up. Then the unexpected happened, Larry closed the door without completely destroying it. He turned around with a ridiculous smile of pride and said. "I told you I got it."

A relieved Will said. "That's my boy, I knew you was good fa' somethin'." Larry nodded full of pride and began to walk off and as soon as his first step touched the marble floor. *CRASH*. The glass collapsed fiercely to the floor making a horrific sound that attacked Will's nerves causing him to cringe with his back towards the scene. A moment of silence followed the crash along with stares of pathetic wonder at Larry from the others. Will turned around slow and with a look of a damned man said. "Now Larry, you know you gotta clean that shit up right."

"Oh yea I got-cha,' don't even worry about it." Larry said and retrieved the broom and dustpan.

"Alright Shawn, do yo' thang." Kevin said with an anxious glare in his eyes.

"What time is it?" Shawn asked staring at the clock, which read eleven-thirty-nine. "Well I guess we can go ahead and get started. Shawn unfolded the paper with Daniel's instructions on it. "Alright first we goin' need the chalk." Kevin and Michael went into the living room and retrieved all of the items off the card table and returned to the kitchen. "Alright MJ since you're the best drawer out of all of us, you need to draw this with the chalk powder." Shawn handed MJ the paper.

"What da fuck is this?" Michael responded in a confused tone.

"It's what chew gotta draw, what's the matter, you 'on't thank you can draw it?" Shawn asked.

"Yea I can draw it, it just that, that symbol. It look crazy, it don't look, safe."

"Man fuck that pretty-boy, just draw the damn thang." Kevin insisted in frustration.

"Alright nigga damn."

"Make sure it's big enough fa' all six of us to sit around it." Shawn said.

"Alright well I need all yall to stand in a circle shoulder to shoulder." MJ requested, the boys followed his instructions and formed a circle. Michael stepped out of the circle, poured a handful of chalk in his hand and began forming a circle around them. When he finished they stepped out while Larry continued sweeping up the glass. "There go the circle, now for the shit on the inside. Yall might wanna give me a minute cause this shit looks complicated."

"Alright we got plenty of time." Shawn said glancing at the clock.

"Let's smoke another blunt while MJ do that." William suggested, they all agreed and made their way outside. They tried walking over the glass particles that Larry was sweeping up but still ended up stepping on some, the glass crackled under their feet as they walked. "Maann, look at this shit." Will said with much disappointment. Everyone except Michael which was drawing the diagram and Larry that was still sweeping up the glass, took a seat on the lawn chairs. Tracy lit up the blunt and began taking pulls from it. He then passed it and the rotation began in silence, a silence caused by deep contemplation.

Tracy contemplated on what they were about to do, he still felt uncomfortable about the whole thing, it did not sit well with him. Shawn contemplated on if it would work or not, he worried that if it did not work, not only would he be disappointed, but it would disappoint his comrades especially Kevin. He also thought about if it does work what would be the outcome, what would it lead to.

Will contemplated on how he was going to get the back door fixed before his parents got home. Kevin contemplated on the information that Lance gave him about his brother and his killer. He couldn't believe that the same person he bought weed from, the same person his mother bought crack from, was the same man that killed his brother. He had plans, a plan if it work and a plan if it didn't.

"A MJ, come hit the blunt." Shawn said peeping into the kitchen.

"Alright, hold up, I'm almost finished."

"Let me hit that while MJ is doing that." Larry said sweeping the glass into a pile." Shawn gave Larry a funny look.

"Hell naw you need to get all this shit up, janitor." Michael finished and Kevin went into the kitchen and stood over the diagram, which look like this.

He stared at it as if he was waiting for someone or something to rise up from it. Shawn walked over to join him. "What chew thankin' 'bout dawg?"

"You know what I'm thankin' 'bout, I'm ready to get this thang started." Kevin said with calm conviction in his voice.

"But what if it don't work?"

"It's goin' work. I can feel it. It's like something is talkin' to me, tellin' me somethin' big is finna happen."

"Ahhh shit, you done gone crazy, you hearin' voices and shit, I'm finna call Serenity."

"Naw folk it ain't nothin' like that, I ain't really hearin' voices and shit, it's more like a feelin', you know what I'm sayin'."

"Yea I see what chew sayin'." Shawn and Kevin was so deep into their conversation that they didn't notice the others had walked up and was staring down at the door on the floor.

"I don't mean to break up yall lil emotional moment and shit but it's almost twelve, we goin' do this or what?" William interrupted. "Cause we ready."

"Yea, so what's next?" MJ asked.

"Now we need the candles. Lined them on the edge of the circle with enough space between them so that we can sit behind them."

Will set up three candles while MJ set up three. "You want us to light them?" Michael asked.

"Naw not yet. We light them at twelve o'clock." While Will and MJ set up the candles, Kevin stared at the diagram with a look of deviant hope in his eyes. Shawn, that stood next to him noticed the expression and said to himself. "Damn, it looks like Kev is really deep into this shit. I hope this don't make him flip." Tracy also stared at the diagram but his thoughts were opposite of Kevin's. "Damn, I can't believe we really finna do this crazy shit." He mumbled just loud enough for William to hear him. Will then placed the last candle on the circle's edge.

"Don't worry folk, this just might work."

"That's what I'm worried about. This shit might work."

Michael grabbed the bowl and asked. "So Shawn, what's the bowl for, we goin' feed the demon some grits or somethin'?"

Shawn gave a short laugh, followed by a sneaky grin and almost an evil stare at his comrades. "Oh now that's the fun part." They all stared at Shawn puzzled except Kevin who was giving a look of waiting and Larry who was still sweeping up pieces of glass.

"The fun part, what chew mean by that?" William asked.

"Yea what chew mean Shawn, what suppose to go in this bowl?" Michael asked again this time with more suspicion than curiosity.

"Guess." Shawn grinned.

"Cuz, we ain't got time fa' no guessin' games it's eleven forty, twelve o'clock is goin' be-done came and went." Kevin interrupted.

"Alright-alright-alright, damn yall lame. Blood."

"What!" Tracy uttered.

"Blood." Shawn repeated. "We gotta put blood in the bowl."

"What da fuck, what kind of blood, chicken blood right?" Michael said.

"Nope." Shawn laughed. "Our blood."

"What! Our blood, man why you ain't tell us this earlier!"

"Cause I knew yall definitely wouldn't want to do it then, so I waited 'til now."

Michael shook his head. "Naw playa, I 'on't thank I can do that shit."

"Yea me either." Tracy said. "I ain't wit' all that self mutilation shit."

"Come on fellas it ain't like we gotta cut off no finger or arm, just a lil small ass cut."

William took the bowl from MJ and began examining. "We ain't gotta fill this mothafucka up do we?"

"Hell naw, just a couple of drops from each of us."

Michael still shaking his head continued to protest. "Man, I'm allergic to pain."

"Yea me too." Tracy said.

"Come on man quit cryin', yall act like yall ain't never been cut befo', yall sound like some whoes." Kevin chastised.

"Yea but I ain't never intentionally cut myself." Tracy said.

"That's physically and psychologically painful."

Shawn looked at Tracy subtly surprised. "Damn professor I didn't know you knew such big words."

"And I ain't know he was such a big pussy." Kevin said.

"I ain't no damn pussy."

"Me neither." Michael said.

"Well quit actin' like one and man up and let's do this shit."

"So what's up? Yall ain't goin' just let me waste my time and money on this shit is you?"

MJ and T-Murray looked at each other then Michael answered first. "Come on man and get this shit over wit'."

"Yes, Will get a knife." Kevin ordered.

William went over to the counter and retrieved a six-inch stainless steel straight edge knife from an ivory and chrome knife holder.

"Hold up cuz-o we goin' need somethin' sharper fa' the lil girls in here." Kevin looked around the kitchen then noticed Larry about to dump his last dustpan of glass. "Hold up Larry." He walked over and examined the pile of glass and picked out a three-inch piece of glass in the shape of a triangle. "Oh yea this'll work. Glass don't hurt as much as steal do."

"I don't even wanna know how you know that." T-Murray said.

Shawn looked at the time on the microwave, which read eleven fifty-five. "Well let's get started. Will you got a lighter?"

Before Will could answer Kevin held up a blue Bic. "I got it."

"You can go ahead and start lighting the candles now."

Without hesitation Kevin began his route around the diagram lighting each candle while Shawn began his instructions. "Alright fellas, yall take a seat behind a candle." They all sat Indian style behind a candle outside of the circle. Shawn sat at what could be considered the head of the circle, to his left sat MJ, next to MJ sat Will, and to Will's left sat an eager Kevin, which was opposite of Shawn. To Kevin's left sat Larry and next to him sat Tracy.

"Alright fellas, yall do what I do and repeat after me. Kevin toss me the glass." Kevin tossed the piece of glass over the diagram landing on Shawn's lap, he picked it up and sat the bowl in front of him and said.

"This is my blood and I give it willingly to bring life to the powerful Zeinoch so that he may strike down our enemies and grant us riches." He then cut an inch long incision in the palm of his left hand and clenched it allowing his blood to drip into the bowl. He then passed the bowl and glass to Tracy. Tracy stared at the glass then at Shawn's blood in the bowl and shook his head in disbelief.

"This is my blood and I give it willingly to bring life to the powerful Zeinoch so that he may strike down our enemies and grant us riches." Tracy then made a half of an inch long cut and squeezed a few drops of blood into the bowl. He then passed it to Larry. Larry said the words, cut his palm then passed it to Kevin. Kevin said the words with emotion in them then over zealously cut a two-inch incision in his left palm and contributed twice as much blood as Shawn, Tracy, and Larry had combined before finally passing the items to MJ. Michael stared at the bloody tip of the glass for a moment then finally said the words and made a small cut in his palm. The cut was so small that he was only able to squeeze two drops of blood from it. He then passed the items to William that said the words, gave his blood then passed the items back to Shawn.

They were so engulfed with what they were doing that they didn't notice the wind picking up outside. "Alright chall repeat after me. Zeinoch, we offer our blood and in doing so we denounce our God above so that you may have power and walk the Earth to do our will." They repeated the words. "So come Zeinoch threw the gates of hell and into our service where you shall dwell."

After they spoke the last word, thunder rumbled and lightning lit up the sky snatching their attention to the outside, as wind howled passed the glassless door. Their hearts raced; Michael's in panic, Shawn's in shock, William's in confusion, Tracy's in dread, Larry's in fear, and Kevin's in pleasurable excitement.

The bowl of blood Shawn was holding began to bubble like a thick boiling soup, gumbo on a hot stove, he then poured the blood onto the eye in the center of the twelve-point star in the circle. The blood began to run its route through the snake like pattern inside of the circle, outside the star. Once the blood ran its full course, a huge horrifying sound crackled in the sky that shook the house and was immediately followed by a bolt of lightning that shot down from the sky, through the roof, and struck Shawn causing him to stiffen up. Then a stream of bluish energy passed from Shawn to Tracy, from Tracy to Larry, from Larry to Kevin, then to Will in the same order the bowl was passed until a complete circle of energy was made. A bolt of energy then shot out of Shawn and into the eye of the diagram followed by a huge. *BOOM*, which shook the house. After the thunder's echoes ceased there was a disturbing silence and they found themselves laying on their backs staring up at the ceiling, disoriented. After a few seconds of dizziness and confusion, they began sitting up. Shawn sat up slow with his eyes squinted as if to regain focus as Michael sat up rubbing his. William yarned as he sat up, and though Kevin was fatigued as the rest of them, his excitement was still strong. "It worked! That shit really worked, did yall niggas see that shit!"

"Yea-hell yea I saw it and felt it." Shawn said in a tired and exhausted tone.

Kevin stood to his feet and began pacing the kitchen in excitement. "It's on now, the shit worked!"

"Damn, my head hurt." Tracy said.

"Mine too." Michael added. "And I'm tired as hell. Kev you ain't tired?"

"I feel kind of weak but I'm too damn crunk to thank about it."

"I'm tired and weak too." Larry said. "I feel like I been fuckin' fa' twelve hours."

William smacked his teeth to Larry's comment. "Naw, more like you been jackin' off fa' twelve hours."

"So it worked?" Tracy asked Shawn.

"I believe so."

"Hell yeah it worked, didn't you see all that shit, it..." Kevin was distracted by Lance standing on the patio deck.

"Yall fellas alright?"

"Yeah, we cool." William answered.

"My power had just went out and I looked out of my window to see if anyone else power was out and saw a big bolt of lightning coming down from the sky and shoot dead into the roof of your house. And the crazy thing about it, it didn't just strike and go away it stayed flowing from the sky into your house for almost a minute."

William slowly limped over to Lance like an old man with arthritic joints. "Oh naw, we alright Mr. Stamps, everythang is cool."

"You sure yall alright 'cause you walkin' like you just got beat up."

"Oh it ain't nothin'." Will said with a slight laugh. "Me and the fellas had a lil Royal Rumbled-King of The Ring type thang goin' on, ain't nothin'."

Lance noticed the boys had a look of guiltiness as if they were hiding girls in the house and their parents had just came home. He also caught a glance of William's left hand. "Well it looks like you lost." He said pointing to Will's hand.

"Oh we just got a lil carried away, I'm straight-I'm straight."

"Well alright, I just wanted to check up on yall after I saw that strange bolt of lightning, but since yall alright I'll head back to the house. Yall be safe and don't hurt yourselves, if yall need anything I'm next door."

"Alright, 'preciate it."

As Lance got ready to walk off he caught a better glimpse of the kitchen, one that wasn't blocked by William. He saw the chalk diagram that was now burned into the marble floor.

"Is he gone?" Kevin asked.

William watched as Lance entered his house before answering. "Yea, he's gone."

"Good, nosey mothafucka. So Shawn what we do now?"

"Yea Harry Potta-I mean, Shawn." Tracy joked. "Now what we do?"

"Well, now we sleep."

Chapter7:
Dream Manifest

"**M**aann, this is some gay-homo shit right here man." Michael complained as he laid out a blanket and pillow preparing his sleep area.

"What chew cryin' about now?" Kevin said.

"This, we six niggas havin' a slumber party."

"Don't look at it like that." Kevin said taking off his sneakers then his white t-shirt. "Look at it like this. We six homeboys that's 'bout to get paid in a strange ass way."

"Yea MJ, look at it like that. And don't worry, I'll tuck you in nice and cozy right befo' you doze off." William said with his impressive imitation of a homosexual.

"Alright Will, touch me and you'll be short two arms."

"Well, I'm fired." Shawn said returning from the kitchen.

"They fired you?" Tracy asked as he took off his sneakers.

"Naw, I just left a message with the security guard but I already know, a call-in on the first week. It's over, I already been wrote up fa bein' late."

"Don't worry 'bout it folk." Kevin said. "After we do da damn thang you won't need no job." Kevin made his bed on the smaller couch while William prepared his on the larger one. Shawn, Tracy, Larry, and Michael made theirs on the soft and expensive carpet.

"So Shawn, how this thang supposed to work?" Tracy asked. "I mean once we go to sleep what's goin' happen next, is the demon gonna be here when we wake up or somethin'?"

"To tell you the truth, I ain't too sure about the details but I do know it's supposed to appear in our dreams and that's when we use 'em?"

"So if everythang is going down in our dreams how we suppose to get the money, I mean we can't do shit wit' dream money." Michael sad.

"I guess we'll find out when we wake up."

"Shit, I'm so crunk that's it's goin' be hard fa' me to fall asleep." Kevin said laying on his back staring up at the ceiling.

"Not me." William said. "That circle got me tired as hell. And I hope that shit come up off my flo'."

"My-bad Will, Daniel didn't say if we should of done it inside or not and I ain't even thank to ask."

"It's straight man."

"I'm tired as hell too." Tracy said.

"You ain't tired Kev?" Shawn asked.

"I'm tired but I ain't sleepy."

"Well how 'bout I fire this blunt up and hit the lights, that might help." Will walked over to the light switch and turned off the lights. Using the light from a bright full moon that shined through the open blinds, he carefully walked back over to his couch. He began taking pulls from the blunt causing the ember of the blunt to glow casting a haunting affect over his face, snoring from the floor caught his attention. "Damn who dat sleep already?" He asked passing the blunt to Kevin.

"Larry's lyin' ass." MJ said.

"Damn that was quick." Shawn said.

"I'm 'bout to take it there too, soon as I hit the blunt." Tracy said. "I thought chew wasn't goin' burn in the house."

"My back door is busted out and I got a demon symbol burned into my kitchen flo', marble too. So fuck it."

Kevin took a few more pulls then passed it to Michael he took a few pulls and then passed it to Tracy, and then from Tracy to Shawn. When Shawn tried passing it to Will he noticed that he was out. "Well, Big Will done passed out." He passed the blunt to Kevin. After every full rotation, one of the crew would fall asleep missing their turn to smoke. Soon only Shawn and Kevin were left awake.

"Here Shawn." Kevin said with his hand extended to pass Shawn the blunt.

"Haauuuauuhh." Shawn yarned. "I'm straight, I'm finna go to sleep."

"Alright folk."

"It's goin' be a whole lot different tomorrow." Shawn mumbled as he dozed off.

"I hope so." Kevin said as he continued to puff and ponder. He couldn't wait to see the results if any from their conjuring ceremony. The blunt was now a five-centimeter roach that burned his fingertips. He put it out in a nearby ashtray, laid back down and adjusted himself until he found a comfortable position. Vivid thoughts began running through his mind like highlighted scenes of a dramatic movie of his life. The first visual thought was of the money he saw in T-Money's closet, he wondered how was on those selves and how good it would be to have it in his possession. The next thought was of T-Money closing the closet and smiling at him, which changed to T-Money giving his mother crack and watching her smoke it as he smiled back at him. The vision was so vivid that he could hear T-Money laughing and the sound of his mother inhaling the crack smoke, he could even smell the stench of it. He then quickly replaced the disturbing thoughts with a more pleasant memory, a memory of his brother in his late teens dribbling a basketball with Kevin when he was a small boy, but as quickly as it came to him, the memory disappeared. It was ended by a gunshot from the back of his brother's head. T-Money stood over Markell's body with a boastfully evil grin and a gun. Hatred bubbled in a drowsy Kevin and though he was now full of anger it didn't stop sleep from taking him, the vision slowly faded to black, and as he dozed off he mumbled.

"I'm comin' fa' ya'."

Then Blackness.

They opened their eyes in a cold and dark room, all of them aware but not seeing each other's presence, unable to communicate. They also felt another's presence, the room suddenly lit up in crimson then back to blackness. It flickered on and off with a second between each flicker. An image appeared on the opposite corner of the room, at first the dreamers couldn't recognize the image but as the room continue to flash the image approached. The dreamers could see that it stood erect like a man, a huge man. As soon as they realize it wasn't human, the creature stood six-inches from their faces.

A hideous beast that stood over nine feet with massive muscles under reptilian skin, huge hands that even with its huge body structure they seemed too large for normal. Each hand had six long fingers with the sixth digit at the base of its palm, similar to an eagle's talon. Its back, arms, the back of its hand, and its head were lightly covered with a thick coarse dark brown hair, its feet matched his hands with the sixth digit opposing from its heels.

Its ears were wolf like, a black slimy nose like a gorilla's and two five-inch black horns protruding from both sides of its forehead. Its eyes were symbols of pure evil, dark yellow with red veins running throughout them with white irises and cloudy crimson pupils. Its bottom jaw resembled a warthog's with two four-inch fangs that were thick enough to be considered as tusk surrounded by two rows of two-inch sharp teeth. Its teeth were covered with a puss colored acidic slim with a black forked tongue the size of a serpent that was covered with razor sharp scales. The creature was truly hellish how-ever, it only struck up a small insignificant amount of fear in them. It stood staring at the dreamers as if waiting for orders, breathing heavy, low but noticeable growls with each exhale.

The room began to spin then stopped abruptly and the dream-ers were now looking from another perspective. They looked down at their feet and their feet were now the creature's feet, their hands were the creature's hands. The dreamers were now in the demon. A minute passed after the transformation the walls fell and they were now standing in the Southside housing projects. The beast stood on the sidewalk scanning its environment in search of some-thing, someone. It fixed its eyes to its right on three thugs deep in a dice game about a hundred yards away. It made its way towards them and despite its massive size it moved with stealth like move-ment, quiet as a cockroach tiptoeing on carpet. It stood over them undetected.

"Watch this-watch this, watch this now!" One of the thugs said shaking the dice in his right hand. "Watch how I brake yall off. Huuah!" He uttered as he tossed the dice. "What dat is five! Okay five, the point is five right watch how I brang that five back on yall ass. Got-damn, J-Dog you farted?" The dice roller asked with his face bald up not realizing the smell came from the hellish creature behind them.

"Hell naw I ain't fart it's dat nigga right there." J-Dog protested pointing at the other thug kneeling next to him.

"Don't try to put that shit on me J-Dog I claim my shit, I'm real wit' mine."

"Yea you're real stank." J-Dog said.

"Who ever let that loose need to be locked up, out here smellin' like gorilla shit, let me roll this five." He stood up and began shaking the dice. "Here we go, come on five wit'-cha' fine ass, come fa' daddy, I'm brakin' both you clow…" There was an abrupt silence, J-Dog and his friend stared at the pile of money waiting for the dice to fall.

"Shoot the dice nigga." J-Dog said impatiently, the dice fell one landed on four and the other on one. "Damn dat nigga won! Go ahead and talk shit man." He said staring at the pile of money, soon after he finished his statement the dice roller's body fell headless on top of the money.

"Oohh shhiiittt!" The two thugs shouted together as they stood to their feet. They were standing at the torso of a hideous creature.

"What da fuck is that!" J-Dog uttered in terror and disbelief, the two thugs could not fathom what stood in front of them: the size, the smell, its face, its eyes all its features froze them in fear until they saw their homeboy's head in its hand, eyes staring at them. J-Dog grabbed the handle of his nine-millimeter but before he could draw it the creature let out a horrific sound, similar to a cough and a growl which it released a puss colored slimy substance onto J-Dogs neck and shoulders and immediately began eating away his flesh. His nine was forgotten he was now trying to wipe away the burning substance but only to melt away his hands as he tried, screaming in agony but only for a few seconds before the scream turned into a gargling as the acidic saliva ate through his neck and larynx. The other thug was paralyzed in terror as he watched his homeboy melt into a puddle of human soup. The creature stared at the terrified goon breathing its stomach-turning breath in his face, which snapped him out of his paralyzed state. He turned and ran but only for two feet, the beast threw the head into the back of his dropping him to the sidewalk. He moved slightly as he fought off unconsciousness, the creature approached and lift the thug slightly by his dreads then folded him anatomically incorrect, backwards in a way his shoulder were against his ankles. There was no more movement, the creature sniffed the air and its eyes fixed on T-Money's door. It walked up the steps and with two massive kicks it took both doors off the hinges into the living room. The ruckus woke up T-Money and a girl that laid with him.

"What da fuck was that baby!" She uttered as she sat up. T-Money jumped out of bed, reached under it and pulled out two tech-nines with extended magazines.

"I 'on't know but they done kicked in da wrong mothafucka doo'. Who da fuck in my house!" He yelled with his guns aimed at his bedroom entrance. "Oh yea yall done picked the right mothafucka to fuck wit'! You fuckin' wit' a G!" He yelled as he approached his bedroom's doorway leading to the hall. He stuck his barrels out and began firing as he moved into the hall. The array of bullets ripped up walls and furniture creating a cloud of debris that at first, camouflaged what he was shooting at but in the midst of his gunfire, he caught a glimpse of what it was. The glimpse of the creature shocked him into a cease-fire to make sure he saw what he thought he saw. "What da fuck is … That!" He began firing again and he realized that the bullets wasn't penetrating the tough reptilian skin. He began backing up as it approached. "What da fuck man! Shit! Die mothafucka die!" Click-click-click-click. T-Money's twin techs clattered empty, he ran back into his bedroom and slammed the door. He rushed to his closet and retrieved a double barrel shotgun. He cocked it, and aimed it at his door shivering from fear in his Gucci boxers like a cold infant with sweat running down his hairy flabby body. The girl sat up in the bed overwhelmed from the ringing in her ears from gunfire, in tears she held the burgundy silk cover against her naked chest, and trembled as she watched T-Money and the door.

"Who is it!" Her frantic voice trembled.

"'On't-'on't-'on't-'on't know!" T-Money said breathing hard.

"Wha-what chew mean you 'on't know, is it the police?"

"Naw!"

"Is it some niggas?"

"Naw!"

"We-well who da hell is it!"

"I 'on't know what da fuck it is!"

"It!"

The door smashed open hanging on by the last bottom hinge, she screamed at the sight of what walked in, she rolled of the bed and bald up in the corner of the wall and the bed. T-Money began firing but just as the tech-nines, it had no affect on the beast, it backed him against a wall. T-Money realized it was over he had nothing to stop this thing, he tried swallowing his fear and show his toughness, his 'G'.

"Fuck you…I'ma' G! I'm a mothafuckin' gangsta 'til I die!" T-Money spat into the creatures face. It grabbed him by his throat completely wrapping its hands around the fatty neck and picked him up eye level, T-Money kicked franticly as he gagged. The creature returned the gesture and spat back in his face landing on T-Money's nose and immediately began dissolving it. He kicked more violently and let out what would have been screams but were only grunts and groans being that the beast gripped his neck so tightly. However, the girl in the corner provided enough screams for the both of them. It stared into T-Money's eyes as his life slowly slipped away, but then decided to change its method of kill. It took its left hand and grabbed T-Money's left ankle and held him upside down. Soon after releasing his neck a violent cough followed by a gasp gave intro to a scream of pain and horror. "Ahhhhaaauuugghhhh!" The beast then took its right hand and grabbed T-Money's right ankle and with one quick tug, the creature ripped him in half down his middle like a wishbone. Guts spilled out onto the floor and blood flew decorating the walls, the creature stared in satisfaction at the piles of entrails on the floor while still holding both halves of his victim. It then looked at the girl that was now spotted with T-Money's body fluids. She was in so much shock that all she could do was tremble, whimper, and stare off into space with a dead look in her eyes. Her arms were now down by her sides being that the shock had killed all the thoughts of defense and self preservation, her caramel colored supple C-cup breast were exposed and glistening with sweat and blood sprinkles that ran down her chest and dripped from her breast. The creature looked over at her then dropped the human halves and made its way around the bed to her. It knelt down then sniffed her, it stuck out its sixteen-inch tongue and it moved and swayed before her as if it had thoughts of its own. The beast then licked her up from her left breast to her chin ripping off flesh in the process with its razor sharp scales on its tongue, easily shaving and plowing through skin and muscle tissue. She did have time to scream before her jugular vein was ripped.

Satisfied with its kills the creature headed to the hallway to the closet door at the end. It opened it and stared at the stacks of money and two black trash bags of marijuana. It began stuffing the stacks of money and bricks of marijuana into the bags until it cleared the entire closet of drugs and money. The beast held the bags in each hand as it left the scene of carnage and disappeared into the night's darkness.

The clock read 1:17 pm when they began to wake up. "Ahhauaah." Kevin yarned as he stretched and opened his eyes, he looked at his comrades on the floor slightly moving, stretching, yarning as they emerged from their slumber. He sat up and mumbled. "Ahhw-man, was that shit real? Damn, that was some crazy shit!" Shawn sat up and stared at Kevin with a grin, Kevin returned the grin and without even saying anything they knew that they both had experienced the same dream. Kevin nodded his head in satisfaction.

"Well I guess we got our answer." Shawn said as he got up and sat on the couch with Kevin.

"I already knew the answer."

William on the other couch turned over and opened his eyes to see Kevin and Shawn staring back over at him. "Man, now that was some sick shit." He said with a groggy voice.

"Hell yea." Shawn agreed.

"Oh so yall had the same dream huh?"

"Yep." Kevin said.

"Ahhawuhh." Michael yarned. "Man what the fuck was that?" He said laying on his back with his eyes still closed.

"That was da damn thang pretty boy, we did it." Kevin said.

"That was some twisted shit." Tracy said in a groggy voice.

"Fa'real." Shawn replied.

"So let me guess, everybody else had the same dream too huh?"

"Yep, well Larry ain't up yet but I'm pretty sure he had it too."

"So I guess that means it was real?" Shawn said.

"Yep. A MJ wake Larry's ass up."

Michael moved over to Larry that was asleep on his stomach. Michael held his hand in the air two feet above the side of Larry's face and then let it drop, it landed hard with a smack.

"What-huh man!" Larry uttered as he jumped to his feet looking around confused. "What the hell is wrong wit' chew, I done burnt niggas fa' less than that!"

"Wake yo' punk ass up." Kevin said laughing. As Larry rubbed his eyes, Shawn accidently caught a glimpse of Larry's erection protruding through his khaki shorts.

"Haaah-haa-hell naw!" Shawn laughed.

"What chew laughing at?" Kevin asked and William and MJ also caught a glimpse of Larry's print and began laughing.

"What?" Kevin said still confused. "What chall... Oh. Okay." Kevin realizing what they were laughing at. "Damn pokey-mon put that away befo' you hurt cho'-self."

Larry looked down. "Oh, my-bad."

"How in da hell do yo' dick get hard in a room full of dudes?" Michael asked. "You tryin' to tell us somethin' LL?"

"Haters, quit hatin'. But on the real, I had a crazy ass-fucked up dream. I was in Southside and..."

"-And you killed T-Money, his girl, and his homeboys then robbed 'em." Tracy interrupted. "We already know, we all had the same dream. So that was the demon. Oh shit, so that means it worked!"

"I guess so." Shawn answered.

"What chew mean, you guess so, it did work the dream was proof." Kevin insisted.

"Wait a minute." MJ said. "How do we know if it really went down like that, it could of just been a dream."

"Come on MJ, how in da hell do six niggas have the same dream in the same night?" Kevin asked.

"I 'on't know."

"Because the shit was real, it felt real to me."

"Too damn real." Tracy mumbled.

"Did yall see how it killed J-Dog and 'nem?" William said. "That was sick how he threw up that acid shit on his head."

"Naw what about when he ripped bubby's head off and threw it at Charles." Shawn added.

"But none of that shit was compared to what it did to T-Money's ass."

"Oh yea, he got fucked up real bad."

Kevin stared at the floor as if to recall a lost memory. "A fellas, I thank I did that."

"What chew mean cuz-o?"

"Let me ask yall this. In the dream when the demon, or should I say us, was walkin' down the sidewalk right befo' it brutalized J-Dog 'nem, how did yall feel?"

"What chew mean Kev?" Tracy asked.

"I mean when Zeinoch was walkin' did you feel like you was walkin', or did you feel like a passenger along for a ride?"

"Oh I see what chew mean." Shawn said. "To me it felt like a ride."

"Yea me too." William said.

"Me too, I felt like I was in a small hot ass car and I was waitin' to see where I was bein' taken." Tracy said.

"I did too." Larry said while MJ nodded.

"Okay then so everybody felt the samethang I felt until I saw T-Money's ass. That's when it changed fa' me. When I saw him I snapped and it was like I snatched the steerin' wheel. I went after his ass and so did Zeinoch, I wanted to choke his ass so I grabbed his neck, so did Zeinoch. It seemed like he spit in my face so I spit back in his. Then I was like fuck it, I felt like rippin' that nigga in half, so Zeinoch did it. It was like I was him and he was me or he was just doin' what I was thankin', somethin'."

Shawn took in the information and pondered on it. "So that's maybe how we control it, with our thoughts."

"So if we thank it in our dream it'll do it?" Will asked.

"I believe so."

"How is that, when dreams take place at an unconscious state, and you can't thank unconsciously." Tracy said.

"Well maybe it's not our thoughts, maybe it's our wants and desires, cause ain't most people dreams are based on what they wish they could do or want to do in their real life situations."

"Yea cause Kev could have been actin' on emotions. I know I would if I was face to face wit' the cat dat killed my folk."

"Damn right I was actin' off of emotions, broke his ass off. Literally."

"Okay well if you got Zeinoch to kill T-Money then what about them other three cats?" William asked.

"Oh I 'on't know about them cats I was just along fa' the ride then. Probably one of yall."

"Not me." Shawn quickly responded.

"Me neither." Larry answered.

"Don't look at me." Michael replied.

"I was just a spectator." Tracy said.

"So if it wasn't one of us then that means it did that shit on its own." Shawn figured.

"I wonder why it licked shawty?" Kevin said which caused a guilty expression to form on Larry's face, Will noticed.

"You nasty, dirty ass nigga!"

"What!" Larry uttered as if he had no clue as to what Will was talking about.

"Ain't no what, you know what I'm talkin' 'bout, it was yo' perverted ass that licked that girl."

"A, shawty was fine as a mothafucka."

"You's-an-ole, horny demented bastard." Kevin said with a grin.

"That's fucked up, you killed that girl." Tracy said shaking his head.

"How was I supposed to know it was goin' lick 'er skin off, shit I thought it was just a regular dream." Everyone picked on Larry and his sexual handicap except MJ who was deep in thought. He had a conclusion.

"Hold up yall. Yall forgettin' the meat on the sandwich."

"Meat, MJ you hungry or somethin'?" Will said laughing.

"Naw man, the money, the last thang I remember was Zee, I'ma' call 'em Zee, was walkin' out of T-Money's crib with big trash bags full of weed and money, where is it?"

"Yea I remember that." Will said.

"Yea I was drivin'." Kevin said. They all stared at Shawn, waiting for an explanation.

"I don't know, remember this shit is new to me too."

"See I told yall that it was nothing but a dream." MJ said as he stood up.

"I 'on't know MJ the shit was real to me." William said.

"A lot of dreams feel real but they ain't nothin' but dreams."

"Well how in da fuck do you explain all of us havin' the same damn dream?"

"Well I 'on't know about that but I have seen somethin' on TV about these soldiers in basic training havin' the same dreams of torturin' their drill sergeant. See what they was sayin', if you take a group of people that's goin' through the same stressful situation, and they all sleep in the same area they'll have similar dreams. It got somethin' to do with brain waves travelin' on the same wavelength, same plane or somethin' like that. I 'on't really remember the details 'cause I was high when I saw it, but that's probably what happened, we all got high together, we all messed wit' that circle together, and we all anticipated somethin' to happen and that's what it is."

"And that's bullshit." Kevin strongly disagreed. "And what makes it mo' fucked up is that you da nigga that came wit' the thug wit' titties story to convince me of some shit, now here you go."

"Fa'-real MJ, we didn't have similar dreams we had the exact same dream." Shawn said.

"Well yall go-head and get cha' hopes up, but me, I'm chillin', show me the money then I'll believe it worked. A Will, can I get somethin' to drank cuz?"

"Yea go-head."

Michael headed for the kitchen and added. "If we end up findin' the money then it's all good but until then we just six broke ass nig-gas that just had a gay-ass slumber party."

Kevin smacked his teeth. "Man fuck dat shit MJ sayin', I'm tell-in' yall, that dream was real. I got this crazy feelin' that's tellin' me T-Money is dead." Kevin's statement possessed a haunting since of truth in the tone, even his jokes were dark. "I really believe that T-Money ain't got his self together. I mean just thankin' about it makes my dick hard."

"Hey man." Shawn said moving away from Kevin. "You can keep that shit to yo'self gay-gangst…"

"-Oooohhhh shit!" Michael shouted from the kitchen. "A yall come here, hurry up! Come look at this!" The yell brought Shawn and Kevin to their feet first then followed Will, Larry, and Tracy. They rushed into the kitchen and stopped abruptly behind Michael who had both of his hands up on the top of his head in shock at the sight in front of him. The two black trash bags from T-Money's closet were neatly placed in the circle, Kevin was first to express his excitement.

"What I told you, what I told you! What I told you!" He repeated himself in MJ's ear. "I told yo' ass-I told yo' ass!"

Will, Shawn, Tracy, and Larry walked over and started pulling out bundles of money and bricks and branches of marijuana. William took huge sniffs of both the weed and the money bundles. Kevin grabbed a bundle of money and walked over to Michael. "Now what I told you!"

Tracy stood next to Michael containing his shock and observing the strange situation. "It worked." He said in his head.

"Shawn you my mothafuckin' folk!" William said between taking a strong sniff from the weed. "I love you man, fa'-real."

Shawn gave a twisted look. "A chill out wit' the funny shit I 'on't swang that way."

"Shut up man you know what I'm talkin' 'bout, on some real shit. I love you fa' introducin' us to the witchcraft thang. I just wish I been knew about this, I would have been doin' this shit a long time ago."

"Shit, me too cuz-o." Kevin said flippin' through a bundle of hundreds. "I definitely appreciate it Shawn."

Shawn felt proud, flattered, important but for only a brief moment, their thanks stirred up the memory of when he thanked Daniel for his help. "Don't thank me yet." He said in a depressed manor.

"What that mean?" Larry asked smellin' a bud as big as his hand.

"Oh, uh-nothin'-nothin'. Let's count up this cheese." The suggestion was easily agreed upon as William picked up and carried the bags to the living room where they unloaded the money onto the card table. "A T-Murray since you be ballin' out in math, how 'bout you do the honors."

Tracy, seeming somewhat distant from the present situation, took a deep nervous breath and replied. "Alright." He walked over and sat at the card table, the bundles were overwhelming but fortunate for Tracy T-Money was well organized and meticulous with his money. There were only three denominations of bundles, which Tracy separated them as. Twenties on his left, hundreds in the middle, and fifties to his right, his comrades gathered around the table too anxious to sit while Kevin paced the floor. After he finished organizing he picked up a bundle of hundreds and stared at it for a moment, disturbed by the eerie feel it gave him.

"What, what's wrong you forgot how to count or somethin'?" Shawn asked.

"Naw it ain't that, it's just that, it seems weird. The shit feels… It just don't feel right."

"What did you expect, we did some weird shit to get it. But it's been done and we can't undo it, so we might as well move forward." Shawn's words were like a small dose of motivational logic to Tracy.

"Yea, might-as-well." He said with a regretful tone as he took off the red-orange 'collard green' rubber band T-Money used. His comrades hovered over him as he began his count except Kevin who was anxiously pacing the living room waiting on the results.

"Damn fellas, I can smell all yall's breath, Larry yours is the worst." T-Murray insulted without losing count.

"That's fucked up." Larry replied.

"Naw, that ain't fucked up, what's fucked up is that you ain't never seen pussy befo' but your breath smell like you been eatin' buckets of unwashed pussy."

"What! Fool I done seen mo' pussy in a month than…"

"Shut up Larry don't nobody wanna here that shit." Kevin interrupting Larry's developing lie. "Let that man count." Two minutes of nail biting anticipation passed before Tracy spoke.

"Alright fellas check it out. I counted five of them bundles of hunneds and it's a hunned one hunned dollar bills to a stack, fifty times ten thousand is five hunned thousand."

"Oh shhiitt, that's half-a-mill!" Will said ecstatic.

"Calm down that ain't it. I counted five bundles of fifties and it's seventy two of them, so that's three hunned and sixty-fo' Gs. The twenties was the same and it's a hunned and fifty so that's three-o-eight. All together it's, one million, one hunned and sixty eight thousand dollars."

"Say what!" William uttered.

"One mill!" MJ shouted.

Shawn stared at the now neatly stacked money. "So that's what a million dollars look like."

"I ain't even know that cat T-Money was ballin' like that." Larry said.

"Shit I heard he had more than that but believe me I ain't disappointed." Kevin said.

"One million, one hunned and…What else?" Shawn asked.

"Sixty-eight thousand."

"And how much that is six ways?"

"About a hunned and ninety stacks a piece."

"A hunned and ninety thousands!" William shouted.

"Well give or take a hunned, more like give 'cause it's goin' be some loose change."

"You get that loose change fa' countin' it up for us." Shawn said. "Yall cool wit' that right?"

"Hell yea, I'm cool wit' it." William answered for the rest of them.

"Naw I'm cool I 'on't want it, let Big Will get it, get that back doo' fixed and the kitchen floo'."

" It's yo' call."

"I ain't never seen this much money in my life." Larry said shaking his head with wide eyes.

"Me neither." Shawn said.

"This shit don't seem real, it feels like the money is finna disappear at any second." Michael said finally taking a seat.

"Yea I feel that too." Will said. "A T-Murray, take out one ninety and put it to the side so we can see what it look like."

"Alright." Tracy separated accordingly. "There you go."

"Damn, it's a lot smaller but it still looks good." Will said nodding.

"If yall fellas don't mine." Kevin said as he nudged Will over a little. "I'll go ahead and collect my share now, yall talkin' 'bout it might disappear and shit."

"Hold up Kev. I gotta be real wit' cha', I only counted a few stacks of each and estimated how much it is. I mean T-Money could of fucked around and put one or two bills too many or less in a stack that I didn't count out. So you or somebody else might be short or over a lil. If yall want it down to the last dollar then I can count it bill by bill but it's goin' take me a while, probably an hour or two." Kevin took in the information and then looked down at the bundles of money he cradled like a newborn child, he kissed it then replied.

"Naw, naw, I trust your estimation, I believe I can live with this."

"Hell yea me too!" William said staring at Kevin's share.

"I can too, do me-do me one!" Larry said with raw impatience.

"Okay now why did that sound gay as hell." Tracy said.

"T-Murray you know what I mean, hook my paper up."

Tracy shook his head and grinned as he began to divide the rest of the money. As he counted out each portion the crew, overwhelmed with excitement, unknowingly formed a line as if they were starving and Tracy was giving out hot meals.

After an hour of celebrating by smoking, some of T-Money's weed and playing with money while they danced and bragged, a realization occurred to Shawn killing his excitement. He stared out of Will's living room pondering unnoticed by his celebrating comrades except T-Murray, Tracy walked over. "What's up Shawn, talk to me, I can tell you thankin' 'bout somethin' serious."

"Yea, I'm thankin' 'bout this, if this money is real, then what happened to T-Money and 'nem is real."

Tracy took in a deep breath as the uneasy reality sat on his chest, he then walked over to the coffee table and grabbed the television's remote. "A fellas, chill out for a minute." He said loud and firm enough to get their attention along with their compliance, he then turned on the TV and to channel two where a flash ran across the screen.

"...We're bringing you news of a horrible massacre that has taken place in the Southside Housing community. We go live to Brad Spiers who has updated details on the horrible event, we want to warn viewers that this broadcast may contain graphic scenes unsuitable for children and some viewers. Brad can you up date us on the details?"

"Yes George. I'm standing here in the Southside Housing division where there has been a terrible multiple homicide. Five bodies were found viciously mutilated this morning by neighbors. One victim Jacob Willis was found decapitated and another Terrell Samuels was found in a way by medical personal as being, torn in half. Another victim, still unidentified, was described as being melted as if a high grade of concentrated acid was poured on the victim. Two other males have been identified as twenty-five year-old Charles Dent, an unidentified body, and a female whose name has not been released being that she was a minor..."

The crew watched the report speechless, all of their faces displaying expressions of tense attention except Kevin's, he smoked a blunt while basking in pride, happiness, fulfillment, and satisfaction. "Hell yea, it's all real!" Kevin uttered with even more excitement while tapping Shawn on his shoulder.

Shawn shook his head then looked over at Will and asked stressfully. "A Will, we need to take a ride to Southside."

To be continued...

To Marty The Sister-in-law

I could and almost had

Take care and thanks

for the support

Marcus Turner

CPSIA information can be obtained at www.ICGtesting.com
225605LV00002B/14/P